Cat proffered her right hand and he turned it over, pressing the stamp onto her palm. The ink burned on contact but the sensation was so brief she thought she must have imagined it. All that showed on her skin was the smudgy black outline of a wheel. He stared at her, unsmiling.
'Welcome to the Game.'

At an exclusive Soho party one rainy night, Cat discovers a dangerous world unlike any other. Soon, she finds it hard to stay away. Because in the Game, though the risks may be real, and the stakes may be high, the prizes are *to die for...*

A fast-paced thriller from an exciting new author.

THE
GAME OF
TRIUMPHS

LAURA POWELL

ORCHARD BOOKS

In memory of my grandfathers.

William Vaughan Wilkins (1890 – 1959)

Newby Odell Brantly (1905 – 1993)

ORCHARD BOOKS
338 Euston Road, London NW1 3BH
Orchard Books Australia
Level 17/207 Kent Street, Sydney, NSW 2000

First published in 2009 by Orchard Books

ISBN 978 1 40830 236 1

10 9 8 7 6 5 4 3 2 1
Printed in Great Britain

Orchard Books is a division of Hachette Children's Books,
an Hachette Livre UK company.

www.hachettelivre.co.uk

The Wheel of Fortune turns,

I go down, demeaned;

Another is raised up;

Far too proud

Sits the king at the summit –

Let him fear ruin!

For under the axis we read

That Hecuba is queen.

From the Burana Codex, *circa 1230*

In every bet, there is a fool and a thief.

Chinese proverb

CARDS PLAYED IN

THE GAME OF TRIUMPHS

★ •• *The Greater Arcana (Triumph Cards)* •• ★

21	Eternity	10	Fortune
20	Fame	9	Time
19	The Sun	8	Justice
18	The Moon	7	The Chariot
17	The Star	6	The Lovers
16	The Tower	5	The High Priest
15	The Devil	4	The Emperor
14	Temperance	3	The Empress
13	Death	2	The High Priestess
12	The Hanged Man	1	The Magician
11	Strength	0	The Fool

★ •• *The Lesser Arcana (Court Cards)* •• ★

King/Queen of Cups
Knight of Cups
Knave of Cups
Ace of Cups   Root of Water
Two of Cups   Reign of Love
Three of Cups   Reign of Abundance
Four of Cups   Reign of Blended Pleasure
Five of Cups   Reign of Lost Pleasure
Six of Cups   Reign of Past Pleasure
Seven of Cups   Reign of Illusionary Success
Eight of Cups   Reign of Abandoned Success
Nine of Cups   Reign of Material Happiness
Ten of Cups   Reign of Perfected Success

King/Queen of Pentacles
Knight of Pentacles
Knave of Pentacles
Ace of Pentacles   Root of Earth
Two of Pentacles   Reign of Change
Three of Pentacles   Reign of Material World
Four of Pentacles   Reign of Possession
Five of Pentacles   Reign of Material Trouble
Six of Pentacles   Reign of Material Success
Seven of Pentacles   Reign of Success Unfulfilled
Eight of Pentacles   Reign of Prudence
Nine of Pentacles   Reign of Sheltered Luxury
Ten of Pentacles   Reign of Wealth

King/Queen of Swords
Knight of Swords
Knave of Swords
Ace of Swords   Root of Air
Two of Swords   Reign of Peace Restored
Three of Swords   Reign of Sorrow
Four of Swords   Reign of Rest from Strife
Five of Swords   Reign of Defeat
Six of Swords   Reign of Earned Success
Seven of Swords   Reign of Futility
Eight of Swords   Reign of Shortened Force
Nine of Swords   Reign of Despair
Ten of Swords   Reign of Ruin

King/Queen of Wands
Knight of Wands
Knave of Wands
Ace of Wands   Root of Fire
Two of Wands   Reign of Dominion
Three of Wands   Reign of Established Strength
Four of Wands   Reign of Perfected Work
Five of Wands   Reign of Strife
Six of Wands   Reign of Victory
Seven of Wands   Reign of Valour
Eight of Wands   Reign of Swiftness
Nine of Wands   Reign of Great Strength
Ten of Wands   Reign of Oppression

CHAPTER ONE

It was his breathing that she noticed first: the hoarse, ragged wheezes of someone who has been running hard. Which was a physical impossibility, seeing as they couldn't have moved more than five paces in the last ten minutes. Two escalators were down at Piccadilly Circus, and at half past nine on a Friday night the Underground station was at a rowdy, jostling standstill.

'Oi, mate, shoving won't get you nowhere, all right?' said a woman ahead as they moved another inch towards the foot of the escalator. The man slid his eyes towards Cat, as if in appeal, but she had her London expression ready – blank and impenetrable. He was just a nondescript middle-aged bloke in a suit, but that didn't mean anything. You met all sorts of nutters on the Tube. 'Please,' he wheezed to no one in particular. 'Please.' He closed his eyes and she caught the scent of his sweat. Must be claustrophobic, she decided. Small wonder, stuck down here in the hot, stale air of the Piccadilly line.

At last they shuffled onto the escalator, their pace gaining momentum as people spilled off it towards the ticket barriers. With a whimper of relief, Heavy Breather pushed past her and was gone. She would have forgotten him already if it hadn't been for a snatch of conversation she overheard a few minutes later. Two men and a woman, in dark clothes, lean and purposeful, had come out of the east exit. 'He must have gone this way,' said the woman. 'It won't take long,' said one of her companions. They set off up Regent Street, weaving through the crowds with practised ease.

They're after that man, Cat thought, and though it was just a hunch she knew it was true. Perhaps he was a criminal, or perhaps his pursuers were.

It had nothing to do with her.

Cat went down Shaftesbury Avenue, turning left at Great Windmill Street and into Soho. Five minutes later she was letting herself into the flat. It was, as usual, dark and empty, although Bel had left a note and a partially defrosted bowl of cooked mince on the kitchen table. Bel worked as a croupier at the local casino, which sounded a lot more glamorous than it was. From the kitchen window, Cat could look across the street to the windows of the gaming floor, blacked out so that punters would lose track of time. A neon sign fizzed below: Palais Luxe, it said, in acid pink. Palace de Crud, said Bel.

Bel was Cat's mum's sister, though she had never called her 'Auntie', and certainly not 'Aunt'. She was always just Bel, like the owner of a saloon bar in some corny old Western. She looked the part, too, with her big red mouth and big red hair and swagger. She was only nineteen when her elder sister and brother-in-law were killed in a car crash, leaving behind them a child of three, but Bel hadn't hesitated. Cat was fifteen now and more Bel's than ever.

'Mind – you'll always be an orphan,' she'd say, squinting at Cat shrewdly, 'and don't you forget it. People like a bit of tragedy. Adds colour.' When Cat was younger, Bel wasn't above improving on this 'colour'. Her eyes would moisten, bosom heave, and she'd be off: 'Struck dumb for a whole year afterwards, poor mite. Even now, she'll wake screaming in the night – doctors say she'll never get over it…' This was Cat's cue to look frail and interesting. All sorts of useful things followed, from hefty discounts to extra helpings.

Bel wasn't feckless, though, just footloose. They'd moved three times in the last five years, much more before that, keeping to small to middling-sized places, where it was possible for Bel to make the most of herself, and for Cat to stay in the background. They both preferred it that way. Then Bel met Greg. Greg, who told her he worked in a big London club and had a flat to rent in the West End. 'A third-rate casino, more like,' she reported the Sunday night she got back from the city, 'and a Soho bedsit. But I tell you what, puss-cat, there's a town where anything could happen.' Three weeks later they had moved there.

So perhaps Bel was a romantic after all; perhaps London was the destination she'd been rehearsing all those other arrivals for. Her big adventure. It should have been the same for Cat. Her eyes were as cool and watchful as Bel's, her mouth just as stubborn. But here in London, Cat's self-sufficiency had deserted her. There was just too *much*, of everything, always shifting and changing, everything for sale or rent or served hot. Even being invisible was exhausting.

Most week nights she headed for the Underground, where she sat tight on the Circle line and just stayed there, going round and round. It felt like she was keeping the city at bay at last, watching the endless blurring of platforms and faces outside the carriage windows. Tonight it had taken three circuits before she changed lines for home, and that was only because she needed to pee.

Cat scowled at her reflection in the window above the sink. Thin, pale face, ragged black hair. 'Nothing but a poor orphan girl!' she mocked aloud, using Bel's voice.

A poor, *starving* orphan, she amended, giving the half-frozen mince a prod. Overcome by a craving for comfort food – salty chips, noodles swimming in soy sauce – she pulled on a coat and went out into the street again.

It was still early in Soho terms, the Christmas lights sparkling among the shop and bar signs; swarms of people cruising from pub to club, merry, mostly, not yet at the puking or brawling stage. Cat decided on noodles from the Vietnamese place, and ducked down the little alley running between Great Pulteney Street and Golden Square. It was when she was turning right at the bottom that she felt someone take hold of her arm. 'Please,' said a voice, very softly.

She tensed: ready to scream, to kick, to run. The place must be bristling with CCTV – there were a couple of blokes chatting only a few feet away – a girl on her mobile at the corner – if she could just – 'Please forgive the imposition,' said her would-be assailant, his voice trembling as he withdrew his hand. 'I didn't mean to alarm you.' It was the heavy-breathing businessman from the Tube.

Cat relaxed slightly, although every nerve was on alert. 'What d'you want?'

'I need help.' His eyes were darting from side to side, his face clammy. 'There – there are people after me.'

It was as if she'd walked onto the set of some cheesy

detective film, though she was finding it hard to imagine this bloke as a fugitive criminal or whatever. He looked too ordinary for that: middle-aged, middle class, middle management. Still, she kept her distance. 'You're being followed…?' she asked, as noncommittally as possible.

'Yes, yes that's right. Ten of Swords, you see. I think I gave them the slip at Argyll Street, but it won't be long now.' He licked his lips nervously and gave her an odd sort of half-smile.

'If you're in trouble, try the police.'

'Oh no,' he said, frowning slightly. 'I couldn't possibly. It's all for the Game.'

'A *game*?' God, there were some right nutters around. Ten to one it was some kinky Soho sex thing. 'Well, have fun then.' She turned to go.

'No, wait. Please.' He put out a hand to stop her, his expression crafty. 'If you were to stay with me, Swords would have to back off. Bystanders can't engage in play, you see.'

'I'm not going anywhere with you—'

'Just for a while,' he wheedled, grabbing at her arm. 'Just to give me some time – one last chance—' His whole body was shaking, but there was a spark of something in his eyes. Fear, yes, but also excitement, and a kind of greed. She swore, and shook him off.

His face hardened into a snarl, then he turned and

disappeared up the alley. And good riddance, thought Cat. But as she turned to go, three people appeared at the north end of Brewer Street. Two men and a woman, dark and purposeful. They moved swiftly down the street, and would have gone past the turning if Cat hadn't caught the woman's eye. 'If you're after that man,' she said, 'he went up the alley.' Serve him right for creeping her out back there.

The three of them stopped dead in their tracks as, silently, they turned their gaze on her. Under their cold scrutiny Cat felt sudden misgivings. But it was too late now…the woman gave a terse nod, and before she knew what was happening, they had swept past her and hastened up the alley in turn.

Daft way to spend a Friday night, she thought, looking after them. Something on the pavement drew her eye, a postcard or flyer that the man must have dropped in his retreat. It appeared to be a playing card, though not from any game Cat was familiar with. One side was patterned with a motif of interlocking circles or wheels, with the roman numeral for ten in the centre; on the other was a picture of a fallen male figure in a barren landscape. There was a cluster of swords stuck in his back. His blood was painted angry red, the clouds lowered blackly above him.

Cat shivered in spite of herself. A game, the man had

said, just a game… But what if there was more to it than that? Her misgivings increased. Not quite knowing what she was doing or why, she doubled back up the alley. She didn't really believe she would catch them up amidst the Friday night bustle, but then she saw one of the men whisk round a corner and found herself quickening into a jog. They were in the heart of Soho now, the maze of narrow streets heaving with people, and the hunt – if a hunt it was – was zigzagging through the crowds at an almost leisurely pace. At one point Cat thought she had lost them, but then she saw the woman's head in profile, eyes scanning the street, before she turned right and disappeared.

When Cat reached the turning point she found herself at a dead end, a little courtyard crowded with rubbish bags and empty beer crates. It was the back entrance to a pub. The others would have gone straight through and out onto the street again. Or maybe this was the end goal and they were downing pints at the bar by now, comparing notes on points and penalties or whatever it was.

Yet this cosy vision didn't quite convince. A creepy playing card was one thing, but there was something about the way those three people had looked at her – so cold and resolute – that felt wrong. Threatening. As Bel always said, *Don't go looking for trouble, else trouble comes looking for you.* But perhaps because Cat was tired of these empty aimless weeks, of feeling so damn *lost*, she decided that now was the moment to get a grip and make a move. She walked past the rubbish bags and through the door.

Inside there was a dark passageway leading to the bar, and a narrow set of stairs to the right. Although she could hear the punters through the frosted glass of the door, the handle wouldn't open. Locked. But those people must have come in here – where else could they have gone? Her stomach gave a growl of hunger, or it might have been nerves. She gave herself a shake, then turned and began to climb the stairs. At the top was another door, with a ragged sort of circle scratched into the wood. Cat hung back for a moment, then opened it and walked in.

She was in a room that looked halfway between some sort of posh, members-only club and a caretaker's closet. There was a stack of paint tins and a battered filing cabinet in one corner, with a small TV on top showing nothing but static. The walls were panelled with wood, badly scuffed and cheaply varnished, but an old-fashioned oil lamp was set on the windowsill and the carpet beneath her feet felt thick and rich. In the centre of the room was a circular table of green baize around which four people were playing a game of cards. They all looked up at her entrance, but not in an outraged sort of way. They didn't even seem that surprised. 'Ah,' said one of the ladies, arching her brow. There was an expectant silence.

Cat knew that she should begin with an apology or excuse of some sort: 'I don't mean to interrupt but…' or 'I'm sorry to intrude…' Instead, she advanced into the middle of the room, holding out the crumpled card. 'There was a man,' she said, 'a man I followed here. I think he's in some sort of trouble. Do you – have you—' She ground to a halt.

The man sitting nearest to her got up in one graceful movement, came across and took the card, glancing at it – the blood, the swords, the lowering storm – with a quizzical smile. 'Trouble? Yes, I should think he is.' He looked to be in his late twenties, tousle-haired, with a boyishly sophisticated face and sleepy eyes. Public-school type, Cat thought with instinctive dislike, newly conscious of her smudged face and cheap uniform.

She tried again. 'He asked for help. Some people were after him. I…I followed them here, that's all.' She found she didn't want to admit that it was she who'd set them onto him. And even as she spoke, she felt the absurdity of her words – wherever those people had gone, it wasn't here. The only intruder in the room was her.

'The player was attempting to cheat. Involving a bystander is an invalid move,' said one of the two women. She turned to gesture at the TV screen and its impenetrable flicker. 'Wands should pay the forfeit.' She was in early middle age and darkly glamorous, wearing an evening dress in burgundy velvet. Of her companions, one was a stern-faced black man, his hair just beginning to grey, the other a blonde in a white trouser suit and dark glasses. Cat thought she looked stupid, wearing shades in a lamp-lit room.

'I disagree with Lucrezia,' said the black man heavily. 'The bystander intervened of her own accord. And since her actions were to the disadvantage of Wands, my player has already paid for his error.'

'Come now, Ahab!' chided the younger man. 'It's clear the intervention would never have occurred if Wands hadn't broken the rules in the first place.'

The dark-haired woman turned to the blonde. 'Odile? What's your call?'

'There is only one rule of significance here,' she replied, sipping daintily from a cup of pale tea. 'And that is, a bystander whose intervention has changed the course of the Game is no longer a bystander. We must issue the usual invitation and await further play.'

'What is this *about*?' Frustration, and suppressed nervousness, had made Cat belligerent. She took another step towards the green baize table and saw that the cards they were playing with were not from a normal deck, but in the same style as the one she had found in the street. Strange images and symbols in rich, harsh colours. Tarot cards, maybe. So what were they doing – fortune-telling? Or had she stumbled into some creepy occult society? She shivered in spite of herself, and looked to the door. The room must be soundproofed, she decided, because there was no sound from the street or the bar below.

'Please don't be alarmed,' said the young man charmingly. 'It's only a game.'

The older woman, Lucrezia, flashed Cat a roguish smile. 'We are perfectly in order, I assure you! Perhaps, Alastor…?'

The young man called Alastor walked over to the TV set and gave it an impatient rap. The static cleared to show a grainy image, as if from CCTV, of the street immediately outside the pub. Among the revellers who had spilled onto the pavement, Cat thought she could see the three people she had followed, drinks in hand, chatting to a middle-aged man in a suit. Reception was poor, and the next moment the picture began to flicker in and out again.

So they must have gone through the downstairs bar after all, and the door she tried had merely been stiff. Now Cat felt foolish, and resentful for being so. 'I still don't get it,' she said stubbornly. 'Who are you people?'

'Me? I'm the King of Swords,' said Alastor, cocking his eyebrow at her and laughing. 'And these are my companions: Ahab, King of Wands; Odile, Queen of

Cups; and Lucrezia, Queen of Pentacles.'

Kings and queens and mystic cards – they *were* one of those daft role-playing groups! For all their posh clothes and enigmatic airs they were just a bunch of nerds, really, huddled above a pub to act out some bizarre fantasy quest. Cat suppressed a smirk.

'I s'pose the royal titles mean you're team leaders in this game of yours.'

'We lead the players in our court,' the black man replied seriously. 'The man you met is one of the knights of the Court of Wands. I am his king, and he plays for me.'

'Right…so chasing after him is part of a competition you've set up? With rules and prizes and stuff?'

'There are rules, and also principles.' The blonde took another sip of tea, its steam perfuming the air with the scent of jasmine. 'The knight in question has flouted both.'

'Admittedly, he was dealt a difficult card. The Ten of Swords' formal title is "Reign of Ruin",' Lucrezia explained in a conversational tone, lighting a cigarette. 'And so Alastor, as King of Swords, sent his knaves to bring him down – or stab him in the back, if you want to be literal about it. Either way, it's terribly thrilling.'

'Knaves? That a fancy word for henchmen?'

'A king must have his servants,' said Alastor smoothly.

'As such, my knaves have served me well. But as a result of Wands' rule-breaking, another card has entered play.'

He slid a card over to her, this time depicting a figure dressed in patchwork rags, poised at the brink of a precipice.

'And what's that one called?' Cat asked.

'The Fool,' said the black man impassively. The blonde waited, motionless as a mannequin. In the sudden silence, the other two were staring at her intently, eagerly even, and her misgivings returned. It was just so odd. They were odd, all of them.

'I'd best be off,' she said abruptly. 'Goodbye.'

Alastor moved ahead to open the door for her. 'I do hope you won't intervene in play again. Second time round, we'd have to impose a forfeit. And *then* where would you be?' He winked conspiratorially as she brushed past, her heart jumping awkwardly, anxious for fresh air, for crowds and noise again.

Once she was out in the street, however, her nerves seemed absurd. Those people were a bit strange, sure, but it was nothing to do with her how they chose to spend their time. King of Swords! Mr Boring Banker, more like. Or one of those super-smooth lawyer types, playing at world domination on his days off.

CHAPTER TWO

On Saturday, Cat woke to find Bel cooking breakfast for her and Greg, and the flat filled with an eye-watering smell of burned toast and cigarettes and bacon frying. Bel's shift usually ended at four and it didn't look like she'd been to bed in the meantime, for her make-up had that lopsided, end-of-the-night look, and she was still wearing tights and a blouse under her dressing gown. Her throaty laughter raised itself above the radio to rattle the windowpanes.

'Check this out, puss-cat!' she called. 'You're looking at the Palais Luxe's new senior croupier! Bacon sarnies and bubbles to celebrate!' She was flourishing a bottle of cava; courtesy of Greg, presumably, who had gone a bashful pink around the ears. Greg had a long, rather drooping face, and small delicate hands, like a girl's. Cat had always thought he looked more like a small-town librarian than the pit boss at a seedy casino.

She eyed Bel thoughtfully over a tumbler of slightly

warm fizz. The Greg-factor aside, this promotion didn't come as much of a surprise – Bel never had to stay long at a place before there would be talk of promotion and perks. Why the big deal? Bel herself had said the casino was a dump. London had gone to her head like the bubbles in her glass. '*Told* you this city was going to work for me!' she exclaimed as she sashayed off to the bathroom.

'Bumped into some right weirdos last night,' Cat said casually.

'Weirdos like what? Perverts?' Greg lowered his voice, with an anxious glance at the bathroom door.

'Nah, these weren't the kinky sort. Bunch of bankers and whatnot playing this card game where you had to run around acting things out. Quests and chases and stuff.'

'Sounds like them *Dungeons and Dragons* fans.'

'Dungeons! Now *that* sounds kinky.'

'Ah, but these are the imaginary kind.' Greg looked knowledgable. 'For imaginary adventures. You're given tasks or puzzles, and you build a story round them. Some people really get into it: write scripts, make costumes… Though I've heard it can turn nasty, mind.'

'Nasty?'

'Ooh yes. There was a murder. Some lad killed another one, see, or got his mate to kill somebody else, I can't remember which, and they said it was all part of this fantasy role-play business. It was in the papers a while back, and I don't reckon it was a one-off, neither… I'd steer well clear, dungeons or no.'

'Fine by me,' said Cat, reaching for another slice of bacon.

The day was cold but fine, and after breakfast Cat went out to mingle with the Christmas shoppers and sightseers. After her weeks of drifting it was almost disconcerting to have a destination in mind, but although her route crossed paths with the one she'd taken last night, the scene of the chase, or game, or whatever it was, already seemed to belong to somebody else's life.

Dark Portal was a sci-fi and fantasy shop on the Charing Cross Road, selling an assortment of books, DVDs and comics, together with film and TV memorabilia. The window display had a signed poster of Buffy the Vampire Slayer, a collection of model dragons holding crystals in their claws and a 'limited edition' Luke Skywalker doll. Cat went inside with the same furtive air as customers at her local porno video store.

Inside, the shop was orderly and well lit, and she was relieved to see her fellow browsers didn't look too dodgy – only a couple of beards between them. She went up to the till, where a bored-looking student type was reading the *NME*.

'Excuse me?'

'Yeah?'

'Do you deal in, er, role-playing games?'

He heaved a long-suffering sigh. 'What're you into?'

'I'm not sure…'

'Space Opera, Western, Wicca, Detective…or maybe you're more the Post-Apocalyptic type?'

'I don't th—'

'Of course, Sword 'n' Sorcery is always popular.' He waved his hand towards a display cabinet full of little figurines. 'I'm told we have a particularly fine selection of hobbits.' Now he was smirking and she stared at him coldly. Weren't these places supposed to be run by geeky enthusiasts?

'Can I help you?' A little man came bustling over.

'I was asking about role-playing games,' she said, turning her back firmly on Mr Too Cool for Tolkien.

The man beamed, practically twitching with enthusiasm. This was more like it. 'Do you know what you're looking for?'

'Not exactly…I wondered…do you know of any role-play games based on, like, Tarot cards?' she asked casually.

'Well, some game masters use them, but usually as a basis for building up a wider fantasy scenario. People either create their own game from scratch, you see, or else they buy ready-made packs and plot-guides to get them going. If you're interested, I could get you our catalogue.'

Was this how those people on Friday night had got started: chatting over the miniature hobbits? Cat was suddenly embarrassed by her questions. She didn't belong in a place like this, none of this stuff had anything to do with her. 'Uh, thanks – maybe I'll look into it.' She was already backing out of the door.

Over the next couple of weeks, Cat stopped haunting the Circle line and spent her evenings and weekends out walking instead. For the most part, the West End had a holiday feel, its lights garish but cheerful, its crowds good-humoured. Cat wasn't stupid, though; she never loitered in the dead hours after the pubs and coffee shops had emptied, the office workers and tourists had melted away, and the older, darker city came to claim its own. Besides, at ten-thirty sharp, Bel would telephone the flat, and all hell would kick off if she wasn't there to answer.

Sometimes Cat would pass a group of girls giggling in the window of a cafe, or a couple, smilingly entwined outside a bar, and feel a fleeting restlessness. Once, when Cat was about eight, she'd had a friend at school, a *best* friend, Tara, and when she'd heard they were moving again she'd cried for a day. Bel had been kind but tough. 'You meet the same people wherever you go and whatever you do. Truth is, most people are replaceable, if you look hard enough.' As she got older, Cat realised Bel was right. The Taras and Gregs of the world were nice enough, useful even, but they didn't last. Whereas Bel and Cat were separate and for ever. That was their pact.

Meanwhile, all schools had become alike to Cat – even if this latest one was more sprawling and chaotic than most – and by now she was adept at putting in just the right amount of effort not to draw attention to herself. It was the same with the in-groups and alliances outside of class.

On the last day of term, she went to hang out in a chip shop with a bunch of girls from her year; they were going on to a party afterwards, but by then she'd had enough. Once she got back to the flat, however, she had time to regret it. After half an hour listening to the thump of drum 'n' bass from the flat next door, Cat gave in. Just because she'd missed her chance with the party didn't mean she had to be stuck at home all night.

Almost without noticing it, she had begun to form an internal map of the district, the ebb and flow of its streets. As Cat neared the entrance to the strip joint at the end of her road, she automatically noted that it was the Saturday blonde on the door, not the black girl who usually took the Friday night shift. The girl gave a brief nod of greeting as Cat walked past, the fan heater by her bare legs blowing sudden warmth across the pavement. Cat shivered, and hunched further into her coat.

The coat was one of Bel's, a fur-trimmed parka that had been living on the back of one of the kitchen chairs pretty much ever since the move. It was warmer than Cat's usual denim jacket, and she was glad of it in the drizzle. Thrusting her hands deep into the pockets, she felt something poking out of the inner lining of the left one. It was a card: thick, gilt-edged, and with a familiar illustration. No swords or blood at least, but the giddy Fool, poised between the light and the dark, the open sky and the abyss.

What the…? Cat stared at it nonplussed for a moment or so, before remembering that this was the coat she'd been wearing two weeks ago, the night of her encounter with the card-players above the pub. The King of Thingummy must have slipped it into her pocket on her way out. Now she saw that there was writing on the back.

Cat walked over to a brightly lit shop window to take a closer look. The reverse of the card was blank, and printed with a bold black script.

THE ARCANUM
Temple House, Mercury Square

⊗

ADMITS ONE
Throw the coin, turn the card.
What will YOU play for?

There was a little icon of a four-spoked wheel, but no date or RSVP, no real information about what it was promoting or inviting her to. Was 'The Arcanum' a game or a society? And what did it mean about throwing coins?

On impulse, Cat felt in her pocket again. Sure enough, a coin had been slipped in there, along with the invitation. It looked more like a counter than any kind of currency: blank-faced, about the size and thickness of a two-pence piece, but heavier, and made of some gleaming black metal.

'Got a light, miss?'

Cat started: she had been too absorbed in her discoveries to pay attention to what was going on around her. An older Asian boy, face half-hidden by a baseball cap, was leaning towards her expectantly.

'Sorry,' she said, moving off. The area always had an assortment of young men with pinched, unhealthy faces loitering on corners and outside doorways, doing furtive business of one sort or another. Up till now, she had managed to steer clear of them.

'Spare some change for the bus, then?'

'No.'

Cat moved more quickly, into the crowds, and he began to follow her. She remembered the businessman fleeing down the alley, the set faces of those in pursuit, though she immediately shook the thought off. That whole thing had been a misunderstanding, she was perfectly safe, there was warmth and light and people were everywhere... Even so she walked briskly, away from her original direction. She glanced back to see if he was still following her. Yes. She turned another corner, this time away from the main thoroughfare, and looked back again.

He had stopped, was standing, staring, on the kerb. The light of a taxi swung round and for a moment he was illuminated in its beam: a dark face and glittering eyes. Then he tugged his cap down low again, turned his back on her and melted away.

Cat was embarrassed to find she was breathing hard, her palms clammy. She must have come further than she had realised, for she'd moved away from the warren of streets around Soho into one of the grand old squares that lie in the heart of the city. At this time of year, many communal gardens decked their trees in ropes of lights, but here the sickly glow of the streetlamps was the only thing to illuminate the rustling shadows behind the railings. It looked as if many of the houses around the square had been converted into offices, now shut up for the night, since the buildings were mostly dark and silent. Except for one, that is, a little way down from her on the left, where the windows glowed richly and the faint hum of talk and laughter spilled into the air.

Cat drew nearer to the pools of light, as if standing in them could make her warmer. She saw then that the front door was invitingly ajar. There was a discreet bronze plaque to one side. Temple House, it said.

She half laughed and felt for the card in her pocket. *The Arcanum, Temple House, Mercury Square.* A sudden wind gusted; the drizzle had turned to sleet and stung her face. Talk about good timing! From the sound of it, there was some sort of party going on. Cat didn't mind large, anonymous crowds; slipping around the edge of things was her speciality. She might as well give it a go: maybe get something to eat, wait until the sleet had eased…and if it didn't, there were probably umbrellas lying about that she could pinch.

The door opened onto a hallway with a marble floor chequered in black and white. A man was seated at a desk immediately in front of the door, while the rest of the hall behind him was shut off by a heavy curtain of gold brocade. The sounds that came from the other side were oddly muffled, though Cat could hear laughter and the chink of glasses.

The doorkeeper was dressed in black and gold livery, the kind that concierges wear at smart hotels. He had a withered face and clouded eyes. 'You're just in time,' he said. 'May I see your card?'

Cat produced the invitation, half-expecting to be

shown the door on the spot. It was still possible she'd got the wrong end of the stick and, anyway, she didn't exactly blend in with the fittings. Her hair straggled damply around her face and she was wearing an old navy V-neck and jeans under Bel's parka. If there was a dress code she was screwed.

She waited as the doorkeeper studied the card and then her face. 'Do you choose to enter the Arcanum and play the Game?' he finally asked.

'There's no membership fee, right?'

'Anyone can join,' he said gravely, 'who accepts the invitation.'

'OK, then.'

'I will need the coin.'

She passed over the metal counter, which the man tossed with an expert flip. 'It comes of use later,' he said, even though he was already tucking it away into his coat. Then he reached for the stamp and ink pad beside him. 'If I may?'

Cat proffered her right hand and he turned it over, pressing the stamp onto her palm. The ink burned on contact but the sensation was so brief she thought she must have imagined it. All that showed on her skin was the smudgy black outline of a wheel.

'Cool. Do I get a plastic wristband as well?'

He stared back at her, unsmiling.

'Welcome to the Game.'

Before she could change her mind, Cat went past the desk, drew back the heavy brocade drapes and stepped through. The building was even larger and grander than it appeared from the outside, for she now saw that the entrance hall was the size of a reception room and swarming with people. It was lit by an elaborate wrought-iron candelabra. A flight of stairs at the far end swept up to a gallery, and there were two doors set into the walls on either side of the stairs. Somewhere a piano was being played, a complicated modern piece with little obvious melody.

If Bel had been at this party she would have lifted her chin, pulled down her neckline, sauntered over to the largest and liveliest group – glass in hand – and just stood there, waiting for their attention to turn. Cat, however, was equally accomplished at keeping a distance. It wasn't simply a matter of skulking in corners; instead, she had learned to hold herself aloof, to stay watchful but relaxed. That way, she could be left to her own devices.

She accepted a drink from a passing waiter, who was wearing the same livery as the doorkeeper, and wandered to the entrance of the room on her right. Inside, a group were clustered around a green baize table, but as far as she could see it was just an ordinary card game, poker, maybe. The guests were a range of ages, and most had dressed up for the occasion in cocktail dresses or lounge suits. A few people looked as if they'd come straight from the office. Nobody gave her a second's glance. Cat went to sit in a window seat and allowed herself to relax.

In some ways, her senses were heightened by her surroundings. The prickle of champagne in her mouth, the scent of the women's perfume rising in the warmth, the click of heels on wood and the chiming of glass… All these things were sharp and clear. And yet there was a drowsy, muddled feeling that she couldn't quite shake off. When she tried to pick up what people were talking about, she found she couldn't concentrate, kept losing the thread. She thought she saw a well-known actress languishing against the wall, and didn't she recognise that jowly, grey-faced man she'd passed in the hall? A politician or newsreader, perhaps. But when she looked again, she couldn't be sure. It was as if her focus had gone.

Champagne on an empty stomach, she supposed, though it wasn't as if she had much experience of the stuff. She put her glass down and wandered through to the room on the other side of the hall, with the vague idea of trying to find the piano. This room had an immense gilt-framed mirror above the mantelpiece, and Cat saw a new glow and softness in her reflection, as if the lustre of the place was rubbing off on her.

The light-headed feeling was definitely getting stronger. She found another window seat, sat down and closed her eyes, trying to trace a thread of melody in the distant music. Every time she thought she caught the tune, it slipped away or subtly altered, so that she was unsure if sweetness or melancholy had been the dominant key. Somewhere a clock chimed; she tried and failed to count the hour. Her watch, always temperamental these days, showed the second hand twitching on the spot like something trapped behind glass.

Even though it couldn't be that late – she was sure the clock hadn't struck for long – it was probably time to leave. But first she wanted to find somewhere quiet and cool where she could clear her head. Cat went back into the hall and, on a whim, climbed the stairs to the gallery above. Another flight of stairs at the end of the hallway led up to a double door inlaid with a decorative design in black and gold. She tried the doors along the corridor at random, hoping to find a toilet or cloakroom.

Through the first, she glimpsed a room with walls lined in crimson silk, unfurnished except for a piano. A blonde in dark glasses and a white ball gown was sitting with her back to the door and playing an old-fashioned waltz. The room next to it was a book-lined study where a group of people were exclaiming over a game of dice. Surveying them from a sofa was the older woman from the night of the Tarot cards. Beside her lounged the lad who'd followed her in Soho; his cap was gone and his face was blank and glassy-eyed. As Cat paused by the threshold, Lucrezia looked across and smiled at her, then, holding her gaze, ran her hand through the boy's black hair.

The door on the other side of the corridor opened into a long bare room that ran the length of the building. Tall windows lined the wall overlooking the square; they had no curtains or shutters and the panes were shining black. The other side of the room was hung with pictures. It was like being in a museum, Cat thought, her steps creaking on the polished wooden floor. Cat didn't know anything about art but these pictures looked old, centuries old maybe, for the colours were rich but faded, and patches of paint were nothing but a cracked blur.

The painting nearest to the entrance was of a man and a woman standing naked among flowers, with a rainbow and flaming sword behind them. The next depicted an armoured knight on a white horse, but where his face should have been was a gleaming skull. Both these paintings, and the two at the further end of the room, were about four feet by five. The central painting, however, was far bigger: a vast four-spoked wheel with fantastical figures climbing or tumbling on its rim and a woman in the centre. After that came a painting featuring an angel with a trumpet and, finally, a desert landscape, with a robed figure bearing an hourglass.

She turned back to the picture of the wheel. Close to, she saw the woman in the middle was blindfold and carried a banner bearing an inscription in a foreign script. Latin, perhaps. Her smile was shadowy, knowing. And now Cat saw that the wheel itself was inlaid with many smaller images: a chariot, drawn by sphinxes. A flaming tower. A man with a cluster of swords in his back... Were these all to do with Tarot, then?

A soft noise at the other end of the room made her turn round, and she saw she was no longer alone. The young man who had called himself the King of Swords was lounging against the door, a cigarette in one hand. 'Hello again,' he said.

She nodded briefly and turned back to the painting, feeling self-conscious. Her head had begun to ache, and she hoped he'd leave her alone, but he was already moving to join her. He was dressed more casually than before, scruffy almost, in a faded grey T-shirt and with bare feet. *Pad, pad, pad* along the floor. He looked younger than she remembered. 'So you found us all right.'

'Yeah.' This was her prompt to say what a nice party it was, how kind of you, blah blah blah. Instead, she frowned, trying to think past the fuzziness. 'Why'd you invite me?' It came out more abruptly than she'd intended, but he didn't seem to mind, just smiled and took another drag of his cigarette.

'Why did you come?' he countered, watching her through the smoke with sleepy eyes. There was a pause. 'I'm Alastor, as you may remember.'

'The King of Swords.'

'And the Cat Who Walks By Herself.'

That rattled her. It was what Bel used to call her, quoting from some old kid's book, she said, though she'd never remembered the title. Had Cat even told him her name, or was it just an uncanny coincidence? She hunched her shoulders defensively and moved away a little, until she was standing beneath the painting of the knight with the bone face.

'The Triumph of Death,' he told her, and gestured towards the painting to its right, the one of the man and the woman in the garden. 'Over the Triumph of Love.'

'Not very romantic.'

He laughed. 'No.'

Cat could feel him watching her, not in a sleazy way, not checking her out, but thoughtfully, as if she was being measured for something.

'The pictures tell a story?' she prompted

'An allegory. It begins with Love or, in a more general sense, humanity,' he explained, sounding relaxed and perhaps a little bored. 'Love is overpowered by Death, who prevails over mortal passions and endeavours. Next comes Fame, the golden messenger who survives Death, and so defeats him. But even Fame, like memory, must fall to Time. Our friend with the hourglass.'

Cat digested this. 'So where does the wheel fit in?'

'The Triumph of Fortune. *Regnabo, regno, regnavi, sum sine regno.*' Now his voice was mocking, though who or what she wasn't sure. 'One could say that Fortune prevails over every other triumph, determining the nature of our loves, deaths, legacies… Perhaps even Time's victory is not so absolute. The Wheel turns, life begins again.'

'And…and the woman at the centre?'

'Take your pick. Tuche. Domina Casus. Queen Hecuba. Fors Fortuna, goddess of fate and luck.'

Cat frowned. 'Fate and luck aren't the same thing.'

'No.' He was playing with his lighter: flicking the flame up and off again. The spark of it danced in his eyes. 'But who's to say what's behind the throw of a dice, the turn of a card? However skilled the player, whatever the stake, those who win their triumph have Fortune on their side.'

'The Game of Triumphs,' she whispered, as if she'd known it all along. She thought back to their first meeting, the Knight of Wands and a card called the Ten of Swords. What had the dark-haired woman said? *He was dealt a difficult card…and so Alastor, as King of Swords, sent his knaves to bring him down…* 'You deal the

40

cards and the other players act out whatever's on them. For what – kicks? Or prizes?'

'Ah, but these aren't ordinary prizes. Love, Death, Fame – they're only the start of it. Believe me, Cat, there's *every*thing to play for.'

Cat sensed he was laughing at her, and felt her initial hostility return. 'Seems to me that you lot have too much time on your hands.'

'Perhaps you're right.' Alastor glanced at his watch. 'And speaking of time, I believe the evening's Lottery is about to begin. I do hope you'll join us.'

'Depends on the jackpot.'

'Our Lottery has different odds: the chance for our players to pick a new card and find a new fate.' He shrugged elegantly. 'Who could resist?'

Left alone in the gallery, Cat spent the next few minutes listing all the reasons why it was time to go home. The longer she stayed, the more confusing the whole set-up became. Not just confusing – absurd. Pompous play-acting for rich screwballs, she told herself, trying to avoid the eyes of the painted figures on the wall. But in spite of her best intentions, when she left the room she let herself be caught up in a crowd of guests who were surging along the hallway; it seemed easier to go with the flow and be jostled towards the stairs, up to the second and final floor of the house. The black-and-gold patterned doors at the head of the stairs had been flung open, and Cat saw that the entire floor was one vast mirrored ballroom.

Soon the room was thronged with people. It was difficult to judge the space, since the mirrors around the walls reflected the scene back and forth and around in a kaleidoscopic whirl of people and lights and sparkling glass. For a moment it was as if Cat was looking through the mirrors into myriad other crowds in myriad other rooms, but then she blinked, and the impression was gone. A hush descended.

At the far end of the room, the kings and queens were seated in a row behind a long narrow table, like members of a board. Behind them, suspended from the ceiling, was a TV monitor showing a silent blizzard of static. In front of them was a wheel.

After the build-up, Cat was expecting something spectacular, studded with gems, perhaps, and a flaming cresset at the centre, but in fact the wheel looked very similar to what any ordinary casino would use for roulette; about three feet in diameter and made from dark polished wood, with numbered slots in alternating checks of black and white. The doorkeeper stood next to it, one hand resting gently on the side.

'The players are assembled,' he announced. 'Who is presented for the Lottery?'

'The Queen of Cups calls upon the Knight of Cups,' said Odile, blank-faced behind her dark glasses.

A man stepped forwards from within the crowd. The doorkeeper turned to face him. 'Speak, Knight, and name the prize that you play for.'

The knight was a lean, scruffy man of indeterminate age, and his voice shook slightly as he spoke. 'I – I'm playing for the Triumph of the Moon.'

Cat turned to the woman next to her. 'What does he mean? Does the moon stand for a reward?'

The woman tutted impatiently and didn't answer. But someone behind her – a boy of about her own age – leaned to whisper in her ear. 'Artistic inspiration,' he explained, though this didn't leave Cat much the wiser.

The King of Swords looked unimpressed. 'Question is,' he drawled, tipping back in his chair, 'will a cure for writers' block do our friend any good, without the Triumph of Fame to enjoy it?'

The crowd laughed, and the knight licked his lips uneasily.

'Which court holds the Triumph of the Moon?' asked the doorkeeper in ritual tones.

'The Court of Wands,' replied the black man, Ahab, who, dressed in a pinstripe suit, really did look as if he was attending a business meeting.

'And which card has Wands dealt to Cups in challenge?'

'Ten of Wands, Reign of Oppression.'

'Which my knight wishes to exchange,' Odile put in, sounding a little bored, 'for a new card, allotted by the wheel.'

'A Lottery may only be held when the Triumph of Fortune has entered play,' the doorkeeper said gravely.

'But of course.' Odile waved towards the knight, who brought out a card from his pocket. In his excitement or nervousness he nearly dropped it as he handed it to the doorkeeper. Cat couldn't see the illustration, but she guessed it must resemble the picture of the woman and wheel that she'd seen in the gallery.

'Fortune's card is hidden in different moves throughout the Game,' the boy at her shoulder said in an undertone. 'Players aren't dealt it; they have to find it for themselves.'

Cat nodded politely, wishing he'd shut up. They were both getting black looks from their neighbours.

'The card has been accepted,' said the doorkeeper, 'and the Lottery may proceed. It is time for the wheel to spin a new fate.'

The Queen of Cups inclined her head towards the King of Wands, who bowed slightly in return. Then she rose to stand before the wheel. The King of Swords stopped swinging on his chair and leaned forwards with narrowed eyes. Even the Queen of Pentacles, who had been toying with the rope of jet around her neck, became still and watchful. Meanwhile, the knight waited to one side. He was visibly sweating.

Odile produced a silk pouch, from which she took out a small gleaming ball that she held up before the crowd. 'A crystal die for Cups, ebony for Wands,' whispered Cat's informant. 'Gold for Pentacles and iron for Swords. The numbers in the wheel's slots refer to the sequence of cards in the deck.' After a brief pause, the queen spun the wheel and, with a graceful flick of her wrist, launched the circular die. There was absolute silence as the wheel whirled and the ball rattled. The whole room seemed to be holding its breath.

At last, the spinning stopped and the ball dropped into its slot. The doorkeeper bent to inspect the number. The wait seemed to stretch on for ever.

'Four of Pentacles!' he called.

At once, the place erupted into a tumult of exclamations and acclaim. It appeared that the Four of Pentacles meant something good, for the knight was grinning dazedly, his face foolish with relief. Even though Cat barely understood what had gone on, she found herself joining the applause.

The King of Swords raised a hand for quiet. 'It has been decided: for his next move, the Knight of Cups will face the Four of Pentacles, Reign of Possession.' He smiled his lazy smile. 'Let play begin.'

This time it was the doorkeeper who spun the wheel. All eyes were fixed on it as it whirled around, gaining rather than losing speed. For a confused second the room seemed to be spinning, too. And when, abruptly, the motion stopped, the Knight of Cups had disappeared, presumably back into the crowd or through some hidden door.

'A fine gamble,' the Queen of Pentacles said appreciatively. 'And now I have news of a winning one.'

Buzzing and rustling from the floor.

'Yes,' she continued, voice raised, 'it is my pleasure and privilege to announce that the Court of Pentacles has won another triumph. After playing all four cards in her round successfully, a Knight of Pentacles has taken the Triumph of the Devil from the Court of Swords.'

Her announcement was greeted with a mixture of gasps, mutters and applause. Meanwhile, Cat shifted uncomfortably. Talk of the moon and fame was one thing, the devil quite another. Once again, the freckle-faced boy leaned in to explain. 'It's the hedonist's card. Sex, drugs and rock 'n' roll,' he said, eyes shining.

The doorkeeper rapped on the edge of the wheel for silence. 'Does the Court of Swords accept the loss of the Triumph of the Devil?'

Alastor's jaw tightened but his expression stayed

carefully neutral. Then, 'Naturally,' he said, as he took out a card from his pocket and slid it across the table to Lucrezia with an ironic little half-bow. 'Though I'm sure it won't be long before we win it back again.'

'Let the Knight of Pentacles come forward and receive her prize.'

A young woman pushed her way out from the centre of the throng: a tall angular girl, her mouth a slash of scarlet and her eyes outlined in startlingly thick swoops of kohl.

'Pass it over, then,' she said.

The doorkeeper looked disapproving. Clearly, this wasn't part of the script. But the King of Swords didn't take offence. In fact, he was looking the knight up and down appreciatively. 'I hope you'll make the most of your reward.'

'Oh, you can count on it.' She held out her hand.

As the other king and queens looked on, smiling indulgently, Alastor handed her a small metal object. A circular die, like the one Odile had cast into the wheel, but made of iron for the Court of Swords.

'Once it passes the threshold of Temple House, the powers of the Devil will be yours. You have played a fine Game and earned your fortune.'

Cat was disappointed. Alastor had told her they didn't compete for ordinary prizes, but it seemed the whole triumph gimmick was just a fancy way of awarding points. Perhaps if you managed to collect enough dice you could exchange them for a sports car or a luxury holiday or something.

And yet, all around her, the faces of the other players were suffused with a mixture of yearning and envy. A kind of reverence, too. As if this moment of victory was a sacred thing. And as the winning knight turned to leave, her hand clenched over her prize, the crowd parted to form an aisle of honour for her to walk out of the room. There was no more applause, just a long, soft sighing sound as the doors closed behind her.

Further speeches followed, but Cat barely heard them. She was still trying to process all the things she had witnessed. Finally, she became aware that the King of Wands was bringing events to an end: '…for the night is young, my friends,' he was saying, 'and the Game is long. May Lady Luck favour you all.'

A final cheer, and everyone began swarming out of the room. As Cat was borne along by the rush she heard snatches of comment. 'The Devil hasn't been attempted for a while' – 'Or won, either' – 'Yes, but if Cups take the Moon, Pentacles may lose the advantage' – 'Wands are pressing hard, but they lost another knight last week…' Meanwhile, the doors swung shut on the kings and queens, leaving them alone under the flicker of the TV screen, the glimmer of the mirrors.

Back in the hallway, Cat stood aside to let the other guests stream downstairs, where the party was resuming with new vigour. Shouts and raucous laughter floated up from the rooms below. The questions massing in her head were like a hundred spinning wheels, but she couldn't think past them. The woozy feeling she'd had at the start of the evening had returned; all she wanted was to go home.

She went to the top of the stairs. As she did so, someone caught her arm. It was the boy who had whispered to her in the ballroom. 'You can't leave now!' he said, his freckled face frowning. Her head ached and throbbed. Somehow she shook him off and hurried on down, stumbled across the black-and-white chequered floor that seemed to sway beneath her feet, clawed her way past the muffling brocade and spun – at last – into the damp night air.

Cat didn't remember much of the walk home or what time it was when she tumbled, fully clothed, into bed. Sleep came instantly, her dreams crowded with feverish images that were at once familiar and utterly strange. There was the knight on his horse, but instead of a skull he had the face of the King of Swords. She saw the wheel in the painting again, spinning, and sometimes the figure in the centre was Bel, and sometimes her mother, and once it was the businessman from the Tube. One last

CHAPTER THREE

'Look what the Cat drags in,' said Bel sardonically. It was gone twelve, and the winter sunlight coming into the kitchen made Cat groan and screw up her eyes. Was this a prelude to a strop? Bel didn't have many rules, but those she did weren't open to negotiation. Curfew was one of them.

'Still,' her aunt continued, 'you sounded perkier on the phone last night than I've heard you for a while. I'm guessing your end-of-term bash was a good one.'

So she hadn't stayed that late at the party after all – not if she'd been home in time to answer Bel's ten-thirty checkup and make up some story to account for her evening. She didn't have any memory of it. Cat wondered if she'd drunk more than she realised, even though she wasn't actually hung-over: just tired and rumpled and out of sorts.

Bel started crashing the kettle and mugs around.

'At someone's house, you said. Any gossip, then?'

'Not likely. Bad music and a load of spotty lads chucking crisps around.'

'Ooh, there's a surprise. Still, always good to put in an appearance.'

Cat grunted noncommittally. She knew Bel would have enjoyed hearing about the real party: the swanky guests, the candelabra, the champagne. Like something out of one of those glossy lifestyle magazines. The weirdo stuff with the wheel and the role-playing would have made a good story, too; there wasn't any reason she needed to lie about it. But as she squinted round the frowsty kitchen, with its clutter of unwashed dishes and Bel's underwear soaking in handwash in the sink, the evening before seemed very far away. Unreal, almost…like the images from the picture gallery that had followed her into her dreams. Glancing down at her right palm, she was disproportionately relieved to see nothing but a faint, greying circle where the wheel had been.

'Right,' she said, 'I'm going to grab a shower. See you in a bit.'

Bel looked disappointed, but she let her go.

There wasn't enough hot water for a proper shower, but Cat still took her time over it, shivering under the tepid sprinkle until the last trace of fuzziness was washed from her brain.

Once she got out of the bathroom, she found a note from Bel to say she was out shopping. Underwear still dripped in the sink, Friday's evening paper was still strewn under the greasy remains of Saturday's lunch. Cat stomped around tidying things away. She was angry with herself for getting spooked, for allowing herself – nearly – to be drawn in. Expensive bubbly, soft lighting, some mumbo jumbo about a load of old paintings… Jesus, it was about time she got a grip. Irritably, she grabbed the last of the newspaper and started stuffing it in the bin. Then her eye was caught by the strapline towards the bottom of the page: 'Businessman's Body Recovered From Thames'. And next to it, a photograph that seemed vaguely familiar.

Police have confirmed that the body pulled out of the Thames on Thursday morning is that of London businessman Anthony Linebeg, 47. The body was found with multiple stab-wounds in the back and had been in the water for approximately two weeks. Investigators do not believe robbery to be a motive for the murder, since the victim's wallet and watch had not been taken. Linebeg, a freelance IT consultant, who lived alone, was only reported missing after he failed to show to speak at a seminar this Monday.

Anyone with information relating to the crime was urged to contact the police. A telephone number was provided.

Cat didn't know how long she sat there staring at the page, smoothing out the creases in the paper over and over. The photograph of the victim could have been of any middle-aged, balding guy in a suit; she couldn't be sure it had anything more than a passing resemblance to the man she'd met. But all the same... Dead two weeks, they thought. She closed her eyes and once more saw the blood, the black clouds, the cluster of blades. The Knight of Wands and the Ten of Swords. How many stab-wounds were 'multiple'?

Cat's hand hovered over her mobile, then returned to fidget on the page again. She both wished Bel was here and felt relieved she wasn't. Bel had no patience with uncertainty: her decisions were instinctive, and absolute. Yet Cat could find no certainties here.

For the first time in a long while, she thought of her parents. Was this something she could have brought to them? She'd been told that her parents were good people, who had loved her and each other, but that didn't amount to much.

Although Bel acknowledged that orphans had a certain romance about them, and that romance could be useful, she wasn't one for dwelling on the past. Her stories about her sister Caroline were nearly always taken from their childhood, not from her life as a wife and mother. Cat could see from photographs that she had her father's black hair, and her mother's grey eyes. But more often than not she thought of her own eyes as being like Bel's.

Sometimes, it was true, she had dreams of being very small and held very close by some unseen, infinitely comforting presence. When she woke up, a sadness would be within her all day, and also the sense that, if she screwed herself up to do it, certain memories could be brought to the surface again, where they would have shape and weight and warmth.

However, that kind of thinking was morbid, and best left alone; that's what Bel always said. It wasn't as if a few soft-focus memories could be of any use to her now.

In the end, Cat folded the article into her pocket and went outside, back to Dark Portal. Where she found Too Cool for Tolkien enthroned at the information desk, ostentatiously flicking through a men's lifestyle magazine.

'D'you have any books on Tarot?'

'This isn't a *New Age* store.' If possible, his expression was even more contemptuous than when she'd enquired about role-playing games. Then, just as she was about to turn away, he cleared his throat in a grudging sort of way. 'Though I s'pose you could try Reference.'

The book section turned out to be in the basement, and was deserted. It was mostly sci-fi and fantasy fiction –

everything from Arthur C. Clarke to the soft porn exploits of space babes with laser guns. There was no reference section. However, the bottom shelf of the last bookcase was labelled 'Misc.', and contained a step-by-step guide to building a model Starship Enterprise, a book on the history of vampires and, stuffed wrong-side up behind an encyclopaedia of Middle Earth, *The Wondrous World of Tarot*. Bingo.

The book was not particularly wondrous in its appearance. Its pages were grubby, the dust jacket – a riot of lurid psychedelic swirls – was torn, and the OTT prose style was as naff as the cover. If the overexcited introduction was to be believed, Tarot cards incorporated myths and symbols from prehistoric Norse tribes to the classical world, from the ancient religions of China, India and Egypt to the medieval courts of Italy and France. One theory was that the first cards were made by the deity known as Thoth to the Egyptians, Hermes to the Greeks and Mercury to the Romans. As the scribe and magician of the gods, he created the Tarot deck from The Book of the Dead, imbuing the cards with the lost magic of antiquity. Cat wondered if the location of Temple House in Mercury Square was an in-joke, or if those people took all this stuff seriously.

In any case, a lot of the references from last night were beginning to fall into place. The Arcanum, she now realised, must be some kind of allusion to the division of the Tarot deck into two sections: the Greater and Lesser Arcana. The Lesser Arcana was fifty-six cards broken into four suites which corresponded to an ordinary card deck: Wands (Clubs), Cups (Hearts), Pentacles (Diamonds) and Swords (Spades). Each suite or court had its own Queen, King, Knight and Knave. The twenty-two trump cards (or 'triumphs') in the Greater Arcana were supposed to depict a journey through one's life, starting with the Fool, designated as zero, and ending with number twenty-one, the World. The Fool was apparently the ancestor of the modern joker in the pack.

The rest was mostly teach-yourself-fortune-telling, or 'divination' as the author preferred it. Cat wasn't much interested in fortunes, but she did spend a while looking at the illustrated section in the middle, which showed pictures of all the cards, as well as a selection of Tarot designs through the ages. She was surprised to find that there were a range of different symbols and even names for the cards. In some decks the High Priestess was depicted as a female pope, The World was called Eternity, Time was transformed into the Hermit and Fame into Judgement. Cat tried to find a match for the paintings she'd seen in the gallery, but although she found similar images there were none exactly the same as the ones she remembered.

She flicked through the last few pages of the book with mixed feelings. In some ways, what had seemed strange, and possibly threatening, a short while ago, was easy to dismiss once she saw its sources laid out in a tacky little book. All that hocus-pocus about Egyptian gods and Cabbalistic cults was the kind of thing she associated with your stereotypical Tarot fan: droopy girls with unwashed hair and too much eyeliner, burning incense in dark rooms. But then she'd always thought role-play games were for spotty nerds living in basements…

Trouble was, she was no closer to understanding how the Game of Triumphs combined the two, or if either of them had any connection to the newspaper in her pocket. There certainly weren't any guides to divination that could tell her what exactly she had seen, or not seen, that Friday night two weeks ago. *I need help,* the man had said. *There are people after me.* She remembered his fear, but also his air of suppressed excitement, how he had clutched at her arm with greed in his eyes. Which should she believe, a half-familiar photograph or a flickering image on CCTV? And what was her real motivation here – her pricking conscience or curiosity?

Lost in thought, it was only when she turned to place the book back on the shelf that she realised someone else had come into the basement and was leaning against the other end of the bookcase, openly staring at her. He was a boy of about her own age with a clever, freckled face and an unruly mop of sandy hair.

'I remember you. You were at the party yesterday.'

She must have heard him wrong, or else it was a case of mistaken identity. 'I don't think—'

'You know, the Lottery. I was giving you tips about the triumphs. Sex, drugs and rock 'n' roll!'

The shock of his words brought home to her the fact that in spite of all her careful rationalisation, she hadn't yet reconciled last night with the ordinary world. She opened her mouth, but no words came.

'Pretty wild, huh?' The boy gave an odd little giggle. 'I'm Toby, by the way.'

'Cat,' she said reluctantly.

Close to, Toby didn't look much like the poised, glossy guests that she remembered. He was wearing a battered tweed hunting-jacket over a Godzilla T-shirt, baggy cords and bright yellow baseball boots. The outfit was hardly radical in this neighbourhood, but there was something a little bit staged, a little bit self-conscious about the way he wore it. He didn't look entirely comfortable anyway, hunched into his jacket, one foot tapping agitatedly on the floor. 'So, how did you first enter play?'

'I'm not playing anything.'

'Of *course* you're in the Game. You were there last night, weren't you?' He gestured towards her right hand

and she felt a brief twinge where the stamp of the wheel had been. Or rather, where it still was. She could have sworn the last of the ink had washed off in the shower this morning, but now she saw a smudgy grey circle still lingered. Reflexively, she put her hand behind her back.

'Look, the only reason I was at that party was for the free booze. Sorry to be rude, but I think your gang's little fantasy world is a load of junk.'

Toby didn't look offended. 'Aw, don't tell me you aren't curious. Why else are you here?'

Cat realised she'd left *The Wondrous World of Tarot* face-out. And of course he was right. 'Maybe I do have some questions.'

'And maybe I have some answers.' He smirked. 'Come here often, do you?'

'No.'

'But you live nearby? You're a local?'

'I guess.'

'Cool,' he said, a bit too eagerly, like he meant it. Then, suddenly, he flung back his head and cried, 'So-HO!', the last syllable drawn out in a kind of howl. Cat started. 'It's a hunting cry,' he explained. 'That's what this area used to be, back in the sixteenth century: the royal hunting grounds. So*ho* was the call used to rally the hounds.'

Cat thought back to the scene of the chase two weeks ago, and wondered if this was some kind of test. But no, he wasn't even watching for her reaction, just fiddling with his watchstrap and grinning to himself. Showing off, that's all it was – trying to impress her with his local knowledge.

'All right,' she said brusquely. 'Tell me about this game of yours.'

'I *knew* it. You're hooked.' He leaned towards her, sandy hair falling into his eyes, and lowered his voice to a dark whisper. 'It's not just a game, you see, it's a way of life – the gateway to another dimension!'

An older man had come into the basement and was looking at the fiction shelves, but he gave them no more than a cursory glance. Cat supposed this kind of conversation was standard-issue for Dark Portal customers. 'Let's stick with this dimension for now.'

Toby took this as an invitation to begin. 'Well, as you know, the kings and queens are in charge of four courts: Wands, Swords, Cups and Pentacles,' he began importantly. 'Each of the courts possesses a number of different triumphs. They're the prizes. When a knight chooses the triumph he wants, he has to play against whichever king or queen currently owns it. The other three draw lots to decide which of their courts he'll play for, then if the knight's successful, he'll win the triumph both for himself and his court.'

'So it's just a competition to see who can collect the most triumph thingies.'

'Basically, yeah. Though while the knights are trying to win the power a triumph represents, the kings and queens just pass them around like gambling chips. You see?'

'Er…kind of,' she said dubiously.

'Anyway, in each round, the Game Masters, that's the kings and queens, take it in turns to deal a card to the knight. They use their knaves – dogsbody servant types – to help act out the moves. Now, a few of the cards represent nice or useful things, but most are different kinds of tests, some of which are a lot harder than others.'

Cat nodded to show she was listening, a fixed smile on her face, as her fingers brushed the crumpled newsprint in her pocket. Perhaps that was what had happened to the Knight of Wands she'd met – some wacko initiation rite that had gone wrong. She was reluctant to bring him up, however. Toby seemed harmless but his enthusiasm for all this gumpf had a whiff of fanaticism.

'Is that what last night's Lottery was about: swapping a nasty card for a nicer one?'

'That's the idea. Of course, knights hope the wheel will give them a better card than the one they've been dealt, but there's always the risk it could be worse.'

'And what kind of, er, knight are you – I mean, which court do you belong to?'

'Ah, but I'm not a knight. I don't play for any court, either. No… I'm a chancer – a joker in the pack!' He gave a nervous giggle. 'And you too, I think. That's why I made contact outside the Arcanum.' He leaned towards her in a conspiratorial manner. 'You see, this could have untold consequences for the State of Play.'

Okaaay. Cat had had enough. 'Right, thanks for the explanation, then. It's been…interesting.'

'You're not going already?' Toby's face crumpled with disappointment. 'But we've got so much to talk about!'

'Sorry and all that, but I really have to go.'

'Oh. Well, maybe we should swap numbers, then.'

She pretended she hadn't heard him. After all, she was already halfway up the stairs. 'I'll leave my details by the Tarot book,' he called plaintively as she reached the top. 'And I guess I'll be seeing you around…'

Not if I see you first, thought Cat.

It took her a while to find Temple House again. The square wasn't off the street she thought it was, and she spent a frustrating half-hour or so wandering about, trying to trace her route from the night before. And when she finally found the right turning, the square was considerably less impressive than she remembered. The buildings looked shabbier in the cold light of day, the grandeur of scale and design let down by ugly office conversions and dingy brickwork. The garden in the middle, which had seemed so abundant and mysterious in the dark, was just a scruffy grass space fringed by droopy-looking trees and a few shrubs.

Temple House wasn't as she remembered it either. The paint on the door was peeling, the plasterwork cracked and stained. On a whim, she pushed the bell, but no signs of life came from behind the shuttered windows. A burger wrapper was half-stuffed into the letter box. If she hadn't known better, she would have thought the place was derelict.

Cat slumped down on the steps, swearing under her breath. Her right hand had pins and needles and she absently rubbed it against her jeans. What had she been expecting to find today, anyway? All this time wasted on tacky books and the ramblings of random nutters... She didn't even know what she was looking for, she thought, glancing over to the garden, where a gaggle of lads in hooded tops were kicking a beer can around in a desultory sort of way. A tramp snored on a bench beneath a lopsided cherry tree.

Once more, she took the newspaper page from her pocket and stared at the dead man's face, trying to imagine what she would say to a police officer. A man she couldn't positively identify, a dead end that wasn't a dead end, a game that might have turned murderous... It was all so far-fetched, and that was before she got to the bit about secret role-playing societies and the Wondrous

World of Tarot. But then if she *was* right, and it was the same man, there were bound to be other CCTV images from that night in Soho. Other people might have seen something. For all she knew, Anthony Linebeg's flat was stuffed with Tarot cards issuing threats or promises or invitations.

Either way, she knew there was only one way to find out.

Coming to a decision didn't make it any easier to leap into action. Instead, Cat idled on the steps, fiddling with her hair and looking out over the square.

Some sort of altercation had started up between the tramp and the lads in hooded tops. She wasn't sure what was going on at first, because her vision was oddly unfocused, as if her eyes were out of sync. Then she blinked, and the unsteadiness cleared. She saw that the tramp had got up from his bench and was flailing his arms about and shouting, his ragged coat-tails flapping in the wind. His adversaries' goading laughter rose to join the gibberish; one of them kicked the can they'd been playing ball with so that it clattered against the man's leg. It was the kind of scene you saw all the time, all over this city, all over any city. A young mother, wearily pushing a pram along the pavement close to Cat, didn't even give it a second's glance. Nor did the smart couple climbing out of an estate agent's car on the other side of the square.

Then something changed. The tramp's voice rose again – harsh squawking, spat like a curse. The youths weren't laughing any more; stood together, hoods down, there was something predatory about their stillness. One of them – there were four, though there was another boy at the other end of the garden, chucking pebbles at a tree-bound cat – raised his arm. It was a strangely formal gesture, half-command, half-salute, and it was only then that Cat saw each of the four was grasping something in his right hand. Not knives: short wooden bats, like truncheons. She scrambled to her feet, adrenalin surging in her blood, her vision blurry with shock. As often happens in such situations, time seemed to slow. Nobody else appeared to have noticed what was happening or what was about to be unleashed. The scene before her had the private leisureliness of a nightmare.

And then the tramp took a card from his pocket and tore it in half. At once, the ground in front of him burst into flame.

It combusted with soft *whump!*, spreading into a ring of fire that lit the entire square with the fierceness of tearing light. The grey air above it shimmered with heat, the cherry tree within was showered in sparks of gold. Cat opened her mouth to scream but no sound came. It was as if her breath was frozen in her throat. She spun around, gesturing in incoherent appeal to the woman with the baby, who was just five feet or so away. The woman looked up at her strangled half-cry, then immediately hunched back over the pram, paying no heed to the conflagration or the circling youths.

'Wait,' Cat croaked. 'We have to – someone – we must – someone must stop—'

But the woman was already hurrying away. Cat stumbled towards the railings, began to shout out something indistinguishable. The grass must have been soaked in petroleum and he'd thrown a match, that must be it... It seemed impossible that the whole garden was not alight, yet both the tramp and his surroundings seemed immune to the flames. Meanwhile, the youths prowled, still tensed for action, and occasionally jumping back as the breeze sent the fire licking towards them.

'No! Please!' Cat begged, although she knew it was futile. A spark blew onto her cheek and she slapped at it frantically. At the far end of the garden the other boy loitered, his baiting of the cat abandoned. He, too, was staring – but not at the blaze or the bats. He was staring at her. So were the couple and their estate agent standing on the opposite side of the railings. The predominant expression on their faces was distaste. A car turned into the square, purred smoothly past, and then out again.

It was then that the true horror of the situation took hold. Nobody else could see what was happening. As far as these others were concerned, the only strangeness in their afternoon was the mad girl, babbling to herself and gesturing wildly at things that weren't there.

Gasping in disbelief, Cat clutched the iron railings so that the cold metal bit into her flesh. As she did so, she felt a twinge on her right palm. The mark of the wheel throbbed as it had in her dream: she could see the trace of it like a silvery, glowing scar. She cried out and closed her eyes and put her hands over her ears as if she could blot everything out, as if she could start over. And when she opened her eyes again, she was looking into a quiet London square. Not so much as a speck of ash remained; the empty beer can had vanished along with the tramp and his adversaries. Cat fell down on all fours and retched.

For what felt like a long time she squatted by the railings, sick to the pit of her stomach. After the heaving subsided, she found she couldn't stop shaking.

'Uh, are you OK?'

Somebody was crouched beside her. She flinched away before she realised that he wasn't one of the hooded youths with the bats, that he must the boy who'd been throwing ordinary pebbles in an ordinary garden. He had a blunt, tough face and his bitten fingernails were grimy, but his expression was concerned. Or maybe just curious.

She licked her dry lips. 'I felt a bit ill, that's all. I'm all right now.' *Get a grip, she had to get a grip…*

'You should go home.'

His eyes fixed hers. They were very dark, and ringed with the bruising of fatigue. He looked like a street kid, with his grubby hands and shapeless clothes, but he wasn't threatening. He was of her world. She felt an impossible urge to clutch hold of him as hard as those iron railings.

But whatever impulse had brought him over was already fading, for he had got to his feet and was slouching away.

The shaking and queasiness passed. Of course it did: Cat was tough, Cat wasn't the type to fuss. She wasn't mad, either. Or dreaming. Or high. That's what was so terrifying… Her cheek still stung from the stray ember; she could smell smoke in her hair. The roar of the flames and the tramp's hoarse cries had been as clear and present as the uninterrupted grind of city traffic or the mewing of the child in the pram.

Toby's excitable voice echoed in her head. What had he called it? Not just a game: a way of life. *A gateway to another dimension.* Cat gave a half-laugh, half-sob. She could have carried on crying or laughing or both, but instead she felt a huge and uncomprehending rage begin to boil within her. Her fury warmed her, she clung to it with relief, letting it surge over the fear until she was able to get to her feet and walk away from the square, her head held high and her fists clenched. Toby, she thought furiously, I'll find Toby.

CHAPTER FOUR

When she got back to the basement of Dark Portal, the book on Tarot had gone. There was, however, an envelope with her name on it tucked alongside the encyclopaedia of Middle Earth. Cat's heart thudded – another Tarot card? But all it contained was a slip of paper with a mobile number and a hastily scrawled line: *Hey Cat, hope you'll get in touch some time(?) Toby.* Did he have any idea what she had just gone through, what she had been about to witness when she'd left him in the basement? Had the little creep been *toying* with her, the whole time? Once again, hot rage began to beat in her head.

She found a bench not far from the shop and dialled the number, trying not to wonder what she'd do if he didn't pick up. But when he answered on the second ring his 'hello' had the alert air of someone who'd been expecting a call. She clenched her fist, hard. 'It's Cat. I need to see you.'

'Hi, Cat! This is so great. I mean, it's great you got in touch. OK, so what do you—'

'I'll be outside Dark Portal. Come now.' Then she hit the off-button, not trusting herself to speak any more. And when Toby did arrive, just over ten minutes later, she found she couldn't speak at all.

They went to a greasy spoon around the corner. Toby was obscurely proud of the place, glancing round at the smoke-stained walls and grubby Formica with an almost proprietorial air. 'This is the real, authentic Soho,' he told her. 'You can't find places like this in magazine listings.'

Cat looked into her cup of over-boiled coffee. Greg had been known to go misty-eyed over the decline of what he called the 'old Soho', and Bel called 'local colour', but since Cat could no more visit a glossy cocktail bar than an ancient pub, and an ad agency held about as much interest for her as a strip-joint, this wasn't something that much concerned her. But what did this boy, with his cultured accent and ironically retro clothes, know about it? He probably lived his whole life according to the back-pages of pretentious mags.

Toby didn't seem to mind her continued silence. His foot tapped nervously under the table, but away from the shop he seemed more relaxed. Pleased with himself. Cat noticed there was a fleck of milk froth on his upper lip. It was impossible that she could sit here in a normal cafe, surrounded by normal people, while the world as she knew it had just been wrenched into some parallel reality. Or Dark Portal. If it wasn't so terrifying it would be ridiculous.

'Aren't you going to ask why I called you?' she said at last.

He glanced at her sidelong, his expression both sly and hopeful. 'Well, I'm guessing it's to do with the Arcanum.'

'I don't know what that means,' she said. Deep breath. 'All I know…is that I, uh, saw something that wasn't there. In the square by Temple House.'

'Mercury Square.'

'OK. Mercury Square. There was a tramp in the garden, see, and he got into an argument with some other blokes. They had these wooden…truncheon things and I thought there was going to be a fight.' She took a sip of coffee to steady her, feeling the hot liquid scald her throat. 'But then the tramp pulled out a card from his pocket, and tore it in half. And suddenly the ground around him burst into flame. A whole wall of it, just like that. The fire was *protecting* him, keeping the others back. The thing was…the thing is, nobody else – the other passers-by – could see what was happening. They thought I was off my head.' She looked into her cup. 'But I'm not, am I?'

'I doubt it,' said Toby cheerfully. 'What happened next?'

'I'm not sure. I think I fainted. When I came round, everything was back to normal and the people had…vanished.'

Toby linked his hands round the back of his head and leaned back in his chair. 'Interesting. Your tramp must've been using the Ace of Wands to defend himself. It's otherwise known as the Root of Fire, after all.'

'What the hell's that supposed to mean?'

'Have a look.' He turned to rummage in his bag. 'I bought this for you anyway, just in case. Check out page thirty-three.'

It was *The Wondrous World of Tarot*. Dumbly, Cat flicked through until she found the page in question. It was an illustrated layout of the Suite of Wands. The Ace was a disembodied hand grasping a flowering branch, from which sparks flew.

'Fire, see? Each ace represents one of the four elements. They're some of the most powerful cards in the deck; in fact, they're the only cards apart from the Triumph of Fortune that knights can collect themselves. Presumably, that's to make a more level playing field – it wouldn't be very fair if the kings and queens kept *all* the cards up their sleeves, now, would it?'

Cat could only stare back at him in incomprehension.

'This should also look familiar.' Toby tapped a card called the Five of Wands, which showed a group of men in combat with thick wooden staffs. 'From your description, I'd say it was the card you saw in play: the King of Wands' knaves ganging up on some poor knight. But somewhere along the way, he found an ace, and their plans – literally – went up in smoke.'

He chattered on some more but Cat barely heard any of it. She had turned to the next page, which was a layout of Swords. 'Wands and Swords,' she whispered. 'That's how it all started.'

'Tell me about it,' said Toby eagerly. And, haltingly, she did: everything that had happened from the moment she found herself standing by the heavy-breathing businessman in the Underground. Everything, that is, apart from the newspaper cutting in her pocket. But Toby didn't seem particularly concerned with the knight's fate. He was much more interested in the debate above the pub.

By the end he was beaming. 'I *knew* it! Ha! You're another chancer, like me.'

'Chancer?'

'The Triumph of the Fool. No offence or anything; it just means you're a bystander who accidentally altered the State of Play. That makes you part of the Game without being, like, an official player. It means you can move around the Arcanum without belonging to a court. Which means—'

'Toby—'

'But what you have to—'

'Toby, wait—'

'We can—'

'SHUT UP. Shut up and listen.' Cat took a deep, steadying breath. 'OK. Here's the deal as I see it. A bunch of messed-up poseurs looking for thrills pick random Tarot cards and then act out what's on them: murder, arson, whatever. Which is sick. Probably the sickest thing I've ever heard. Even so, I *get* it. I can see how something like this is started and how it works. But what I *don't* get is how all this is taking place in some kind of crazy parallel dimension that the rest of the world can't see.' To her shame, her voice had started to crack. 'Meanwhile, you're chatting away like we're swapping tips on bloody *Monopoly*. You say we're the same but how do I know that? How do I know *anything*?'

Toby looked stricken. 'I'm sorry. Sorry. Hell – I can see I've gone about this all wrong. I'd forgotten what a shock it is – finding out, I mean. And I'm not psychotic or anything… I promise.' He blushed furiously beneath the freckles. 'Invitations turn up at random, you see, so it's not as if any player, even a knight, could ever *plan* to join. But in my case, I'd been dreaming of finding something like the Arcanum for most of my life.'

Cat bit her lip. 'The Arcanum – is that what you call

the…the…place where I saw the tramp and the fire? And the inside of Temple House?'

'The Arcanum is where the Game is played: the Game's board, you might say. It's going into the Arcanum that brings a player's card to life. If it'll make you feel any better, it's not technically a different world to ours. At least, I don't think so.'

'But—'

'Picture it as the reverse of a card.' Toby sounded relieved to be returning to practical matters. He picked up the greasy menu on the table and turned it over in demonstration. 'Or the two sides of a coin. The same thing, just a different view.' He looked at her shyly. 'You know, it might be easier to explain what you saw if we went back to where it happened. But I don't want to, er, traumatise you or anything…'

'I'll cope.'

Toby had clearly resolved to be more considerate of Cat's fragile mental state. At any rate, he made a big deal about paying for her coffee and rushed to hold the door open for her on their way out of the cafe. Once outside, he kept darting her quick, nervous glances when he thought she wasn't looking. In any other situation, Cat would have found it funny.

The afternoon had got progressively gloomier, and when they reached the square everything looked even more dingy than before. Cat felt chilled by the ordinariness of the scene; in the time that had passed since she'd last been here, it had become easier to believe she was merely delusional.

She slid her hands over the iron railing. 'If the garden I was looking at belonged to the Arcanum side, I don't understand how I was able to see it without... I dunno...saying the magic words, or going through the magic door or...'

'Sounds like you weren't actually in the Arcanum proper, more like looking in. I expect that's because of being so close to Temple House, which is common to both our side and the Arcanum – and not wholly belonging to either. There's bound to be an overlap, especially if a card's in play there.'

'So how do you get in...properly?'

'Toss a coin.'

'Seriously.'

'I *am* serious. Find a threshold, then toss the coin that'll appear – you know, like the one you got with your invitation. Thresholds aren't doors, you see; they're more like switches to flip you over to the other side. You come across them wherever there's the sign of the wheel. The Arcanum throws them up randomly for the knights to find and play their cards.' He held up the palm of his right hand, and she saw that he too bore a faint circular mark divided by four spokes. 'This gets going when you're close to one; like a compass, almost.'

Cat stared at her palm, remembering how it had burned as she'd clutched the railings, and looked into a world that shouldn't have been there. She shook her head in frustration.

'But when I met the knight, the knight being chased in Soho, I wasn't in the Arcanum – I couldn't have been. Neither was he.'

'You first saw him in the Tube, right? Well, there must've been a threshold to the Arcanum somewhere in the station. My guess is that as soon as the knight got to the Arcanum, and realised what the Ten of Swords had in store for him, he lost his nerve – and crossed right back. But it was too late, and the Knaves of Swords came after him anyway. Once you play your card, you see, you have to finish the move; the knaves'll make sure of it.'

'Ugh. From what I've seen of them, they're a right bunch of gangsters.'

Toby looked solemn. 'Knaves are players who've tried to cheat. They might have got bystanders involved or attempted to sabotage other players, caused trouble at the Lotteries…that sort of thing. They have to pay the forfeit by acting as servants to the kings and queens. In fact, I don't even think they're allowed to leave the Arcanum except on Game business. But don't worry, knaves don't bother with chancers. Nobody does.'

Cat frowned. She'd decided to trust him – she didn't have much choice – but her brain felt blurred by the enormity of what was happening. 'Did you know I was one of these chancer types right from the start? When you spoke to me at the Lottery, I mean?'

'Pretty much. I actually arrived at Temple House just behind you. I saw you hand over your invite – the Fool – but lost you after I entered the party. As you may remember, that place is pretty disorientating.'

'You seem to be a bit of an expert on it.'

'But I'm not,' he said earnestly. 'I'm an amateur, really, trying to pick up stuff here and there. That's why it's so great I met you. Chancers are *seriously* rare, but now that there's two of us…'

She laughed sourly. 'If you think I'm getting any more involved, then you're even crazier than those royals of yours.'

'What?' Toby was incredulous. 'Look, I realise you're probably still in shock and everything, but you really need to give the Arcanum a chance, to see things for yourself – there's so much more to it than what I can explain.'

'Magic? Mystery? Adventure?'

'Absolutely.' Toby didn't seem to notice the sarcasm in her voice. His cheeks were flushed and eyes bright, his breath coming in enthusiastic puffs of frosty air.

'Chancers don't have to play the cards like knights do, or serve the courts like the knaves. We're free agents. We can come and go as we please.'

'Well, I don't please. Sorry.'

'So you're going to pretend none of this has happened? You're just going to *walk away*?'

Cat eyed him coldly. 'Why not? It's got nothing to do with me.'

For once, Toby didn't shuffle or fidget, but stared back at her levelly. 'That's a load of bull and you know it.' She opened her mouth to protest but Toby swept on. 'People find their way to the Arcanum for a reason, Cat. You *chose* to get involved. You followed the Knight of Wands. You went to the Lottery. You asked your questions. When I found you in Dark Portal, don't tell me you were there to look for an encyclopaedia of Middle Earth. Because I don't think you're nearly as detached from things as you pretend to be.'

'Yeah, well, if I'd known what I was getting into I would've detached myself a hell of a lot earlier.'

'Would you? Can you look me in the eye and tell me that this isn't the most amazing thing that has ever, *will* ever, happen to you in your entire life?'

'That's not the point,' she said, but her voice was uncertain.

Toby's face was alight with missionary zeal. 'Let me

prove it to you. Come with me into the Arcanum. One quick trip. In and out. And if after that you still don't want to be involved I'll leave you alone. I swear.'

There was a long pause. 'I'll think about it,' said Cat, and then she walked away.

CHAPTER FIVE

It was still early in the afternoon when Cat got back to the flat, and she was sure she was too wired even to sit down for more than a minute at a time. But the moment she closed the door of her cupboard-sized room behind her, she sank onto her bed and into a dreamless sleep. When she woke up, groggy and disorientated, it was to find she'd been out for nearly six hours.

By the sound of it, the Saturday night revelries were already well under way: music throbbed, engines revved, cat-calls and laughter floated up from the street below. For a moment she lay there drowsily, and it was as if she was still the old Cat, the Cat from before. The feeling only lasted for a few seconds though. Knowledge came jolting back and she sat up, breathless.

'Well then,' she found herself saying out loud, 'I guess it's time I made a move of my own.'

She didn't quite know how she'd reached this decision,

but it came as a relief. *The Wondrous World of Tarot*, Toby's present, was poking out from under her bed and she gave it a contemptuous kick. Sod Toby – she didn't want a chaperone; she needed to make up her mind her own way, and on her own terms. I'll be quick, she promised herself. In and out. New energy surged through her and she found she was humming a recent chart hit in the bathroom, grinning to herself as she rummaged through the fridge. What did she need to take with her? The usual collection of wallet, keys, travel pass, phone? God, the whole thing was *mad*… 'Mad, mad, mad,' she chanted to herself as she clattered out of the flat and into the street.

After half an hour of wandering about, however, her new-found recklessness began to desert her. She kept checking her palm but the skin was unmarked. She felt cheated. If, like Toby said, thresholds weren't fixed, what if there wasn't a way into the Arcanum in this part of the city at all? The obvious thing to do would be to try Temple House again, but the remembrance of the ring of fire filled her with dread.

Then, finally, she felt it. A pins-and-needles sensation in her palm as she approached Seven Dials, a small junction between Covent Garden and Soho. The streets running off it were busy and brightly lit, and the column in the centre of the crossroads served as a gathering point for people swigging from cans and chatting on phones. She walked up to the pillar, heart thumping. It was in fact a sundial about fifteen feet high, on a circular base with shallow steps. Just above the base she saw that the mark of the wheel, three inches or so in diameter, had been carved into the stone pedestal. Now what? Toby had said a coin would just 'appear', but the only money she could find was a penny lying beside a discarded cinema ticket. Feeling slightly foolish, she gave it a flip, and didn't know whether to be relieved or disappointed when nothing happened.

Cat looked at the carving again. The closer she got to it, the more her palm tingled. Hesitantly, she reached out a finger and traced the lines of the wheel. Four spokes, and a circle. As she closed the circle, she had to snatch her hand away, as if burned, for the print of the wheel on her palm was now a glowing silver scar. Instinctively, she straightened out her hand. And then, so quickly that she didn't even have time to cry out, the circle on her flesh throbbed, merged and solidified into a disc of metal.

The metal was strange – heavy, gleaming and dark – but she recognised it all the same. It was like the counter she'd found with her invitation to Temple House, and which she'd passed to the doorkeeper. That coin, however, had been blank, whereas this was marked on one side with the icon of a sword.

Cat knew that if she hesitated now she would lose her nerve, perhaps for good. And so before she had time to think or marvel or regret, she tossed the coin, high into the air.

Though she'd thrown the coin clumsily, it still landed in the centre of her palm. The wheel there burned beneath it: in the blink of an eye, flesh and metal merged into one. The next moment, her hand was both empty and unmarked. She looked up and saw, with a sickening jolt, that the world had changed.

It appeared to be dawn, for a primrose light was just breaking overhead. After the wintry night she'd come from, the air felt softer, fresh. It was eerily quiet – no traffic, no people, not even any birdsong. She still had the sense of being in the heart of the city but without the unceasing background surge of the place, the energy generated by the comings and goings of millions of people.

Her surroundings corresponded almost exactly to the ones she'd left behind. Even the shop fronts were alike, though their signs were unpainted and the windows bare or else boarded up. And yet... Her mother had had a kaleidoscope, like a little bronze telescope, which was now Cat's. She had been fascinated by it as a kid, the way the shifting glass beads transformed into a myriad of different patterns as you turned the wheel. Looking at this other street, in this other city, was like giving the kaleidoscope the gentlest tap, the tiniest turn – the pattern of things was almost imperceptibly altered, yet irrevocably different. Like the column: on her side, the stone was a light and rather grubby grey, here it was black marble and had only four dial-faces at its top. But the carving of the wheel was the same, and when, with a trembling hand, she began to trace its lines, the burning in her hand told her the same dark coin was ready to appear, and take her home.

Cat took her hand away before tracing the final curve of the circle, and before the silvery scar on her palm could merge into metal once more. Then she clenched her jaw, lifted her chin, and stepped down from the column into the cool summer's morning of the Arcanum.

It was then that she realised she wasn't alone after all. A woman was standing under a lamppost about ten yards away, eating a chocolate bar and watching Cat through narrowed eyes. She had a shrewd, snub sort of face and was wearing a navy skirt and jacket with running shoes, like a commuter on her way home from the office. Now she tossed the chocolate wrapper to the ground and came over. 'What are you?' she challenged.

'I'm, uh…' How had Toby put it? 'I'm a chancer.'

At this, the woman's eyes widened, and she gave a bark of laughter. 'Well now,' she said, 'there's a rarity.'

'What are you, then?'

'Knight of Swords, of course. The mark on your coin could've told you that.'

So the coin didn't just flip her over to the Arcanum; it also told her which of the four courts was in play there. 'I see. So are you...do you, erm, have one of those cards?'

The woman stared at her as if she was an idiot. 'How else would I have got here? It's us knights who're dealt the cards, so we're the players the Arcanum throws up its thresholds for. It's *my* card, *my* gamble, which has made this move. You're just a bystander. One of the Game's little accidents.'

Cat ignored her sneer. 'Do you enjoy it?' she asked curiously. 'The Game, I mean?'

The Knight of Swords didn't reply at first, but stood gazing at the sky, a faraway look on her face. 'There are marvels,' she said at last. 'Things most people can only dream of: angels and demons, blood and glory... So many wonders, so many hazards, and I've prevailed every time. The truth is,' she added in a confiding tone, 'I'm on a winning streak.' She put her hand in her jacket pocket and drew out a card. 'The last card before I end my round and win my triumph. They stay blank till you change sides at the threshold. But look at it now.'

Cat backed away. She didn't much like the sound of angels and demons, nor blood and glory, for that matter.

'There's nothing to be afraid of, girl – one of the luckiest cards in the deck, it is. Six of Cups, the Reign of Past Pleasure.'

Cat reluctantly took the card. It did seem to have a faint glow about it, or perhaps that was just the hazy morning sunshine that had begun to fill the street. And the picture on it was an inviting one. Two children played in the garden of a great house. They were smiling, surrounded by jewelled cups that spilled over with flowers. The walls of the house behind them were high and golden, the sky a radiant blue. As she looked at the scene, memories of lost and half-forgotten happiness began to stir. She found she was reluctant to give it back.

'Lovely, isn't it?' said the knight, glancing up at the sundial. 'And now's the time.'

'Time…?'

'To face the odds and take my gamble. As we all must do.' She gave Cat a brisk nod, then walked down the street, to a door that Cat hadn't noticed before. It certainly wasn't there on the home side: made from ancient blackened wood, and set in a narrow strip of wall between two of the empty shop fronts. It looked as though it hadn't been opened for years. But it swung open at the Knight of Swords' touch and a moment later she was gone.

The place felt even more silent and deserted afterwards.

Cat looked back at the sundial, but it would be lame to go home now, before she'd really seen or done anything... Her anxieties had faded away; somehow, the mere sight of the card had left her with a sense of peace, of good times just around the corner. And the door had been left ajar.

Its wood was warm to the touch, as if it had been baking in the sun for a long time. Behind it, she could hear children's laughter, high and clear, and her throat ached with some nameless longing. *The Reign of Past Pleasure...* She pushed it open and stepped through.

It was as if she'd walked into the card itself. She was standing on a smooth lawn enclosed by high, golden walls. Pale flowers bloomed everywhere, their scent so rich she could almost taste it. Facing her was the front of a great and ageless house built of honey-coloured stone. Its windows glittered, but where the rest of the garden should have been reflected, there was only the blue dazzle of sky.

It was beautiful. The most beautiful place Cat had ever seen, better even than that time, years ago, when she'd been on a school trip to one of those National Trust houses with miles of park and a garden the size of a tennis court just for roses. But even so, she wasn't able to concentrate on it properly. What she really wanted was waiting for her in the house, calling her name, and the further she walked into the garden, the larger the place seemed to grow. She knew that this didn't make sense; that there was a city surrounding its walls, and another city somehow beyond that, but it didn't matter. For the first time since the strangeness of the Game of Triumphs had begun, she felt that she really could be in a dream.

At last, she reached the terrace. There was a glass-fronted door ahead but, like the windows, the view it reflected was disorientating; fragments of brightness where her own image should have been. As she walked up to it, the sweetness of the flowers and the humming of the bees, the warm blue air and distant laughter, surged over and through her. And somehow the glass surged too, a liquid dazzle that sparkled outwards and drew her in.

Then, suddenly, she was home. Her first home, her *real* home, with her mum and dad. The little terrace house that had faded to the memory of a memory, except for a few snapshots and a fleeting reference or two of Bel's. She was sitting at her mum's feet in the lounge, and there was a toy truck nearby, but it didn't interest her much because she was busy peering at the carpet. It had very fascinating swirls of cream and brown. Like ice cream. She pushed her finger into the nap and then sucked its tip hopefully, just in case. Something tickled and it was her mum, bending to kiss her, her long hair swinging over Cat's face, shiny and soft and smelling like apples.

'Where's my kitty cat?'

She stumbled to her unsteady toddler's feet and ran to Daddy, who was standing at the door and swung her up and blew into her neck until she was breathless with squeals. And over his shoulder, she could see the hallway and the little strip of garden beyond, with her orange plastic slide and Mummy's flowers. Only they weren't there, there was just a muddle, shining, and so bright it hurt to look at. But it didn't matter, nothing mattered, because she was safe at home with Mummy and Daddy like they always were and would always be, always, always, always…

And then it was Christmas, Christmas with a real live tree all goldy-glittery with chocolate money, and a rainbow of cards on every shelf. The money and the cards reminded her of something, but then Mummy came over with lots of boxes, and she forgot again, because the paper was slippery and rustling and she could stomp through it like puddles…and after that it was her birthday, and more boxes, with a fat pink cake and candles she wasn't allowed to touch but were the prettiest things she'd ever seen, so Daddy lit them again, and blew them out, and lit them, and blew them out, again and again and again, just for her.

So many times…some of them flashing past quick as lightning, others languorously prolonged, but all of them, always, the best and most perfect… Sometimes she was

Kitty, tumbling about on the floor, and at others she was Cat, watching herself from a very great distance. Something about this bothered her, but only a little, like an itch she couldn't reach. She knew that if she shut her mind to the itching it would go away, but this didn't feel right, almost as if she needed the itch to be there...

And at last there came an afternoon when she was playing in Mummy and Daddy's room, making hidey-houses under the bed. But someone had been there before her, doing their own hiding: a matchbox tucked into the slats, with something round and dark and shiny inside. Secret treasure!

There was something important about this treasure, something she wanted to remember, and so she took the coin to the window, though the light was usually too bright and muddly to look at. But she did it anyway, and this time she looked through the glass to somewhere different, somewhere wrong. And after that the shining became so bright it hurt all over, and she dropped the coin and squeezed her eyes shut and put her hands over her ears but even that didn't help because when she opened them again everything had changed.

At once, she knew something terrible was going to happen, so terrible she couldn't bear it. She tried to tell her mummy and daddy but they didn't understand, they kept on tickling her with shiny-soft hair and swinging her over their shoulders and bringing her boxes and blowing out candles again and again and all the time she knew the terrible nameless thing was coming, just round the corner, and there was nothing she could do. Until there she was, Kitty, huddled on the stairs hours past bedtime, and watching through a gap in the door as three people talked in the lounge.

'This isn't a game,' Mummy was saying, and her voice had a crack in it.

'It is the *only* Game,' replied a voice Kitty didn't know. A murmuring voice, with a slight stammer. 'And I intend to w-win it.'

'What do you mean by that?' her daddy asked.

'I mean that I'm going to t-take what's due to me,' said the stranger. 'Starting with the c-coin. So you see, the odds are ag-gainst you.'

Then Mummy and Daddy began speaking at once, high and quick.

'Please. There's been some mistake,' Mummy was saying. 'We can't—' And Daddy began to shout, shouting at someone she couldn't see, but there was a flash and two cracks and a burning smell and Kitty crouched on the stairs and Cat floating at a great distance both screamed. Because hair had spilled across the carpet, the hair that smelled like apples and the carpet with the ice-cream swirls, both of which were now speckled with hot sharp red. And her screaming went on and on and into a terrible silence that became a surge of blackness and blindness and splintering glass.

The house reared up behind her, grey-faced, its windows gaping darkly. The stones of the terrace were cracked, and greasy with rain. She began to sob. She was still sobbing as she lurched across the tangle of yellowing grass and briar that had once been a lawn, and shouldered her way through the shards of rotting wood that had once been a door. And she sobbed yet harder as she stumbled up to the sundial and spun her cold hard coin, up, over and away.

CHAPTER SIX

For a while, it didn't look as if the bouncer at the Palais Luxe was going to let her in. Not that she could blame him: quite apart from the fact that anyone under the age of eighteen wasn't supposed to set foot inside a casino, she was finding it extraordinarily difficult to string any sort of sentence together. But after repeating Bel's name for the fifth or sixth time, he did a series of mutters into his walkie-talkie and, suddenly, Bel was standing in the musty lobby. Saying her name. Asking if she was all right. Was she hurt, was she sick, was the flat—

'No,' she said dazedly. 'I'm not hurt. I just…I really need to talk to you.'

Bel gave her a long look and a short nod. 'In you come.'

The bouncer was still grumbling about regulations and licences but Bel shooed him away with one hand, and hustled Cat up the stairs with the other. The next thing she knew, Bel was shepherding her into the tiny kitchen by Greg's office. There she set about making two mugs of sweet, dusty-tasting tea. It was only after she'd watched Cat take an obedient gulp that she spoke again. 'Now then,' she said. 'What's all this about?'

Cat stared at the clock on the wall. One forty-five. She had been in the Arcanum for less than three hours. The clock ticked, the tea steamed, murmurs and exclamations came from the gaming floor below. Cat had hundreds, thousands, of thing she wanted to say, all of them impossible.

'I…I want to know about Mum and Dad.'

'Your…?' Bel frowned. Whatever she'd been expecting, it wasn't this.

'Caroline and Adam Harper. My parents.' The clock ticked on: *twitch-tock, twitch-tock.* 'Because they didn't die in a car accident, did they? Somebody shot them.'

Twitch-tock, twitch-tock, twitch-tock. Bel made a small muffled sound. She put her hand to her throat. 'How do—? Where—? Who've you been talking to?'

'So it's true,' Cat said dully. She saw the spill of the hair and the bitter blood, swirls of brown and cream. The Arcanum hadn't lied.

Bel's hand was still fluttering at her neck. 'I'm sorry. Cat, I… God, I – I thought it would be better, you see. Better for you not to know. You were so small…'

'Tell me what happened.'

'Christ.' Underneath the fluorescent strip that lit the kitchen, Bel's face was sallow and tired; the tight polyester shirt she was wearing had damp-patches under the arms. She took a wavering breath. 'It was a burglary, see. A burglary gone wrong. Some smackhead went robbing, off his head most likely, and lost it. Your mum and dad… Well, they got in the way.'

'Did – did they catch the person who did it?'

'No. Could've been any old street scum. Odds on, whoever did it was lying dead in a ditch before the year was out. That's what I like to think, anyway.'

Cat pushed her mug away, feeling sick.

Bel went on quickly, nervously. 'Maybe I should've told you the truth, but how do you explain something like that to a *three*-year-old? I didn't want to go scaring you witless about men with guns and whatnot. Jeez, I was practically a kid myself… I did mean to tell you, when you got older, like, but you seemed to be doing all right and I thought, best leave it. Best to let it go.'

Twitch-tock, twitch-tock, twitch-tock.

'But I saw it happen,' Cat mumbled. 'I *saw* them get killed, Bel. I – I remember now.'

Bel was very gentle. 'No, love,' she said. 'No, you couldn't have. You were staying round a neighbour's that night, thank God. You probably just…I dunno… overheard someone talking about it when you were little.

Must've been repressed all these years and now…well, something set it off. False memory and that. The brain can play all sorts of tricks.'

Cat found she was crying again, a dry, almost mechanical heaving, that nonetheless she couldn't stop. After that things became blurred. She had a hazy impression of Bel in whispered conversation by the door, of being gathered up and taken back to the flat, where Bel undressed her and tucked her up in bed like a little kid, murmuring her name over and over, like a lullaby. And although Bel's hug smelled of cheap perfume and cigarettes, it was the scent of apples that drifted after her into dream.

The next morning was the most painful waking she had ever had.

The truth was, if she'd found out about her parent's deaths in the ordinary course of things – overheard gossip, an ancient newspaper clipping – she wasn't sure how badly it would have affected her. She would have been angry, of course, and sad, but it would almost have been like overhearing a story from somebody else's life. After all, she'd worked hard on forgetting her loss, until she became used to telling people that she couldn't miss what she'd never known. She'd almost believed it, too. But the Six of Cups had given back memories that were too glowing and exaggerated, too abundant with love, to ever be lost again.

And if she trusted those memories about Christmas trees and cake and the rest of it, she had to trust the other one. The one she shouldn't – couldn't – have. The memory of the third person she'd heard in the lounge that final night, the man with the stammer. *It is the only Game. And I intend to w-win it.*

Cat knew that whatever the police or Bel or anyone else believed, her parents hadn't been killed by some thieving druggie. It had been done by someone in control of themselves and the situation. Someone looking for an Arcanum coin.

If she closed her eyes, she could see the cosy darkness under her parents' bed again, and relive the thrill of discovery as her chubby toddler's fingers closed on the matchbox with a treasure inside. What was the coin doing there? Her own parents, players in the Game? The idea sickened her. Because their life had been *perfect*, the Six of Cups had proved that. Caroline, Adam and Kitty Harper had everything they could ever want. Her parents wouldn't risk all that happiness in pursuit of some weird otherworldly prize.

No. Toby had told her that invitations to the Game turned up at random, so in all probability, she decided, one or other of them had stumbled on the coin without knowing what it was. *There's been some mistake,* that's what her mother had said. How the stranger knew about the coin, and what had become of it, was another matter entirely.

Three-year-old Kitty and fifteen-year-old Cat…neither of them would have seen the murder if it wasn't for the kaleidoscopic shiftings of the Arcanum. And because the crime had been committed in the Game's name, by one of its players, then Cat's only hope of resolving it lay in the Arcanum, she was sure of it. If she wanted to go on looking for answers, that's where they were.

Seven Dials at eight o'clock on a Sunday morning had the same air of abandonment as it had on the other side of the threshold. The shop fronts and windows were all shut up and the streets deserted apart from the occasional taxi, or all-night reveller plodding off for breakfast and bed. When Cat approached the column she found she was shaking all over. Grief and anger, but longing, too: the dreadful hope of returning to that golden house. Of going home.

So when her palm remained as blank as the stone on the column, she refused to believe it. But no matter how many times she circled the sundial, alternately cursing and pleading under her breath, nothing changed. In the end she had to face the one thing – and obvious possibility – that she hadn't prepared for. The threshold had gone, taking the Six of Cups with it.

Toby wasn't as irrepressibly pleased to hear from her as she'd expected. In fact, their initial exchange was a series of grunts on his part. Cat thought she heard muttering in the background. 'A *friend*,' Toby said, away from the phone. 'Yes, I *do* have them, OK?' The background voice grew querulous in tone. 'It's none of your business who I—' Crackle of static. Footsteps, a slammed door. 'Sorry about that. Parents, y'know?'

Cat bit her lip. 'Uh, anyway…I was thinking about yesterday and stuff and I think maybe you're right. About going into the Arcanum, I mean.'

This time, his response was as excitable as she'd been expecting. 'So,' he said in a hopeful rush, 'do you want to come over to mine? We can throw some ideas around, draw up an action plan…'

Well, maybe that wasn't such a bad idea. If she was going to get any further, she needed a native guide. And right now, Toby was all she had. She took down his directions and agreed to meet him in an hour.

'Just one other thing.'

'Yes?'

'How do most people join the Game? If us chancers are really rare, how do normal players – knights – get involved?'

'Aha!' He sounded pleased with the question. 'There've always been rumours about the Game: hints and gossip, speculation on the internet, even. Plenty of people spend their whole lives trying to find a way in. The trouble is, invitations turn up indiscriminately, so it's completely down to luck.'

'First you find a spooky card and then, hey presto, a coin?'

'That's the idea. Chancers are invited with the Triumph of the Fool, but a knight begins with the Triumph of Eternity – to show the eternal nature of the Game, I suppose. The card only gets you as far as Temple House, however; it's passing the coin to the doorkeeper that lets you into the Arcanum.

'I heard there's one book on this one shelf in the Bodleian Library in Oxford, right, which has the Triumph of Eternity tucked in its pages. And there's a story that every time a certain painting comes on the art market, whoever buys it finds an invitation stuck on the back. I don't know if either rumour's true. On the other hand, there must be people who get a card and coin but don't follow them up.' He gave a disbelieving laugh. 'As if a ticket to the Arcanum was just another bit of junk mail!'

Well, that might account for how an Arcanum coin came to be under her parents' bed. Even though it didn't quite explain why the coin had been placed in a matchbox, and tucked so carefully into the slats… After she said goodbye to Toby, Cat stared at her palm, thinking of the throb and burn that conjured metal out of flesh, and spun the ordinary world out of reach. What was junk to some was a prize worth killing for to others.

Bel shuffled into the kitchen just as Cat was getting ready to go out for the second time that morning. She didn't look as if she'd slept much and she wore a hesitant, most un-Bel-like smile. Would Cat like to get a coffee? Do some shopping together? Go for a walk? Or…? Cat felt bad, saying thanks, but no, she kind of fancied being on her own for a bit. But as she went to leave, Bel hugged her, fierce and hard, and suddenly things were better.

Toby lived at the top of a red brick mansion block in north London. As Cat stepped out of the creaking lift she prepared herself for olde-worlde splendour, but the flat that Toby showed her into, although large, felt cluttered and uncared for. Books were everywhere, stacked high in teetering piles; dirty mugs, bric-a-brac and bundles of paper covered every surface. 'Writers, both of 'em,' said Toby, with offhand pride. 'It's OK, though. Ma's gone to the library and Pa's holed up in his study. We won't be disturbed.'

Cat followed Toby through the hallway into his bedroom. It was much tidier than the rest of the flat, with pride of place given to a table-top model landscape on which a horde of miniature knights and goblins were arranged in battle lines. Some kind of war-game, she guessed, remembering the figurines from Dark Portal. There was a shelf of books, most but not all sci-fi and fantasy titles, and a collection of 1950s B-movie posters on the walls. Like Toby's quirky clothes, however, Cat felt there was something a little studied about the display.

Her attention moved from a poster for *Revenge of the Mutant Swamp Blob!* – buxom babes vs toxic slime – to a black-and-white print of a fantastic city. The city was a labyrinth of crazy angles and dizzy perspectives, where lizard-like creatures scuttled up stairs that led to nowhere, windows opened to impossible views, and figures sleepwalked off precipices.

'A postcard from the Arcanum?' she asked flippantly.

But Toby took the question at face value. 'Could be. The Game of Triumphs has been going for centuries. All sorts of people have played, so why not Escher?'

The idea that this thing had been going on throughout history sent a chill down Cat's spine. Still, she reassured herself, this was exactly why she'd come over. Toby was the expert.

He was looking at her expectantly. 'OK, so when and where shall we start? And what do you think we should take with us?'

'Hang on. Before we start planning any day trips, I want to know exactly what I'm getting into. Basic stuff right through to Advance Level.'

'Oh, right. Good thinking.' Toby cleared his throat importantly and put on what she was already thinking of as his 'lecture face'. 'Basically, then, a knight has to play four cards to complete a round and win a triumph. The hardest card will be dealt by the Game Master in possession of that triumph, because they obviously want the knight to fail. And of course the luckiest card will be dealt by the Game Master of the knight's own court, because they want him to win.

'The other two GMs – the ones who aren't in direct competition for a triumph – could either give the knight another difficult card or another nice one. It depends on their wider strategy. The thing is, a knight won't know what card he's been given until he's crossed a threshold and the Arcanum brings it to life. That's what creates the move. Until then, the cards stay blank.'

Cat nodded. She'd already worked this much out. 'Fine. What I'm not so sure of, though, is how the cards are organised. Because there are two types, aren't there: triumph cards like the Devil and the Moon and suchlike, and the cards which are named after the courts. Six of Cups, Five of Wands, Blah of Bleurgh…'

'That's right. The triumph cards are collectively known

as the Greater Arcana, while all the court cards belong to the Lesser Arcana.'

Cat groaned.

'It's not that hard to remember,' he told her. 'Triumph cards are Greater, because they're prizes as well as moves. Court cards are Lesser, because they're just moves, and you don't win anything from them.'

'Triumphs are moves as *well* as prizes? Does that mean a knight can be dealt a triumph by a king or queen, as one of the four cards they have to play in the Arcanum?'

'Oh yes. The power a triumph represents only becomes a prize after a player's won their round. Then when they leave the Game, a share of its power is theirs to keep.'

Cat thought back to the prize-giving after the Lottery, when the Knight of Pentacles had been given an iron die by the King of Swords. *Once it passes the threshold of Temple House, the powers of the Devil will be yours.* She knew now that this wasn't a symbolic gesture, and that the Devil, whose picture in *The Wondrous World of Tarot* was of a monstrous half-goat, half-god, was a reward, not a punishment. A knight who won its triumph won the hedonistic power the Devil characterised: the freedom to indulge in all the pleasures of the flesh, all the thrills of addiction, and never have to pay the consequences.

'So apart from triumph cards representing prizes, is there any difference between them and the court cards?'

'Well, the court cards don't change hands, so you can only get dealt a pentacles card from the Queen of Pentacles, a sword card from the King of Swords, and so on. And the knaves can't enter moves involving triumphs. But when you're a knight playing a round, I should think your only concern is how lucky or unlucky a card is, not whether it belongs to the Greater or the Lesser Arcana.'

Cat found that she was getting interested in spite of herself. 'All right. Let's get on to the players. Say a knight wants to be a king. How'd he get promoted? Is it even possible?'

'*Everything's* possible in the Arcanum.' Toby lowered his voice in the way he did when he was trying to come over all dark and mysterious. 'The kings and queens claim to be bound by the rules of the Game along with everyone else. So there's a rumour that if you catch one of them cheating, you can take their place. The most popular theory, though, is that to become a Game Master you have to win all twenty-one triumphs in the Greater Arcana – but give every single one of them up as you go along.'

Cat was beginning to see how some people might think that winning a triumph was worth the risk of the Game. But she could hardly imagine what it would take to win *one* triumph, let alone the whole of the Greater Whatever.

'Mind you,' Toby continued, 'once you got to GM level,

you wouldn't have much need for love and fame and the rest of it. Not when you have the power to lord it over the Arcanum. And who knows what the ultimate aim of the Game is, anyway? Perhaps it doesn't have one. Perhaps something so random can't ever be properly lost or won.'

She almost laughed at this. 'Random has nothing to do with it! Not with those four royal psychopaths pulling everyone's strings.'

'They aren't in total control, though,' Toby said earnestly. 'That's the *point*. Yes, they deal the cards and, yes, they enforce the rules. But they can't win the triumphs by themselves: it's up to the knights in their court. And how the cards come to life, and how the knight reacts to them, is completely out of their hands. What if a knight calls a Lottery? What if he finds an ace? What if a chancer intervenes in a move?'

Cat's head was spinning. It was all too much to take in – and she still had so many more questions to ask. Meantime, Toby rambled on.

'We're part of a noble tradition,' he was saying dreamily. 'An immortal contest! Poets, soldiers, madmen, geniuses…'

'Madmen sounds about right,' she retorted. 'What *is* it with you people? The Knight of Swords was the same. Gushing on about what an almighty privilege it all is.'

'Knight? What knight?'

'Oh. Yeah. The thing is…I went into the Arcanum yesterday.'

'You went *without me*?' He sat there gawping at her, all shocked and wounded-looking. 'But I thought we—'

'Look, I just wanted to see it for myself, OK. No big deal.'

'What happened?' he asked breathlessly. 'What was it like? What did you do? What was the card in play?'

'The woman I met, Swords, had been given the Six of Cups.'

'A lucky card! No *way*! Isn't that the one to do with good times and old memories and stuff? Did you…?'

Cat had no intention of sharing what had happened with Toby. All she wanted from him was information: how to play the Game, how to get back into the Six of Cups, and how to navigate what she found there. She struggled to sound offhand. 'It was a trip down memory lane all right. Like being a little kid again. Tell you the truth, it's a bit of a blur.'

Toby's face glowed. 'Sounds *amazing*. I can't wait for my first go.'

'What do you mean, "go"?'

'My first trip into the Arcanum, of course.'

Cat thought she had misheard. Or misunderstood. 'But you've been doing this for ages. I mean, you first saw me at that Lottery party.'

'Yeah, but the thing about Temple House is that it's neutral ground.'

'I don't understand.'

'Neither one side nor the other, remember? I haven't tried my luck in the Arcanum proper, not like you.'

She still didn't believe it. 'But – but – you must have...you know how everything works, what to do...'

Toby smiled modestly. '*Theoretically*, yes, I like to think I've worked things out. You can pick up a lot from hanging around the Lotteries and I've spent ages looking for clues and pointers and stuff. I've even raised a coin at a threshold, though I haven't gone as far as actually throwing it – the time's never been quite right. But now there's two of us, we can go in together, be a proper team.' He looked at her solemnly. 'It was lucky you had such a nice gamble on your first time. You could have got into real trouble.'

It was all she could to do to stop herself from hitting him. Instead, she got to her feet, face taut with anger. 'What's the matter?' Toby asked, sounding genuinely shocked. 'Don't be mad. Look, I'm sorry if you got the wrong idea—'

'Only because you gave it to me. I thought you had answers. Experience. I thought you were a person I could trust.'

'But you can! We're in this together, Cat.'

'No we're not.' The surreal city on the wall, the fantasy

books, the toy armies of knights and goblins… Never mind his elaborate explanations: the Arcanum really was just a game to him. An adventurous daydream. And what about those big motivational speeches about taking a chance and seizing the day and all that junk? He's nothing but a cheat, she thought furiously, a gutless, hypocritical, lying cheat. 'You have no idea,' she hissed, '*no idea* what it's like in there.'

But Toby didn't rise to the bait. Instead, he was looking at her curiously. 'The Six of Cups…it must have uncovered something. Something buried in your past that you don't understand. And you think the Arcanum is your only hope of making sense of it. Am I right?'

'What I may or may not have seen is nothing to do with you.'

'Even though you came to me for help?'

'That was only because you'd conned me into thinking you were some kind of Game Guru.'

'I can still help, Cat.'

'Can you? Can you look me in the eye and say that the little how-to guide you just gave me is anything but guesswork?'

'Er, no, but it's very *educated* guess—'

'Can you tell me how to find a threshold that's vanished? How to get into the Six of Cups again? What to do when I get there?'

'Um, not exact—'

'No. You can't help me. Nobody can. I don't trust the Arcanum. I don't trust the Game. I don't know how any of it works or what I'm doing. And neither do you.'

'C'mon, give me a break! Please!' When Cat moved towards the door he stood to block her path and looked at her pleadingly. 'Wait. What if I said I could find you someone who does? Know how to get back into your card, I mean.' Cat paused and he carried on hurriedly. 'Because there's this girl I know from Temple House. She's the only other chancer I've come across – except for you, obviously.'

'So?'

'Well, from something she said I reckon she's been in the Game for years, even though she can't be much older than us.'

'Then why aren't the two of you a team? I would've thought you'd be wearing matching T-shirts by now.'

'Because she's even more stroppy than you are! Seriously, I have tried, but she doesn't want to know. Maybe if you tell her your story, though, and ask for help or whatever, she'll change her mind. Female bonding and all that.'

Cat gave an exasperated snort, but she moved away from the door. 'All right.' She thought for few minutes, while Toby watched her anxiously. 'All right. It's better

113

than nothing…I suppose. D'you know where to find her?'

'As a matter of fact,' he said, 'I do. How do you fancy going to church?'

Toby was confident that he'd come up with a winning plan. The girl in question, Flora, attended Mass at a Catholic church in west London every Sunday at five o'clock, and according to Toby, making contact would be a simple matter of intercepting her as she came out. When Cat asked him how he knew to find her there, he looked a bit shifty and confessed that he 'might have' followed her 'on a couple of occasions'.

'You stalked her, you mean.'

'No! There's nothing *sleazy* about it. It was just …research.'

She narrowed her eyes. 'Have you tried to follow me? As part of your "research"?'

'Um, well, after the first time in Dark Portal, I was kind of curious to see where you lived. But don't worry – Soho's such a warren I soon lost track.'

Cat sighed. She was still angry, but part of her recognised that she was being unfair. The fact remained that Toby did seem to know a great deal about the cards and how they were played, even if his knowledge was mostly hypothetical. She wondered what this church-going chancer would be like and if she somehow managed to combine religious zealotry with the dark arts of the Arcanum.

Toby was vague on the subject, either because he didn't really know the girl or because he didn't want to put her off. One thing was for sure: if she'd been casually flitting in and out of the Arcanum for years, she was bound to be odd. Cat found it hard to imagine why anyone would get involved in this world any more than they had to.

But on the way home, she was confronted by just how difficult it was to keep a distance from the Game, even if she had wanted to.

It was lunchtime, and the north London streets were almost as quiet as the ones around Seven Dials that morning. As her bus wheezed to a halt at the traffic lights at the beginning of a long grey road to Holborn, Cat found that she was sitting parallel to the first floor of an office. It was part of an ugly modern block whose front was mostly made up of panels of tinted glass. On a Sunday afternoon, the place should have been deserted. But there were two people in there. A pale blonde and an older black man.

With trembling hands, Cat pressed the request-stop-button. She was able to get off the bus only a little way down from the office; a few minutes later, she was standing outside the main entrance, peering up at the first floor. Could she have been mistaken? But no, the woman had moved nearer to the window, and was looking out over the street. She was wearing dark glasses and a white suit. It was unquestionably Odile.

The Queen of Cups tilted her head so that she was staring directly down at Cat. Then she turned back to speak to her companion, brushing something – a speck of dust, perhaps – off her sleeve as she did so. The gesture struck Cat as deliberately contemptuous.

Something snapped. At once, all the anger and fear and confusion of the last few days came crashing back. She began to repeatedly jab the bell for the main reception. After a while she began to hammer at the door, interspersing kicks with obscenities. Then there was a click, and somebody buzzed her in.

This was the last thing she expected. Her assault on the door was an act of protest; it hadn't occurred to her that she might actually be admitted. And now here she was, once again hovering on a doorstep she was half-afraid to cross. But the thought of those other entrances, the treachery of their thresholds, only made her more defiant. She marched through the reception and up to the first floor.

It was a big open-plan office, furnished in shades of beige, its blocks of desks heaped with papers, mugs and Post-it notes waiting forlornly for Monday morning. In the centre of the room, the Queen of Cups and the King of Wands were observing one of the monitors. '…I think she would be unwise to make a break for it,' Odile was saying. 'The Emperor's not even reached the river.'

Cat saw that all the computer screens in the office were filled with images of indistinct shapes moving through fuzz and crackle. Scenes from the Arcanum, presumably, though she couldn't tell if they were of separate moves or different views of the same move. From the tingling of her palm, she sensed a threshold was near.

'I hope whoever it is is giving you a run for your money,' she said.

Leisurely, they turned to look at her. The black king and the white queen. Like two pieces on a chessboard – and just as inscrutable.

'Not at this juncture,' Ahab replied, heavy and hard as granite. 'But things could change. It appears that another of your kind has arrived on the scene.'

Cat glanced at the nearest monitor, where the formerly impenetrable static cleared enough for her to see a figure walking in some kind of rocky landscape. A male figure. Another of your kind…did that mean another chancer? Did that mean *Toby*? Perhaps after she'd left, he'd gone out and – but no, this person looked taller than Toby, and moved differently. A long-legged, slouching sort of walk, which nevertheless had a sense of purpose about it.

'Ah yes,' said Odile in her light, precise voice. 'I remember. He claims to be in pursuit of one of your knights.'

'It appears he is persistent, if nothing else.'

Cat's bravado was already beginning to seep away. Still, she was determined not to let it show. 'Gripping stuff. Tell me, how's the State of Play shaping up these days?'

'As of this round, the advantage lies with Swords, though Pentacles are only two triumphs behind,' Odile replied coolly. 'Cups gained one triumph but lost another. Wands follow in fourth place.'

'And what happens when Swords nabs all the triumphs?'

'Naturally, the King of Swords would be the one and only Game Master. As the single ruler of the Arcanum, he would direct the course of Fortune itself, and decide other players' fates however he chose.'

Odile didn't seem much concerned by the prospect, however. Her next words explained why.

'The scenario is purely speculative,' she said. 'Should one court show signs of being over-dominant, the other three unite against it.'

'See, this is what I don't understand,' said Cat, struggling to keep her voice steady. 'Your little competition doesn't count for squat. None of it matters – not to you, anyhow. You're not the poor saps risking life and sanity out there. It's just point-scoring for you lot. One-upmanship. What's the point of a game that can't be won?'

'Oh, the Game can be won,' Ahab replied seriously. 'It is the founding principle of the Arcanum.'

'But she just said that whenever one of you starts to be top dog, the other three gang up to stop them!'

'Until now, certainly. But who's to say what the next turn of the Wheel might bring? I am not the first King of Wands, nor, perhaps, the last. The Game is old, its players countless. Other means of winning might have been known once, and then lost, or simply transformed with time. Victory might require a single cataclysmic change in the State of Play, or else an imperceptible series of small ones.

'Yet this we know: a time will come when one Game Master surpasses all others. And once they have won, a new Game will begin, under their sole rule.'

Ahab's austere manner hadn't got any less intimidating, but it struck Cat that in one respect, at least, the kings and queens weren't all that different from the punters at the Luxe. They too were hooked on the lure of the big win that was always just around the corner. 'I see. You four reckon that if you stay in the Game long enough, the odds'll change.'

Odile pushed her glasses to the back of her head. It was

the first time Cat had seen her without them; the eyes revealed were a milky blue so light they were almost colourless. Set in the perfect pallor of her face, the effect was uncanny.

'The odds are of little account. Even if none of us are to have the final victory, our place in the contest is reward enough. For as long as we reign our courts – and a Game Master does not age – the whole Arcanum is our chequer-board. That is a prize above any triumph.' She moistened her lips delicately. 'Though I imagine you might feel differently…'

And suddenly all the monitors were showing pictures of her, Cat, standing before the door to the garden in the Six of Cups. This time the image was in colour and crystal clear. The expression on her face as she moved across the lawn and towards the house – her glow of hopeful happiness – was somehow shameful in its intensity.

The picture moved to a brown and cream swirly carpet. A pink birthday cake. Her mother's face, smiling, as she reached out her arms. A hand raising a gun.

Cat let out an animal whimper. She reached out, futilely, to touch the screen. And as she did so, the blur of static returned with an ear-splitting crackle.

'You *bastards*,' she choked.

Ahab regarded her levelly. 'Do not make the mistake of thinking the tricks and truths that you see in the Arcanum have anything to do with us. We may umpire the Game, but the Arcanum works according to its own mysteries. What you find in them is your affair.'

Odile put her hand up to her mouth, making a small smothered sound. Laughter. They were toying with her, that was all. Cat had achieved nothing by being let in here; in fact, she'd only succeeded in giving them yet more power over her, as they reeled her in with their ghostly screens and their enigmatic comments. And now they were watching, waiting, for her to crumble.

It was at that point that Cat made a resolution.

Enough.

No more tears, no more dramatics. She wouldn't give them the satisfaction. Not now, not ever. She was going to leave these people with her head high and her step steady. Grief and rage would be replaced by cold hard calm. Only then would she be able to do what she had to do.

Whatever it takes and whatever it costs, I will get my answers, Cat told herself as she walked out of the building. Starting with the girl at the church.

CHAPTER SEVEN

Cat was getting the hang of navigating London, but on her way to St Bernadine's she got off at the wrong Tube stop and arrived at the church nearly fifteen minutes later than she and Toby had agreed.

She found him hovering by the railings, his tweed jacket accessorised by a skull-and-crossbones beanie and an immense purple-striped scarf. 'I was beginning to think you weren't coming,' he said plaintively. 'And that maybe it was a mistake not to get here early and actually go to the service.'

'Please. There's a limit to the number of creepy ancient cults I can cope with in the space of one weekend.'

Somewhat to her surprise, he laughed. 'You know, when you're not being uptight, you're quite funny.'

She thought that was a bit of a cheek, coming from someone as twitchy as Toby, but she let it pass. And in the next minute, the doors to the church were opened and people started straggling out into the courtyard.

St Bernadine's was in a smart residential district and built in the elaborate Gothic style beloved by Christmas cards and biscuit tins. Its congregation was mainly elderly, all were well-heeled, and Cat was uncomfortably aware of how out of place the two of them looked. It didn't help that Toby had edged behind a nearby postbox, and was combining chewing his nails with peering around in a furtive manner.

'That's her,' he whispered excitedly, nudging Cat in the direction of an elegant middle-aged couple and a blonde girl who had just come out of the door. But now that the moment had come, Cat found herself overwhelmed by the sheer embarrassment of the situation. Staking out a church! What was she supposed to do now? Rush up to this stranger and start babbling about the Wondrous World of Tarot?

Making contact, however, was easier than she'd expected. It was nearly Christmas, the service had been well-attended, and people were disposed to linger over the season's greetings and farewells. While their target's parents stayed to talk to the priest, she went ahead to wait by the railings. Cat seized her chance.

''Scuse me,' she said, 'but are you Flora?'

The girl turned and gave a cautious smile. 'Can I help you?' She was blandly pretty; blue-eyed, blonde, with a small heart-shaped face, and was wearing a long wool coat with a fur collar. Cat thought the fur was probably real. She looked the type.

Toby cleared his throat. 'Uh, hello there. I – uh – you remember me, right? Toby? And this is Cat.'

'Toby,' repeated the girl vaguely. 'Oh yes…I thought you looked familiar.' There was an awkward pause. She glanced over at her parents but they were still deep in conversation. The pause lengthened.

'Sorry to interrupt and that,' said Cat, 'and I know we haven't got much time, but I was wondering if maybe… since we all… Well, it's about the Game.'

'And what game is that?' asked Flora, knitting her brows in polite bewilderment.

Cat's eyes flicked to her right hand. Flora was wearing gloves. She tried again, more brusquely this time. 'Look, I know you don't know me and there's no reason why you should help, but Toby here says you know a lot about the Arcanum and I was wondering—'

'I'm frightfully sorry,' said Flora, with what sounded like sincerity, 'but there seems to be some mistake.'

'I don't think so. We all know what I'm talking about.'

'You've got the wrong person. I'm sorry I can't help.'

Cat met her eyes. Their expression was as cool and steady as her own.

'Everything all right here, sweetheart?'

A distinguished-looking man with greying hair and an easy smile had just arrived. 'I'm fine, thanks, Daddy.' Flora twisted a strand of honey-blonde hair around her finger. 'Let's go.'

'That's what she's always like,' said Toby gloomily, as soon as they were alone. 'All glossy and impenetrable.'

Cat grunted. Although she didn't want to admit it, Flora had impressed her. There was steel behind the sweetness. Even without Toby's introduction, Cat felt that she would have recognised her as someone who had also walked the Arcanum's streets, and that an implicit acknowledgement of this had passed between them. 'It's not over. If she won't talk to us here, she can't keep playing dumb among the wands and cups and whatsits. You said you first saw her in Temple House, right?'

'Yes. She's nearly always there for the Lotteries.'

'Then we'll try that next. But – wait – how will we know when one's happening?'

'Aha…sooner than you'd think. Look at your palm.'

'It's normal. There's nothing there.'

'Look at it. Focus.'

Cat stared at where the sign of wheel had been imprinted on her flesh. She found that by concentrating, she could bring it up through her own will: a grey circle, faint as smudged ink. But this time, the four spokes had been replaced with an 'X' in the centre.

'Fortune's the tenth triumph in the deck. Clever, huh?' Toby's expression was as smug as if he'd put the mark on her hand himself. 'You'll get into the habit of checking for it, after a while. And it's much easier than signing up to a mailing list.'

There was just no escape, Cat thought, rubbing her right palm resentfully. Even when she couldn't see or feel it, the knowledge that the mark and coin of the Arcanum was always there, *lurking*, set her on edge.

'Lotteries are fairly frequent,' Toby was saying, 'but even so, another one coming so soon after—'

'Let me get this straight. There's another of these gigs tonight and you reckon Flora will be there?'

'Most likely.'

'Then why the hell didn't you say so before? Duh! All this time we've wasted skulking in churchyards!'

But Toby looked troubled. 'The thing is…Flora…well, she's different when she's in the Game. The Arcanum brings out different sides to people. Hidden sides. I'm not sure it would be such a good idea—'

'Whoa there. *You* were the one who was so desperate to recruit some buddies to the cause, but now we have a chance to make a contact you're bottling out on me?'

Toby flushed. 'I never said anything about bottling out.'

'Fine. In that case I'll see you outside Temple House at eight.'

This time it was Toby who was late. His parents had been delayed leaving for a book reading, and he was in full-fret about being back in time for their return.

Cat had scant sympathy. She herself was feeling guilty about going out again since Bel, who had Sundays off, had proposed a girls' night in and had even arranged to borrow Greg's DVD player. And yet when Cat said she was off to the cinema with someone from school, she got the sense that Bel was relieved. The emotions of last night were too raw for either of them to feel entirely comfortable around each other.

Not that she shared any of this with Toby. She wasn't planning to report her encounter with Ahab and Odile, either. It was her own affair – if he wanted to help her, well and good. That didn't mean she was under any obligation to spill her secrets, or confide feelings that were better left undisturbed.

But as soon as she and Toby turned into Mercury Square, all other preoccupations were forgotten. It was like Friday all over again. Warm light spilled onto the pavement, the hum of talk and laughter drifted down the street. She could even hear the piano, which this time was playing a sprightly jazz number.

The same withered doorkeeper was on duty at the entrance, but gave no sign of either recognition or challenge as they passed through the curtain and into the hall beyond. The place was as grand as Cat had remembered, if not as crowded, and the echoing buzz of party noise was just as disorientating. She tried to shake the cloudiness from her head, and said with more energy than she felt, 'Right then, Flora. Here we come.'

They started with the room to the right of the stairs, where Cat had watched the poker game on her previous visit. There were only two people in there now, a couple murmuring in a corner, and Cat went straight to the windows. Outside, the scene had changed from the bitter December night they had come from to a purplish midsummer's dusk. The trees in the garden were in full-leaf; tiny white lights twinkled in their branches and along the railings. It appeared the majority of the guests were outside strolling in the street, or idling beneath the trees.

Cat turned to Toby wonderingly. 'Can *we* get out there?'

'Course. I'll show you.' They went back into the hall and past the golden curtain. The front door was ajar, revealing a glimpse of the wintry London square. Toby turned to the doorkeeper. 'Hi there, do you think you could please let us out? Into the other side?'

The doorkeeper stared at them impassively but didn't

say anything. Instead, he drew a blank card from the stack to his left. When he passed his right palm over the face of the card it left an illustration in its wake: three figures dancing and drinking in a bower of fruit and flowers. 'Three of Cups, Reign of Abundance. It's the party card,' said Toby with a grin. And this time, the door opened onto a view of leafy trees and a purple-dappled sky.

It might have been the world's most exclusive club, but their fellow guests were more varied than Cat remembered from her previous visit. Just inside the gate to the garden a Goth girl with multiple piercings was talking animatedly to an older gentleman in a morning suit. A group of young men with close-cropped hair and baggy trousers were sprawled on the steps of one of the houses, swigging from bottles, and watching the scene with bright quick eyes. Two glamour-model types, one in a sequined cocktail dress, one in denim hot pants, pouted by the railings.

Players in the Game, yes, but ordinary people too, Cat reminded herself. Real men and women with real lives in the real world. Like Anthony Linebeg, the IT consultant who lived alone...or her parents, she thought, with a twist of her gut. Not for the first time, she wondered what ambitions and desires had led these people here, and what strange trials by ordeal awaited them.

Cat glanced back at the lads on the steps; they had a

predatory sort of look, and she wondered if they were the knaves of Wands she'd seen the afternoon of the fire and the tramp. Toby had said that there was often a degree of overlap between the two sides of Temple House, but this time she could see only a flicker of the other square and the other night: the beam of a car's headlights, the bare branches of a shrub, a pedestrian struggling with a broken umbrella…

'So, Toby, you haven't said how you got inv—' she started to say, when her eye was caught by a waiter in black-and-gold livery, proffering his tray of drinks to a girl nearby. The girl accepted a glass, and twirled a strand of blonde hair round her finger.

'Look – over there,' Cat hissed, clutching Toby's arm. 'We've found her!'

But it took another few moments of scrutiny for her to be sure. Flora looked older, for one thing, perhaps because she had put her hair up and was wearing make-up and a flimsy camisole. Nothing surprising about this, it was a party after all, but there was something a bit dishevelled about her appearance that was very different from the artfully Bohemian look posh girls sometimes went for. Her eyes were outlined in smudgy black, and she had a flush of red high on her cheeks.

When she caught sight of Toby and Cat she downed her drink in a quick, angry jerk. 'Oh. It's *you.*'

'I'm glad we've found you,' said Cat quietly.

'Stalked me, you mean,' Flora retorted, shooting a black look at Toby. She helped herself to another drink and raised it as if in toast. 'Today *is* an anniversary, after all.' A private joke, presumably, for the smile she now turned on Cat was a parody of social charm. 'But dear me, I'm forgetting my manners… I gather you're a new recruit to our delightful little club. Isn't it all too, too, utterly *mah*-vellous?' She flung out her arm to encompass the party, slopping the liquid in her glass as she did so.

'Not particularly,' said Cat.

'Hmm,' Flora looked at her in a speculative if fuzzy manner. 'A sceptic. Oh well, you'll soon get used to it. *Regnabo, regno, regnavi, sum sine regno,* as the saying goes.' Then she gave a sneering sort of shrug and walked away.

'I did try to warn you,' Toby muttered.

Cat was about to go after Flora and try again, when a bell began to chime, and she saw people stop what they were doing and look around expectantly. The chime was high and very sweet, and a sense of excitement began to shiver through the air. Flora, too, was standing still and looking up, her mouth slightly open.

The doorkeeper had come out at the top of the steps to Temple House, and raised both his arms to address the scene. 'Ladies and gentlemen, princes and vagabonds, players all,' he began, his old cracked voice carrying with surprising force, 'I bid you welcome and announce that the Lottery is about to begin.'

Applause broke out, along with murmurs and coos of anticipation, and everyone began moving towards the house. Flora was among the first to the door.

'Come on,' said Toby.

'I don't want to see it,' Cat replied.

'Why not? Nobody does anything while a Lottery's taking place. All play is suspended; it's the rules. And anyway, it's exciting.'

'So were those old Roman shows with gladiators.' Now that she knew what was at stake, the idea of watching some knight sweat as the wheel spun made her feel queasy. 'You go keep an eye on Flora. I'll wait by the stairs and we can corner her as she comes out.'

Toby didn't need telling twice, bounding up the steps of Temple House to catch up with the other spectators. Cat moved more slowly. She came to a halt on the first floor and watched as the big black-and-gold doors swung behind the last arrivals.

No sound escaped from the room once the doors were shut. Cat felt uncomfortably exposed in the deserted hallway, like she was trespassing. Playing truant. She decided there would be enough time for her to poke around for a bit, and tried the door to the gallery, hoping for another look at the painted wheel and its shadowy mistress. But the door was locked. Instead, she wandered into the book-lined study.

There was a small fire burning in the grate and a faint, not unpleasant aroma of cigars. A game of chess lay abandoned on a table beside a still-warm coffee pot. Cat helped herself to a cup and went to look at the shelves. Perhaps this was where the secrets of the Arcanum were housed. There didn't seem to be much order to the collection, however, with battered paperback detective stories shoved haphazardly among leather-bound, gilt-edged tomes. A slim book called *The Queen of Spades* looked promising, but it was just a boring novel about Russian aristocrats. A collection of poems called *The Waste Land* was propped next to a first edition of *Alice in Wonderland*. After that came two Latin texts, *De Casibus Virorum Illustrium* and *De Consolatio Philosophiae*. Cat yawned, and began to flick through an instruction manual for bridge.

Sudden clatter and chatter from outside made her start. The Lottery was over more quickly than she'd expected. She hurried to the hallway just as Toby arrived. His face lightened when he saw her, and he pointed to where Flora's blonde head could be seen at the top of the packed staircase. Progress downstairs was slow, and their quarry remained only a few feet in front. But there was a sudden rush as people reached the ground floor and began to disperse into the reception rooms or out to the square, and they remained stuck in the queue as Flora slipped through the crowd and ducked around the corner under the stairs. Cat began to push ahead, dragging Toby in her wake. 'Hurry up,' she said impatiently, 'we can't lose her now.'

Flora had gone through a little white-painted door that Cat hadn't noticed before. The corridor behind had a shabby, neglected sort of air and led to the back of the house and a wide paved courtyard surrounded by high walls. Incongruously, there was what appeared to be an old-fashioned slot machine in the middle of the yard. But no Flora.

'I can't believe it! I could've sworn she came this way.'

Toby looked nervous. 'She did. Um, I think she's gone into the Arcanum.'

'But we're already…'

'I mean that she's left Temple House to enter play.' He pointed to a door at the end of the courtyard. 'I don't know where this exit leads. But if Flora just wanted to go home, I reckon she'd have left by the front.'

A lilac glow lingered over the roof behind them and Cat could still hear the piano somewhere deep inside. But past the high walls of the courtyard was the sludgy orange of London's night sky, where the lights of an aeroplane were winking towards Heathrow. Temple House, the threshold of all thresholds…

And yet the courtyard seemed designed both to keep intruders out and visitors in. The tops of the walls were lined with a thicket of iron barbs, and the door was solid steel. It was also locked.

They went back to inspect the slot machine. It was an antique model and rather beautiful, made of dark wood with an ornate wrought-iron trim. There was a slot at the top for a coin, a row of three mechanised reels, each printed with a strip of assorted symbols, and a lever to set them in motion. A Wheel of Fortune had been painted onto the pearly glass panel above the reels; the tingling on Cat's palm confirmed the design wasn't merely decorative.

Close to, she saw that the circular space within the painted wheel and its spokes was divided into two bands. The one forming the outer rim was marked with roman numerals from zero to twenty-one, while the band around the axis was divided into four sections, each showing a different image: a pentacle, a sword, a cup and a wand. In addition to this, there were two bronze indicators, like the hands of a clock. The smaller one was aligned along a spoke, and didn't appear to be pointing to anything, but the other was positioned on 'XVIII'.

'Eighteen! That's the Moon: the eighteenth triumph in

the Greater Arcana,' Toby exclaimed. 'Because, look, if you wanted to indicate a card in the Lesser Arcana, you'd use the little arrow hand to select its court.'

'So why the Moon?'

'It'll be the move behind this door. Has to be. And what's more, I bet we have to play the machine to get the door open.'

Cat pulled a face. She should have guessed their progress wouldn't be as straightforward as simply following Flora out of a door, or even over a threshold. This contraption was just another test in the endless Arcanum obstacle course.

'Do you know how these things work, Cat?'

'We need the pictures on the three reels to line up, I should think.' She pointed to the two little wheels and a pentacle currently on display. 'That's how most basic slot machines pay out, anyhow. First you feed in your coin. Then you pull the lever to rotate the reels. If all the pictures match when they've stopped spinning, you've hit the jackpot – or in our case, the door opens.'

'And what are our chances of hitting the jackpot?'

'Depends on how the reels are set up. My aunt told me how your chance on an ordinary machine is over two hundred thousand to one.' Cat grinned to herself; it felt good to be explaining something to Toby for a change. 'But the odds must be loads better on this one, else what would be the point? And Flora's already used it to pull off her vanishing trick.'

'Yes, I think this is Temple House's way into *all* the cards in play in the Arcanum. You just have to turn the indicators on the wheel to select the one you want. A kind of super-threshold!'

Hope flooded Cat, and she immediately reached to turn the smaller hand to the picture of a cup, and the longer one to 'VI'. They wouldn't budge.

'I suppose it was too good to be true,' Toby said with a shake of his head. 'It's probably only the Game Masters who can select the cards. But at least we know what's behind the door.'

'Isn't the Moon triumph to do with artistic inspiration and creativity and stuff? That can't be too bad.'

'Yes, but the Moon's also got some spooky associations, too. The illustration shows a landscape with two towers and – hey, what are you doing?'

'Playing the one-armed bandit.' Cat was already tracing the painted wheel's lines, feeling the throb as an Arcanum coin materialised in her hand. At this point, beating the odds, and proving herself against the machine, had become almost as important as catching up with Flora. 'Here goes.'

As soon as the coin went into the slot, the glass panels above lit up. Cat pulled the lever and the reels began to spin with a soft clicking sound.

The final line-up was *wheel, sword, wheel.*

'*Hell.*' She kicked the machine's base in frustration.

'Doesn't matter – keep trying.'

But Cat wasn't able to raise the coin again, no matter how many times she traced the wheel's markings. Her palm had stopped tingling, too.

'I guess we only get one shot at a time,' she told Toby. 'Now it's your turn. And hurry up – for all we know, Flora's back home eating tea and crumpets by now.'

He didn't need telling twice, almost dropping the coin in his eagerness to get it into the slot. And this time, after the level had been pulled and reels clicked round, the symbols revealed were *wheel, wheel, wheel.* Toby whooped. At once, the panel above the reels began to flash.

Cat hastened over to the door. Sure enough, its handle turned.

'Right,' she said. 'I'm going through. Thanks for helping, and all that, but there's no reason for you to come. This is my business.'

'Are you kidding?' Toby's foot was tap-tapping, and he had ruffled his hair into little agitated tufts, but he gave her a lopsided grin. 'Of *course* I'm coming with you. You were right, that stuff you said about research not really counting. It's just…well, this is a big thing, y'know? I mean, wow, I've been dreaming about this for such a long time, right, and now it's actually here—'

She grabbed his arm and pulled him through, before either of them could change their minds.

At first, Cat thought they had got it wrong and the door led to somewhere in the 'home' side after all. The dank overcast night belonged to the evening she'd left behind when she'd entered Temple House, just as the concrete jumble hemming them in had a mundane familiarity. Walls and columns of grubby grey reared up to either side, their windows stretching from earth to sky. In spite of the pallid glow of an occasional streetlight, and the scribbling of graffiti across the walls, the place seemed utterly abandoned.

'Jeez,' Toby muttered, 'I thought it would be a bit more, y'know…'

'Glamorous?' Cat said it sarcastically, but actually she knew what he meant. She thought of the soft primrose morning the other side of Seven Dials, the glowing rooms of Temple House.

Not entirely to her surprise, the door they'd come through only opened one way. Here it was at the base of one of the tower blocks, with a narrow grille at the top and a row of buzzers to the left. 'I wonder if there's a way back to Temple House in all of the moves,' Toby speculated. He was going to try the buzzers but Cat, made uneasy by the CCTV camera above their heads, stopped his hand.

'Doesn't matter. We'll just keep walking until we find a proper threshold.'

'And look who's here in the meantime. Result!' Toby pointed across the scrubby open space, slightly smaller than a football pitch, which lay before them.

Sure enough, it was Flora, walking unsteadily but determinedly towards the underpass of a wide concrete bridge. As they watched, she stopped and took a swig from the bottle of champagne she was dangling from one hand.

Toby and Cat exchanged glances, then hurried to join her. Large greasy-looking puddles pockmarked the yard, and, as they crossed its expanse, the concrete seemed to swallow them up, the towers growing higher, the forecourt wider. But at least one of their problems had been solved: feeling the pins and needles on their palms as they approached the bridge, they knew a threshold must be near. Perhaps that was what Flora was heading for. When she saw them coming, she shook her head slightly and began to laugh. 'Batgirl and Robin ride again. Haven't you two got a garden party to go to?'

'Hey, Flora. Sorry to, uh, keep bothering you, but we could really do with some advice here. You see, Cat wants—'

Cat cut in. 'I'm looking for something.'

'Aren't we all.' Flora's eye make-up had run down one

cheek, her voice was slurred and she was shivering in her flimsy camisole. Still, her insouciance made Cat envious. Envious and irritated.

'It's true though, isn't it, that you've been coming to the Arcanum for years?' Toby asked eagerly.

'Sure. I used to divide my time between here and Narnia – till I got tired of the talking lions, that is.' Flora took another swig, and hiccupped. 'Oops.' She smiled coyly. 'These days, there's just the one world in my wardrobe.'

Cat had tired of the All-Knowing Badass act. 'Leave it, Toby. She's too wasted to talk sense even if she wanted to.'

'*Excuse* me?'

Cat shrugged expressively, and turned away. As she did so, her eye was caught by a blurred figure hastening across the yard, towards the corner of the tower block on the left, where he or she seemed to crawl up the wall. Then she realised that whoever it was must be climbing a ladder attached to a fire escape.

'What's that?' Something in Flora's voice made her turn round again.

The three of them were standing in front of the bridge. To the left was a set of steps leading up to the road, to the right was a lone streetlamp, whose glow barely penetrated the mouth of the underpass. But now Cat could see a pair of yellow eyes gleaming in the sour-smelling dark within. There was the click of nails on concrete and a heavy panting sound.

Instinctively, the three of them moved closer together. 'Just a dog,' said Toby, but he sounded uncertain.

Though it was hard to tell in the gloom, it looked a bit like an Alsatian, but bigger and shaggier. From deep within its throat came a low soft growl.

Cat felt Flora's arm tremble against hers. In unspoken agreement, they began to back away, while the dog crept forwards, slunk low on its belly, its teeth bared. The snarl swelled and throbbed. Yet when the animal reached the threshold of the underpass it went no further. Crouched as if to spring, it nonetheless waited motionless, staring after them with baleful yellow eyes.

Every nerve, every muscle screamed *run*. Cat could hear the others' ragged breathing. *Steady. Steady...* The three of them continued to move backwards in a clumsy, almost comical half-walk, half-jog, that gathered in speed the further they got from the bridge.

Then, just as they were in the shadow of the tower blocks, and were beginning to feel calmer, the animal leaped into the light of the streetlamp, flung back its head and howled – a long, shivering cry that echoed through the blood.

At once, they burst into a scrambling dash, and would

probably have scattered if Cat hadn't remembered the figure she'd seen only a few minutes earlier. 'This way!' she choked out. 'Up!' In a frantic swerve, already imagining the beast snap at their ankles, the other two ran after her towards the lower bars of the fire escape. At the last moment, Flora stumbled. She gasped, lurched forwards, tripped again, before Cat came back and dragged her on.

Toby got to the ladder first, swinging himself onto the platform above with a screech of rusting iron. Together, he and Cat half pushed, half pulled Flora after him. Cat scrambled up last, expecting to feel hot breath and stinking jaws close in on her at any moment.

But the wolf hadn't come after them. Huddled on their perch, about six feet off the ground, they watched as it prowled before the bridge, ears pricked.

'The Triumph of the Moon,' breathed Toby. He gestured at the two towers, the grey waste before them where rainwater had pooled, and the wolf lifting its muzzle to the sky. High above, scudding clouds briefly cleared to show the white disc of light. 'Look, Cat – it's *just* like the picture on the card!'

Cat stared at his rapt expression in disbelief. Flora too seemed to have recovered her composure. Sticking her twisted ankle out in front of her, she leaned back against the railing with a wince and a sigh, as if settling in for the night. She took another swig from the bottle, which she'd somehow managed to hang onto. Catching Cat's eye, she passed it over.

The champagne was flat and tepid, and a sudden clanging noise from above set her spluttering. Whoever had come up the fire escape before them was climbing higher. Craning her neck, she saw a smudge of face looking down on them, before the figure swung into an open window three or four flights up.

'Is that the knight, d'you think?' Toby asked, still unfeasibly chirpy.

'No,' Flora said, pointing. '*That's* the knight.'

There was a woman running along the top of the bridge, her figure in silhouette against the sprawl of city lights beyond. As they watched, another howl shivered through the air, not from the wolf they had seen – which had disappeared into the night – but from somewhere further off. Further, but not far. The woman froze at the sound, then staggered on. Briefly, she disappeared from view, then there was movement in the darkness to the left of the bridge, and they saw her head bobbing as she descended the steps.

A moment later, and she had reached the forecourt. Although the moon had gone behind the clouds again, they could see that she was incongruously dressed in a long white nightgown. Her dark hair had come undone from its knot, and her bare feet kept tripping on the hem. In the vast silence of the place, they could hear her sobbing breath; on the crest of the bridge, black shadows massed.

Cat scrambled to stand up, to call out to the fugitive so she could head for the safety of the ladder. Before she could open her mouth, sharp nails dug into her arm.

'Don't move,' Flora hissed. 'Don't say a word.'

'But we have to help her! She'll be torn to pieces by those animals – Toby!' Cat looked to him for appeal.

'She's right. We have to do something,' he whispered back, wide-eyed.

'Idiots,' said Flora in an urgent yet contemptuous undertone. 'Don't you understand? We're chancers. We're not allowed to intervene. You do anything else to alter the State of Play and you'll be forfeit.'

As they were talking, first one, then two, three, four wolves had slunk out from the underpass and darted ahead of their prey, cutting off her flight. Meanwhile, those on the bridge poured down the steps, as swift and silent as smoke. Eyes gleamed, tongues lolled, hot animal breath steamed in the air. The knight was encircled. Cat's whole body crawled with horror.

Flora still had her arm in an iron grip. 'Wait,' she said. '*Wait.*'

For the woman's face was suffused with a kind of

radiance as she gazed up at the sky. With a cry, she plucked at the neckline of her gown, raking her throat and breast with her nails, as she swayed and muttered. The next moment, the clouds parted to reveal the moon and the landscape was flooded with cold dead light. The woman lifted up her arms, let out another wail, and sank to the ground.

She seemed to shrink into the drapes of the material, twitching and shuddering, her long black hair spilling over her face and down her back. It grew longer and shaggier, shot through with shimmers of grey. There was a terrible moaning noise. And somehow, in a matter of seconds, the tangle of folds and hair and flesh had vanished, leaving a great silver wolf baying at the moon.

At once, the rest of the pack surged to meet it. It was twice the size of the other animals and its cry was louder and wilder, and more desolate, than any they had heard before. With one mighty bound, it leaped ahead, racing across the forecourt and between the two towers.

Cat, Flora and Toby shrank back on their platform, hardly daring to breathe, as the wolf-pack streamed after it and under them and beyond. And sometimes Cat saw the wolf, and sometimes it was the woman, with bare feet and flying hair, running ahead, and urging them on.

*

For a long, long while afterwards, nobody spoke. It felt as if they were eternally locked into this horrible dead landscape, the creaking iron and the damp wind.

Eventually, Toby cleared his throat. 'What do you think will happen to her?' he whispered.

'Depends,' Flora answered wearily. 'Could be that changing into the wolf was her only chance of survival. Or it could be integral to the success of her move.' She looked at the other two meaningfully. '*Her* move, remember. Whatever the outcome, it's nothing to do with us.'

'That's pretty harsh.' Cat was thinking of the first scene of Arcanum violence she'd witnessed, and how differently she would have acted if she'd known what was at stake. *You've got to help me,* the man had said.

Flora pursed her lips. 'I don't make the rules. A chancer can only enter the Arcanum on the condition we don't do anything to help or obstruct the knight in play. Intervene in the Game again, and you'll pay the forfeit – as a knave in one of the courts.'

'But – but for how long?' Toby asked.

'It's said that if a knave catches a knight cheating, or a chancer intervening, they'll be set free. Otherwise, a forfeit can last for as many rounds as the Game Masters choose. And that *is* harsh.'

There was another long silence.

At last, Cat swung around so her feet were dangling off the edge of the platform. 'Well, I'm going down,' she told the others with more firmness than she felt. 'We can't stay holed up here for ever.'

Leaving the comparative safety of the fire escape was a drawn-out process. They all halted on the final rung of the ladder, ears straining for the sound of padding feet or panting breath, and once they were on the ground nobody wanted to be the first to break away from grabbing distance of the rails.

Given the choice, Cat would have preferred to make a run for it, one final sprint across to the bridge. But Flora's ankle, though not badly sprained, meant they had to compromise on a scuttling sort of shuffle around the edges of the forecourt, flinching at their own shadows, hardly daring to breathe.

Somehow, though, they made it. Once more they stood in front of the mouth of the underpass, feeling the sign of the wheel prick their palms, and fear prick at their necks. But this time the darkness within appeared to be as lifeless as the wasteland they'd just crossed.

Toby felt in his pocket and drew out a pocket torch attached to a key ring. 'Thought it might come in handy,' he said, a bit self-consciously.

First Toby, then Cat and Flora stepped under the arch and followed the torch's thin beam. They had gone about seven or eight paces when Flora made a small, exclamatory noise.

'Are you OK?' Cat asked, struggling to keep her voice steady. Flora was further behind her than she'd realised and she could barely make her out in the darkness.

Silence.

'Flora?'

'Yes... Sorry.' Her face suddenly loomed into the glow of Toby's torch, pale as a wraith. 'Look, we've found it. There.'

Sure enough, the slope of the wall to her left had been spray-painted with a fuzzy red outline of the wheel, its curves vivid against the tidemark of graffiti all around. Flora was already reaching out a hand to trace the markings. In a few seconds, her palm gleamed metal. 'We only need one,' she told them, peering down at the disc. 'But you have to be touching me.' And in a flash of her coin, it was all over.

The home side of the underpass wasn't much of an improvement, smelling of toilets and littered with old chip wrappers – but after where they'd come from, the motley row of off-licences and discount shops ahead looked almost welcoming. All three hastened out towards the street.

Just before they got there, somebody shouldered past

Cat, so roughly that she stumbled. 'Hey!' she called out to his retreating back, and he momentarily turned, his face a blur of grey beneath his hooded top. She remembered the youths in Mercury Square, the slouching boy glimpsed in the static of a computer screen, the climbing figure in the Arcanum. But he was already gone.

According to their watches, it was only half past nine. Even on a Sunday night there was plenty of traffic about, and a kebab shop over the way was doing brisk business. Cat glanced back at the bridge and saw the two tower blocks rear into the night, their storeys spangled with lit windows.

'Whoa,' said Toby, shaking his head. 'I mean, *wow*. How cool was that?'

'Cool?' repeated Cat. '*Cool?*'

'Aw, c'mon, I thought it was meant to be one of those female fantasies: "women who run with the wolves" and all that. You know – empowering.'

Cat looked at him incredulously. He coughed and changed the subject. 'Er, right, we need to think about getting home. That's Canary Wharf over there, so I don't reckon we're that far from – hey, where are you going?'

Flora was limping across the road, in the direction of a minicab office. 'Taxi,' she said without looking back. Then, reluctantly, 'I suppose you can get in too, if you want…'

They went to join her. Flora was a mess, her hair straggling, make-up smudged, bare arms covered in goosebumps, but she gave instructions to the cab driver with crisp assurance. Then, as soon as they'd got into the taxi, she sank back into the seat and fell asleep. Toby, meanwhile, wasted no time in getting into an animated – if one-sided – chat with the driver about the local trip-hop scene.

Cat couldn't believe it. Flora's indifference was one thing, Toby's carelessness quite another. She remembered his airy – and, as it turned out, completely false – assurances that chancers were free to do anything they liked within the Game. Yet once faced with the realities of the Arcanum, he seemed more inclined than ever to treat it as one big adventure. Not for the first time, Cat wondered how the other two had joined the Game. But to ask would mean more questions about her own initiation. About how she had helped a man go to his death.

She leaned back in her seat, half-listening to Toby's chatter, interspersed with grunts from their driver and the burbling of the radio. Outside, the quiet Sunday streets slid past, streaked quicksilver in the rain.

'This is me,' said Toby, and Cat blinked, realising that she had been close to nodding off herself. His voice seemed to come from very far away, though she was blearily aware of him saying that he could get a bus home from here, that he'd see them soon, wasn't it great, bye guys, bye, bye…

'We can get the driver to drop you off wherever you want,' Flora offered, once they were on the move again. Her voice was no longer slurred, just very sleepy-sounding. 'I've got plenty of cash.'

I'll bet. 'I can get out at Oxford Street,' Cat said shortly. 'We're nearly there.'

Flora was about to say something else, but the trilling of a phone interrupted her. She extracted a slim metallic-pink mobile from her trousers. 'Yes? Oh, Georgia, hi…'

Cat closed her eyes and tried to zone out again. The conversation ended on a brightly social note – 'Martingale's at eleven, then. Brill. See you tomorrow!' – and the next moment, the cab driver was pulling up beneath a set of Christmas lights, whose flashing reindeers formed an arch between two department stores.

Cat climbed stiffly out of the car. Flora was now setting her smeared face to rights with the aid of a pocket mirror. She raised a hand in brief farewell, then went back to combing the tangles from her hair.

And soon, thought Cat, as she began the chilly trudge back to the flat, Flora would go home to where her parents were waiting. It would be a big old house, most likely, where light glowed from behind expensive curtains, and the streets were quiet all night long. The blonde woman from the church would open the door, and put out her arms. 'Thank goodness you're home,' she'd say. 'Everything all right, sweetheart?' the kind-faced man would ask.

'I'm fine, thanks, Daddy,' Cat whispered into the darkness of the city. 'Everything's fine.'

CHAPTER EIGHT

The next morning, Cat had three or four calls from Toby. She ignored them, just as she ignored Bel's anxious looks over the breakfast table. More fool him if he imagined yesterday had been the beginning of mutual magical escapades. Even so, she was – on balance – grateful to the guy. Flora too. For all its craziness, last night had been very instructive, she reminded herself as she flicked through the Yellow Pages. Martin House, Martina's Bar, Martingale's…

It turned out to be a coffee shop just off the King's Road. Flora and her friends had taken over most of the ground floor, sprawled elegantly on the over-sized sofa or perched on the chairs. The girls' lattes were skinny to match their jeans, their lips as glossy as their hair. There were a couple of floppy-haired, drawling boys, dotted among them.

Flora, sipping daintily from a glass of water, didn't

seem any the worse for wear from the night before. Her skin was peachy-smooth, her eyes a clear and guileless blue. She was wearing a cream cashmere sweater, and a tiny gold cross glinted around her neck.

'Hello, Flora. Got a minute?'

Conversation halted and glances were exchanged. The atmosphere wasn't exactly hostile but it was far from welcoming. 'Do you *know* this girl, Flo?' frowned the fair-haired boy sitting next to her.

Flora gave a sweet, helpless shrug. 'Well…we do seem to keep on bumping into each other.' She blinked up at Cat with the polite bafflement she did so well. 'You know, I'm afraid this isn't a good time.'

'But the future of the world is at stake!' Cat turned to the others and grinned broadly. 'See, we're both members of the *Lord of the Rings* Role Playing Society. Flora here is one of our most adventurous gamers. But now we're coming up to a critical strategic point…'

Flora's eyes flashed. Two of the girls were spluttering into their lattes; the rest of the crowd looked torn between confusion or belligerence. Cat pressed on remorselessly. 'Orcs against Elves: the final showdown. So, Flo, are you coming? Or maybe I should just pull up a chair and—'

'No need,' said Flora smoothly. The boy next to her caught at her hand. 'It's fine, Charlie. Honestly. I just need to sort out this…mix-up. I won't be long.'

She followed Cat out of coffee shop, limping slightly, and over to a bench across the street. They both sat down warily, not quite looking at each other.

'I really don't appreciate being put on the spot like that,' Flora began. 'How did you find me, anyway?'

'Your phone call in the cab. How's the ankle?'

'It's not too bad, thank you.'

'Could've been worse. You could be picking werewolf teeth out of it.'

Flora wrinkled her pretty little nose, as if to say she found the remark in bad taste. 'I don't mean to sound rude, but what do I have to do to get you to leave me alone?'

'Talk to me. About last night…among other things.'

'Last night? Really? I wouldn't have thought there's much to be said.'

'It was lucky for you we came along, though, wasn't it? Else I'm not sure you could've got up that fire escape. Dodgy ankle aside, you were so smashed you could barely walk straight, let alone outrun the beasties.' Flora's breath hissed but Cat just smiled blandly at her. Two could play at that game. 'Is that what the Arcanum is to you?' she continued, still in a conversational tone. 'Party central? A place to get off your face where Mummy and Daddy need never know?'

If Cat was hoping to get a rise out of the other girl, she was unsuccessful.

'I wouldn't have lasted very long if that were true,' Flora replied tightly. She began fiddling with the tassels of her scarf. 'Not that it's any of your business but...Sunday was a bad day, that's all.'

An anniversary, Cat remembered. She pushed the thought to one side. 'You're right: it's not my business. Fact is, I couldn't care less about what you get up to in there. I'm just here for your expertise.'

'Your sidekick seems pretty well-informed.'

'Toby? He's an amateur. Not like you.'

Flora didn't say anything for a while, staring out at the street with unseeing eyes. Then she sighed. 'What do you want to know?'

Cat took a deep breath.

'The first time I went into the Arcanum, the Six of Cups was in play. But when I went back to find it again, the threshold had gone. I want you to tell me how I can get back into the card.'

'It is a dangerous card.'

'I thought it was a lucky one.'

Flora made a small, impatient gesture. 'Even lucky cards can have their traps. That one in particular. People vanish into it, wandering endlessly around in the past until they forget their present selves... After all,' she said quietly, 'there are few things more seductive than lost happiness.'

157

For a moment, Cat caught the sound of distant laughter, the scent of flowers and sun-baked earth drifting in the air. Once upon a time, there had been a family: Caroline, Adam and Kitty Harper. But their happiness hadn't been lost – it had been stolen. Ripped out and thrown in bloody ruin on the floor.

She clenched her jaw.

'I don't want to go there so I can be a rose-tinted kid again. I want to go back because I saw something there that I don't understand. Something important. Unless… unless it's just a trick?'

'It shows the truth.' The other girl's face was very blank. Cat wondered if Flora, too, had walked across that velvet lawn, into the maze of memories beyond.

'So how do I get the threshold back?'

'You can't – a threshold disappears once a move is finished and the players have left; once one is ended, another one appears somewhere else, at random. What lies on the other side will depend on the card dealt to the knight who went before you.'

'Well, once I've got into the Arcanum can't I just keep going from one card to another?'

'No. Each move is played within its own self-contained space. Like the squares on a chessboard. If you kept on walking, before long you'd find you were hitting dead end after dead end.'

'But the Six of Cups is my only chance—'

'Then you have two options,' Flora replied evenly. 'Either you keep going into the Arcanum, time after time, threshold after threshold, in the hope that you stumble on what you're looking for, perhaps in the Six of Cups, perhaps in some other card. Or…'

'Or?'

'You walk away. Forget any of this ever happened, ignore the prickling on your palm, shut your eyes to the signs on the thresholds. Look for your answers in the real world.'

'I can't do that.'

'No.' Flora gave a half-smile. 'None of us can. It's ironic, really. A chancer can't play for a triumph. We're part of a game we're not allowed to win. And yet the temptation's the same.'

'What temptation?'

'Of finding your heart's desire, of course.' She spoke with bitterness.

There was a burst of laughter from across the street: Flora's friends had come out of the coffee shop and were taking up the pavement in a lively gaggle. She got to her feet and straightened her clothes. 'It's time I got back.'

'OK then. Thanks and…uh, see you around sometime.'

Flora gave another of her polite, bland smiles. 'Maybe.'

Cat watched as she walked back to her friends, who

pulled her in, laughing, exclaiming, shaking out their glossy hair. The boy called Charlie slung a careless arm around her shoulder. The group moved on.

When Cat got back to the flat that afternoon, she realised she was too exhausted to think, even to feel. After everything that had happened, the numbness came as a relief.

She spent the next couple of days holed up in her bedroom with *The Wondrous World of Tarot*, trying to familiarise herself with the cards so that she could recognise their Game of Triumphs equivalents. Some were easier to remember than others. The Fool was the chancers' card; Fortune, the one that called a Lottery. Four aces for each of the four elements. The Greater Arcana's triumphs and the Lesser Arcana's court cards… Cat presumed that the court cards which showed groups of people in various activities, often involving combat, were the moves where knaves were likely to be involved. But many of the court cards' images looked just as fantastical as the triumphs, and it was impossible to guess what kind of strange life the Arcanum might give them.

There was one triumph that she kept coming back to, which was illustrated by a stern-faced woman holding a sword and scales. Justice. Cat knew that the Game could make Justice real, and bestow its powers of disclosure, judgement and punishment. Yet because it was a triumph and she was a chancer, these were powers she couldn't win.

Please, her mother's voice entreated in her head, *there's been some mistake*. And the other voice, the third voice, the one that was just out of reach...

Out of reach in the ordinary world, yes, but in the Arcanum it was a different matter. Here, where time and distance blurred, she might find all kinds of impossible things – forgotten voices, secret truths, her past happiness. She might even find the person who had taken it from her. In which case, Cat wouldn't need any triumph. Cat would deal out justice herself.

She told Bel that she felt she might be coming down with something. Neither of them had yet made any direct reference to the revelations of Saturday night. It was as if they had suddenly become shy of each other, Bel especially, and Cat found her nervousness deeply unsettling. For the moment, Bel could understand that she was still coming to terms with the true circumstances of her parents' death, but Cat knew that from here on, the enormous, impossible secret of the Arcanum would always be between them. Thinking of this made the numbness inside grow heavier, and cold.

By Wednesday afternoon, however, Bel had decided enough was enough. When Cat slunk into the kitchen to get some toast, it was to find the place festooned with tropical fruit fairy lights. Luridly glowing bananas, pineapples and bunches of grapes dripped from the walls; a fringe of red and green tinsel hung in the doorframe. Her aunt was sitting with her feet up on the table, wearing a paper crown from a cracker and eating brandy butter from a jar.

'God almighty,' she said, looking Cat up and down, 'you look like crap.'

'Compliments of the season to you too.'

'How d'you like the bling?'

'Tinsel-tastic... Can I have some of that?'

'Help yourself. It's about time we had a bit of Christmas spirit round here. And speaking of spirit,' Bel continued sternly, jabbing her spoon for emphasis, 'you, puss, are growing old before your time. Old and dull. And I'm no better. We need to get out of this hole of a flat and have some fun.'

Cat grinned through a mouthful of brandy butter, mostly from relief that things appeared to be back to normal between them. 'What kind of fun?'

'The high-rolling kind.'

Bel explained, gleefully, that Greg had used his connections to wangle them tickets to a charity poker tournament being held in a plush Mayfair hotel. There would be bright lights and glamour. Free booze and designer canapés. Cat couldn't think of anything worse.

'Sounds like a bit of a busman's holiday,' she tried. 'For you and Greg, I mean. And gambling's for mugs, everyone knows that.'

It was true Bel thought of the Luxe's clientele with a kind of genial contempt. 'Poor old sods,' she'd say, 'down to their last chip, hoping their final throw's going to save the mortgage or the marriage or whatever it is. And even if it does, the next round takes it off them all over again.' But she always added that pity was a waste of time, given the way punters got abusive when their numbers didn't come up.

Now she waved off Cat's remark. 'Yeah, but this is different – a good cause and all that, for people who can afford it.'

'Sounds heart-warming.'

''Sides, you and me are going for the social scene, not the bleeding poker.'

It occurred to Cat that maybe that was what the evening was about for Bel: a fantasy version of her job, where the champagne fizzed and the music played, where everyone was a winner and nothing important was at stake. Which made it all the more difficult for Cat to explain why she didn't want to go.

It wasn't just that the thought of anything involving games or cards made her skin crawl. She was afraid to leave the flat in case she felt the telltale throb on her palm and – what? Fled the site of a threshold in terror? No, her real dread was of going from fearing and resenting the Game to being horribly fascinated by it. Because Cat knew that in her heart of hearts she no longer wished for things to return to normal. Her listless half-life of the past weeks – years, really – didn't feel any more or less real to her, now, than that lurid dream-world of the Arcanum.

Greg's connections weren't high enough to get them through the front of the hotel; instead, they were sneaked through a service door at the back. Since the entrance fee for the event was three hundred pounds for players and two hundred for spectators, they could hardly complain, although Bel, who'd been hoping for marble and chandeliers, seemed a little disappointed by their surroundings. Everything was sleek and minimalist, luxuriously restrained.

As they entered the reception area, Cat found herself thinking back to Temple House. The party-going hum was the same, and the air tingled with the same sense of privilege and expectation. All around them, women were greeting each other with cooing air-kisses, the men exchanging slaps on the back and barks of laughter.

She could see Bel sizing the place up with amusement. Her cheap dress and clashing brightness should have been incompatible with everything else about the evening, and yet the heads she turned were mostly admiring. The male ones, anyway; Cat was oddly touched by the proprietorial way in which Greg ushered her to a table in the bar. His dusty tux made him look more drooping than ever. Not that she could talk. In her plain black shift – one of Bel's cast-offs, hastily assembled for the occasion – she could almost have passed for one of the hotel staff.

Cat had known from the start that she was feeling too fidgety to sit down and too prickly for company. She told the other two that she was going to the main room to check out the tournament, but it didn't take long for her to realise that as a spectator sport, poker came somewhere between indoor bowls and watching paint dry. From there, she wandered into another lounge area, where a jazz band was in the process of setting up.

It was also the place where the few guests who were near her own age had assembled. The way they looked and talked reminded her of Flora's friends. In fact, there was a blonde girl in a lace cocktail dress who—

'Cat! I can't *believe* it! I'd been so hoping I'd run into you again!'

Cat had seen Flora the sweetheart, Flora the wild child, but this was a different Flora again. Flora the effusive, bright-eyed and beaming. As if she was thrilled to see her. As if they were old friends.

'You have?'

'Absolutely. What luck you turning up tonight!' This made Cat uneasy. She didn't trust luck, or coincidence. Not any more. Flora prattled on. 'Are you here with your parents, too? Daddy's on the board of the trust. Last year they raised over a hundred thousand pounds, you know! Anyway…I was thinking that we should meet up. Toby as well. There's something I think you'll be really interested in, to do with what we were talking about the other day. Something I've found.'

'To do with the, er, Game?'

Flora laughed merrily. 'Of *course* it's about the Game! Listen, how are you fixed for tomorrow? I know everyone's madly busy at this time of year…'

Ah yes. The giddy social whirl. 'I'll have to check my diary.'

The other girl either ignored, or didn't pick up on, her ironical tone. 'Well, if you're free, perhaps you and Toby should come round to mine. Say, six-ish?' Flora scribbled her address down on a piece of paper and Cat found herself folding it away in her pocket. 'Brilliant. If I don't see you later, enjoy the rest of the evening!'

Cat was left frowning to herself. Part of her was tempted to tell Flora to shove it – why should Cat come running when she called? But underneath the charm, there had been something a little feverish about Flora's enthusiasm, a kind of urgency, which was very intriguing.

For even though Cat might not want to admit it, she'd been waiting for something like this. Her next cue...

Bel's voice cut into her thoughts. 'There you are! Who were you talking to back then?'

'Just this girl I kind of...bumped into, once.'

'Looks a right little princess,' Bel sniffed. 'One of those trust-fund types.'

'Looks like it.'

'Listen, puss-cat, have you seen Greg anywhere?'

'The last I saw, he was getting cosy with you in the corner.'

'Yeah, but then he went off to have a word with his mate, the one who got us into this place. I don't suppose you'd be a star and go look for him...'

'Why can't you?'

Bel rolled her eyes humorously. ''Cause I'm busy networking, aren't I?' She lowered her voice. 'See him over there? Goatee, cigar? Well, he's only the manager of that flash new casino off Trafalgar Square; Alliette's, it's called. This could be my big break.'

'I don't see why you need Greg, in that case. Won't he just cramp your style?'

'Ah, but he's my boss, don't forget. He's bound to big me up, isn't he? C'mon,' she wheedled, 'he'll not have gone far. Try the night-porter's room – we passed it on our way in.'

Cat shrugged. Looking for Greg was marginally more interesting than watching poker, after all. But retracing their back-door route to the party was trickier than she'd thought. Perhaps she should have gone right rather than left at the end of the hall, or maybe her first mistake was going past the last set of double doors. At any rate, before she knew it she was adrift in the back stairs and service corridors, whose cheap lino and dull paint was a world away from the sleek interiors front of house. She passed a laundry-sorting room, full of weary dark-faced women; glimpsed a cramped office lined with pigeonholes; heard clashes and roars from the kitchens. Eventually, she found her way to the delivery entrance at the back of the building. A couple of porters were on a break, smoking by the wall.

She was about to go and ask them for directions, but as she turned she stumbled into someone who'd come out with a sack full of rubbish. It slipped from his grasp, disgorging a glut of plastic food wrappings. Cat went to help but he gestured her away, swearing under his breath, and stuffing everything back in with irritable jerks. As he looked up their eyes met. There were dark circles under his, their expression hard, and mistrustful.

'I've met you before.' The words came out before she could stop them.

'Yeah? So many girls, so little time,' he said shortly,

pushing back a hank of dirty brown hair. She remembered his bitten fingernails.

'From Mercury Square. Outside Temple House?'

'Can't say I've had the pleasure.'

He had his back to her as he slung the bag into a skip. He was taller and broader than she remembered, and wearing an apron over ill-fitting overalls. Tall, and slouching. What had Odile said to Ahab as she looked into the screen? *He claims to be in pursuit of one of your knights…*

'You're after a Knight of Wands,' she said.

At once, he whipped around. They faced each other, his face startled, and angry, hers questioning.

'Oi, Blaine!' Someone inside yelled at him to hurry up, followed by a barrage of expletives. And the next moment Blaine was pushing past, back towards the steam and clamour of the kitchens. The way he shouldered her out of his path was familiar, too.

Bel was still talking to the man with the goatee. She was doing her special laugh, flinging back her head to display a swoop of throat, and shaking out her hair. They both appeared to be enjoying the performance. However, as soon as Bel saw Cat, she moved away from the bar to join her.

'Cat! I thought we'd lost you! I felt dead guilty; Greg turned up just after you left.'

'Where's he gone now?'

'Oh, he'll be back in a sec – he had to take a phone call. Are you all right? You look a bit peaky.'

'Yeah, I think I must be still fighting this virus thingy. Um…you don't mind if I head off, do you?'

Bel's face fell. 'Listen, I know it's a bit poncy here but Leo,' – she jerked her head towards the goatee man – 'says he'll introduce us to some people. You should come over and say hello. And there's a band just started up, and we've hardly touched the nibbles.'

'Please, Bel, I'm just not in the right mood. Not for this sort of thing.'

Now her aunt looked guilty. 'No. No, of course. After the shock you've had… I thought a bit of distraction might do you good, but there're some things you need to work through in your own way, your own time. I should've known not to push you. It's only because I hate seeing you like this, puss-cat.'

The sympathy was nearly Cat's undoing.

'I hate *being* like this,' she burst out. 'I hate being confused and angry and helpless. I hate being so *weak*… Bel, have you ever blundered into something you didn't understand? Something you were better off not knowing? But then you charge in anyway, and what you find out is the worst, worse than anything, and you wish – *God*, how you wish – that you could forget it all, that life could go back to before, but it's too late, everything's changed. And you have to do something about it, to make things better, to take back control, but you don't know how, and – and—'

She ground to a halt at the sight of Bel's stricken face.

'God knows, if I could make things right, I would. I…'

'S'OK.' Somehow, Cat managed to smile. 'Don't worry, I'm all right really. Not like me to go all hysterical; it's the virus talking. Honest.'

'You don't look all right to me. You don't sound all right, neither.'

'I'll be fine. I just needed to have a rant, that's all. In fact, I think it's done me some good.'

'No, Cat, I've screwed up, I can see that. I haven't been straight with you and now, like you said, everything's changed.'

'Things haven't changed between us. That's not what I meant. And anyhow, I won't *let* us be changed, not by *anything*.'

'You really mean that – not anything?'

'I swear it.'

Bel looked at her fierce expression, and this time she laughed, relievedly. 'Right you are, puss-cat. I'll swear to that, too. Look…let's go home, anyhow. Have some peace and quiet.'

'No! There's no reason for you to leave as well. I'll only feel worse for making you miss out.'

Cat overruled all Bel's protestations and insisted that she stayed: it wasn't late, and the Excelsior was in walking distance of the flat. Right now, she needed to be alone.

She left through the main entrance. A ten-foot Christmas tree dominated the lobby. It was a real tree, though so symmetrical it looked false, its baubles arranged in rigidly co-ordinated tiers. As Cat brushed past, she caught the spice of pine, a dark sap scent that made her throat ache. For a moment, her vision blurred, and she was three years old again, reaching into the prickling branches for the gleam of chocolate coins.

CHAPTER NINE

'Think about it,' Toby was saying. 'We can be like the Famous Three or something. The Prom Queen, the Lovable Geek and—'

'You're not lovable.'

'Aw, c'mon, haven't you ever heard of Geek Chic? Instant x-factor. Anyway, as I was saying. Team Arcanum: the Prom Queen, the Lovable Geek and the Goth.'

'I am not a Goth.'

'OK, not technically speaking, no. But you have to admit, you're on the pale and prickly side,' Toby said cheerily. 'I suppose you could be the Enigmatic Loner, if you'd prefer.'

'I'd prefer it if you shut the hell up.'

Cat quickened her pace so she could carry on pretending they had nothing to do with each other. She couldn't think why she'd agreed to go along with Flora's stupid invitation. It's my own fault, she told herself savagely, for getting mixed up with these people in the first place. Given half a chance, I'd have worked things out by myself. Now, I'm stuck with them. Spoilt Madam and the Annoying Git.

Her mood did not improve when they arrived at Flora's house, a big white-columned affair on the edge of one of London's most fashionable parks. It was the kind of street where even the exhaust fumes reeked of money.

The door was opened by a blonde woman in a silk dressing gown. She raised a perfectly-plucked eyebrow in interrogation.

'Yes?'

'We're here to see Flora.'

'Are you *sure*?' The woman continued to look them up and down in a slightly unfocused fashion.

'Mummy.' Flora's voice came from the hall beyond. 'It's all right, I'm expecting them.'

Her mother shrugged elegantly, the movement making the ice in her drink tinkle, then pinned a well-practised smile onto her face. 'Marv'llous, darling. You know how I love meeting your friends... Sorry to be a touch *dishabille* – running late, as usual. I swear the party season gets more exhausting by the year.' She laughed, a little too loudly, and raised her tumbler as if to make a toast. Cat remembered Flora in the garden at Temple House, her parody of social charm.

'We're going up to my bedroom. Have fun at the Avoncourts'.' Flora wasted no time in ushering her guests upstairs. Cat, her feet sinking into thick carpeting, had only a vague impression of the rest of the house, which appeared to be done up in varying shades of expensive white.

Flora's bedroom continued the theme. The bed had a gauzy white canopy and a gas fire flickered in a white marble fireplace. The pin-board above her desk was covered with snapshots of Flora and her friends at parties, on ski-slopes, city breaks and country weekends. A night breeze ruffled the curtains by the window, which looked over the garden and the park beyond.

Their hostess perched on the edge of the bed, hugging a cushion to her chest. 'Oh,' she said, 'I should have asked. Would you like anything to eat or drink?'

'Why, are you going to ring for the maid?' asked Toby, smirking.

'We don't call her that. Mina's like one of the family.'

Cat turned from the window. 'Toby thinks you're the prom queen,' she said abruptly.

'I beg your pardon?'

'You know. All the best hero-squads have one. You're the token blonde cheerleading type, Toby's the geek and I'm the Goth.'

'It was only a *joke*,' Toby said, reddening. 'There's no need to keep going on about it.'

'It's a joke with a point, though. Right from the start, you made it clear that you wanted as little as possible to do with me or Toby or anyone. Now you've called a team meeting. What's changed?'

'Well, there's no need to make a drama out of it,' Flora replied mildly, twirling her hair. 'I just came across something that I thought the two of you should know about. Whether you choose to take it any further is entirely up to you.'

'So what is it?'

'Something I found – well, stumbled on, really – in that horrid tunnel under the bridge. When we were trying to find the threshold.'

Cat watched as the other girl walked over to her dressing table, took a silver key from one of the drawers and passed it to Toby. It was plain and slim, and the bow – the handle-like part at the gripping end – was a design of a circle enclosing an oval.

'It's a zero! No *way*!' He turned to Cat to explain. 'That's the number for us chancers, because the Fool is outside the sequence of triumphs. Do you know what the key belongs to, Flora?'

'Not for sure.' She hesitated. 'But…there's a door in Temple House that's always locked. I haven't tried the key in it yet, though – I wanted to tell the two of you first.'

Cat frowned. 'And why's that?'

'Because of the circumstances in which it was found. When we were in the Triumph of the Moon, there was somebody else there apart from the knight, remember. The other person on the fire escape. Now, there's only ever one knight per move; what's more, the Moon is a triumph, not a court card, so no knaves would be involved. And whoever that person was, they were as anxious to stay out of the action as we were.' Flora took a pound from her pocket and tossed it from one hand to the other. 'Here's the thing. You know when you reach a threshold and raise the coin, it's always marked with a sword, cup, wand or pentacle, to show which court is in play? Well, when I got us out of that move, my coin came up marked with a zero. That's never happened before: after all, chancers are outside the courts and barred from active involvement in the Game. Yet the coin showed that the focus of the move was on *us*.

'So I believe that as well as the knight, there were four chancers there that night, in that one move. A rarity – definitely. A coincidence? Perhaps. But then a key designed for us, or something to do with us, literally appears on our path. And that, I think, is no coincidence at all.'

'Like an omen,' said Toby in awestruck tones. 'Do you know how many chancers there are in the Game?'

'No. Until I met the two of you, I never encountered

more than one other at any one time. Mind you, there must be a few knaves who began as we did.' She gave a slight smile. 'It's only when we break the rules that we make a difference; I think that's why the kings and queens like to have us in the Game. There's always the possibility we'll slip up, or the temptation will get too much, so that we interfere in such a way as to tip the balance of power from one court to another.

'Now, I could be wrong about this key business. It might not fit the door I'm thinking of. It might have nothing to do with anything. But I thought you should know.'

Cat was still frowning. Why hadn't Flora seen fit to mention any of this when they were talking outside the coffee shop? It was true the workings of the Game appeared to tread a fine line between calculation and accident. But if the arbitrary nature of the Arcanum was frightening, Cat was even more disturbed by the notion that its superficial randomness was a disguise for some Higher Plan. In which case, whose? The kings and queens? Or the Lady of Luck and Fate, who smiled so knowingly in the centre of her wheel?

There was also the fact that Flora's offhand tone didn't quite tally with her agitation last night. Cat was careful to make her voice sound casual too. 'OK. What do you want to do next?'

'Well, if you're still interested, I thought the three of us could go and try the key.'

'In Temple House? Right now?'

'Sure. You see, I know a shortcut—' There came a noise from downstairs, raised angry voices and a crashing sound, and she stiffened. 'Wait here a sec.'

As soon as she'd left, Toby, who had been fidgeting in his chair, got to his feet and began to pace the floor. 'This is a *major* development, you know. Perhaps we'll find some ancient prophecy! Or a secret weapon. Anything's possible.'

'That's what scares me.'

He didn't seem to hear her. 'And then there's the mystery of the fourth chancer…'

For the moment, Cat decided to keep her encounter with the boy called Blaine to herself. They already had more than enough to think about. And in spite of her misgivings, she was just as curious as Toby about this latest development. What if the key really did lead to something important, something that could literally unlock the secrets of the Arcanum?

'Hey, Cat, if you could win any triumph, what would it be?'

'Dunno. Haven't really thought about it.'

'Yeah, *right.*'

'Whichever's the one for being filthy rich, then,' she said, to keep him quiet.

'Ah, the Empress. It's a popular choice. Me, I'd go for one of the more unfashionable ones. Something like the Chariot, maybe.'

'What's that for?'

'Heroism.' He grinned sheepishly. 'I quite fancy being the Clark Kent of the Arcanum.'

'The last thing the Arcanum needs is men in tights. It's already quite frightening enough.' Flora was back. 'Look, my parents have just left so… Do you still want to do this? Because we might as well get a move on.'

The other two nodded, trying to suppress a flutter of nerves. Their hostess, however, looked utterly composed as she slipped the key in her pocket and made her preparations to leave.

They followed her downstairs and into the drawing room at the back of the house. This was as polished, pale and orderly as the rest of the place, except for the mirror above the fireplace, which had a crack running across the centre as if something had been violently hurled against it. Flora made no comment, however, as she led them through the French windows and into a garden glittering with frost.

A gate in the wall opened onto a tree-lined path that ran alongside the inner railings of the park. The noise and lights of the city were not far away, but the expanse of grass unfolding through the darkness felt as other-worldly as any scene in the Arcanum. It was bitterly cold.

'We're not supposed to be here after hours, obviously – they lock the main gates at six,' Flora told them. 'You have to keep your eye out for the park wardens, and sometimes a tramp gets in.'

Before they could ask her where they were going, she had ducked under the rails, her footprints black in the silver grass. She was heading for a summerhouse, built like a toy temple with slender white columns and a domed roof, and set on a small rise.

As the other two hastened to catch up, they felt a familiar prickle on their palms. Flora was waiting for them by one of the columns; close to, they saw the decorative relief around its base contained the moulding of a wheel.

'A threshold's always been here,' Flora said casually. 'Well, for as long as I've been in the Game, anyway.'

'And how long have you been playing?'

'Since I was ten years old.'

God. Cat tried to picture a blonde girl-child, adrift among the monsters and marvels. No wonder Flora was a bit schizo. 'I thought thresholds disappear once a move is over.'

'Obviously, then, the move in play here is still incomplete.' Flora bent towards the base of the column, feeling for the wheel. 'Remember, you each have to be touching me when I throw the coin. Are you ready?'

Almost immediately, their surroundings flipped over to the Arcanum, where the night frost had been replaced by a misty autumnal morning, and the primly planted trees of the park spread out into open countryside. The other two, still unused to these rapid changes in scene, stood about blinking while Flora yanked open the door to the summerhouse. 'Like I said, it's a shortcut.'

They stepped into the summerhouse but out into the courtyard behind Temple House. Even more confusingly, it seemed that they were back in London's frosty evening again.

Toby looked at the door admiringly. 'Wow, Flora! Talk about local convenience!'

'It only works one way, unfortunately. As you know, if you exit the courtyard from this side of the door, your destination's fixed by that contraption.' She pointed to the slot machine, where the wheel's indicators were set to the Seven of Wands. 'But I expect there are ways back to Temple House in most of the moves, if one could only find them.'

Cat was still digesting the news that Flora had been in the game for five years. 'You must've been through a lot of cards by now. Does that mean you know what you're in for as soon as you switch sides at a threshold?'

'I haven't been into all that many moves, as it happens.

Regular trips to the Arcanum are bad for the health. And anyway, the Arcanum never brings a card to life in the same way twice – there might be fundamental similarities, but no two moves are exactly alike.' Flora's tone was impatient. 'Shall we get on?'

Temple House appeared lifeless, its windows shuttered and air musty. As they passed through the back corridor and into the rest of the house, the sense of abandonment became even more complete. In the hall, the gold curtain had gone, and the mat in front of the door was littered with junk mail. The room to the right of the stairs had been stripped bare; in the one on the left, dustsheets sagged in lumpy mounds.

Their guide led the way up the stairs to the second floor and into the mirrored ballroom. The last time they had been there it had been brightly thronged, now their reflections in the glass were as dim as ghosts. All the same, Cat wasn't sure she trusted the deserted feel of the place. Eyeing the blank TV screen suspended from the ceiling, she wondered who could be watching them, and from where. Languid Alastor, chilly Odile. Lucrezia with her dark opulence; Ahab, sombre as a tombstone.

Flora seemed to know what she was thinking. 'It's fine; Temple House belongs to all players. No one's going to interfere. Now, look at this.'

They were standing in front of the mirrored wall that

faced the doors. Its glimmering surfaces looked as uniform as the others lining the room, but Flora guided them to the central panel where, peering closely, they saw there was a small keyhole to one side, with an oval – a zero – etched around it in the glass.

'I've been over every inch of this house,' she said, 'in every room, down every corridor, at times when the place has been heaving with people or as derelict as today, and this is the only door I've never seen open. I've never even seen anyone attempt to go through it, or found so much as a thumbprint on the glass.'

'So what are we waiting for?' Toby asked.

Flora didn't waste time on ceremony or second thoughts. She fitted the silver key to the lock and turned it with one brisk movement; there was a click, and the panel sprang open, sliding smoothly over to one side. It revealed a narrow flight of stone stairs.

There was a slightly breathless pause as they took in the steepness of the steps, and the darkness of the waiting shadows. Toby was the first to recover. 'Can I go first?' he asked, like a little kid.

It must be his every dream come true, thought Cat as she went after him. Hidden chambers and secret passages. Dungeons and dragons…! Then there was a click from behind, and the stairwell plunged into blackness. Flora had closed the door.

'Are you crazy?' Cat hissed. 'Now we can't see a thing! And how will we get back?'

'We have the key,' Flora replied composedly, 'so we can get out any time we want to. I'd just prefer to reduce the possibility of anyone creeping up behind us.'

Fair point. They shuffled on down the steps. And down, and down, and further down again. The only way forwards was by feel, but though the walls pressing on either side were cool and smooth, Cat's heart banged heavily against her ribs. She soon lost track of how many floors they must have passed. It seemed as if the blindness would last for ever, a descent without end.

But at last the black turned to grey, grew softer and warmer, until they stumbled out into a lit room. The floor was chequered black and white, the walls were wood-panelled and set with alcoves where old-fashioned oil lamps burned. On the wall to their right was a large gilt frame that reminded Cat of the paintings in the gallery upstairs; its canvas, however, was so dark with age or grime that it was impossible to tell what was depicted. Facing the stairs was an archway hung with a curtain of gold brocade; the lettering above read *regnabo, regno, regnavi, sum sine regno.*

' "I shall reign, I reign, I have reigned, I am without reign," ' Flora said softly. 'It's the inscription around the spokes of Fortune's Wheel.' Unlike the other two, she showed no outward sign of nerves or even excitement. Her face was calm, intent.

The only furniture in the room was a circular table of green baize, displaying a triangular die, and four cards set around the corners of a fifth. The faces of the die were blank, and the cards were similarly featureless, both sides patterned with a design of interlocking wheels. It was as if, thought Cat uneasily, they were waiting for a game that hadn't yet been made, let alone begun.

When they drew back the curtain, they saw how far they had come. They were below even the foundations of Temple House, among roots of ancient stone. Through low arches and squat pillars, a maze of chambers lay before them, lit by more oil lamps set in alcoves along the walls. A faint scent, as of incense, sweetened the air.

'We must be in some kind of crypt,' Toby marvelled. 'Come to think of it, we've already had werewolves, so we're probably due a vampire or two.'

'Oh, drop the melodrama,' Cat growled. She was damned if she'd let Toby get to her. 'If it was a crypt, there'd be inscriptions. Tombstones. Bimbos in black leather doing kung fu and waving crucifixes.'

'Sounds good to me.'

'This is a sacred place,' said Flora quietly. 'Can't you feel it?'

'Yes! It's like that Mithraic temple they excavated

under the City.' Toby was determined not to be outdone. 'I read a book about it once. The ancients built it underground for secret rites. Maybe we're going to meet a pagan god!'

'Yeah, and maybe we'll have to offer you up as a blood sacrifice.'

'*Quiet*, both of you.' Flora paused, making a visible effort to regain her poise. 'Just…show a little respect, OK?'

They moved on, slowly and cautiously, among crude columns and under shadowy vaults, following the path lit by the lamps, until at last they came to a circular chamber with a high domed roof. In the centre of the room a tree was growing. At the end of one of its branches was a noose, from which hung the motionless body of a man.

All three drew in their breath. The tree sprang strong and green from the bare stone. Its glossy leaves were rustling, although there was no breeze here in the depths of the earth, and the flame in the lamps burned straight. The limp body weighed down its branch like some kind of monstrous fruit.

Then the man opened his eyes and smiled. '*Ave, Fortuna, Imperatrix Mundi!*'

Cat tasted blood. Without realising it, she'd bitten hard into her lip. Beside her, Flora was rigid as a statue. Even Toby was, for once, lost for words.

'Do not be afraid,' the man said, his voice as peaceful as his smile. 'I can do you no harm.'

After the initial shock, Cat realised that although his body hung unsupported from the cord around his neck, some invisible force must be holding him up. He was suspended in the air, as if weightless, about three feet off the ground.

The eyes that regarded them were astonishingly wide and a vivid blue, set in a gentle, childlike face. His skin was drained of all colour and his hair, which came down to his shoulders, was neither the blonde of youth nor the white of age, but something in between. His clothes were plain black, of indeterminate style, and his hands were bound behind his back.

Toby had recovered the power of speech. 'Er...shouldn't you be upside down, like on the card?'

Now the man looked amused. 'Since the Lot of the Hanged Man was first conceived, my fate has known many representations.' He sighed, and the tree's leaves murmured as if in response; in the dim light of the chamber they had acquired a coppery tint. His eyes shone innocent and blue. 'Would you like to know,' he said softly, 'how the Game of Triumphs came to be?'

CHAPTER TEN

'There was a city,' he began. 'Long, long ago, like in the fairy tales – though it was real enough. A city of art and power and learning, much of which has been lost. And each year, on its great festival day, the city held a lottery, when the people would pay to receive a token. Most of these tokens were blank, but a number of them could be exchanged for prizes. Some of these were practical and others decorative, but a few were precious.

'Many citizens played this lottery, but the leisured classes did not, considering it beneath them. Until one year the authorities decided to introduce something different. The four leading guilds within the city, the ones who administered the lottery, announced that they were going to include forfeits among the prizes. Just a few. Small fines or trials, to be performed in honour of the gods. And to their surprise, subscription to the lottery doubled. To play now required an element of daring and so became a matter of prestige.

'The next year, the lottery was not open to all. Invitations were issued at random. The rewards were more glittering, the penalties more dangerous. As a result, the guilds were obliged to form an order whose sole purpose was to enforce the fulfilment of the lots, and who pledged themselves to the service of Fortune and her Wheel.

'And with time, the workings of the lottery – or Game, as it was now called – grew yet more elaborate. The heads of the four guilds met in secret for its operation. The symbols on the lots became so complex it was no longer clear what was a penalty and what was a prize, for their making was steeped in mystery. So too was the fulfilment of the fates decreed. Over the years, it was rumoured that the gods themselves took their chance in the Game, that in joining it you could walk through men's dreams and see into other worlds.

'More time passed, and the power within the city shifted away from the guilds, the old religion too. Some people began to say the Game had become a shameful thing and a wickedness. It ceased to be spoken of, though it was still played.

'Until at last there came the day when the city fell to its enemies. There was great destruction, and most people assumed the Game had perished also. It became a myth. But, somehow, something survived. The symbols devised by its first makers began to appear in different forms – in decks of playing cards, in poetry and prophecy, things sacred and profane. It was whispered that the Game had found new cities, and new players ready to venture all.'

There was a long silence. In the time he had been speaking, the tree's green had changed to brittle brown and gold, and now the first leaf fell, quivering, through the air.

Toby swallowed nervously. 'But – but if you were there when the Game began then, er, why are you down here?'

'It had become essential to the nature of the Game to have one player whose move was eternally suspended, here, on the threshold of all thresholds. And so the Lot of Sacrifice was drawn.' He smiled his gentle smile. 'I am the axle around which the Arcanum whirls. I am this temple's cornerstone. As long as the four courts have dominion over me, their domination of the Game is complete. For all who seek to win from the Arcanum do so in fulfilment of their stratagems.'

'So if we were to set you free, it would be the end of the Game Masters,' said Flora abruptly. Since entering the chamber, she hadn't taken her eyes off the man's face.

'We can't, though,' Cat muttered. 'We can't intervene. We're powerless.'

The Hanged Man laughed softly. 'Not so. Accidentals and blunderers you may be, yet the Fool is the agent of Fortuna, Imperatrix Mundi, who presides over all. Her laws are the Arcanum's laws; all other rules are lesser, and false. That is why the four masters have no choice but to open the Arcanum for you and guide you to the Game. They know the Fool is as integral to its workings as the Wheel, for you too may change the course of a move, shaping a court's luck and a player's destiny.'

'But only by paying the forfeit. By being taken as knaves.'

'It was not always so, nor need it be.'

'What do you mean?'

'I mean that a move to win my freedom would lead to the freedom of greater and lesser alike.'

The three chancers exchanged glances.

'I do not ask this for myself alone. Once the rule of the courts was overthrown, the Game Masters would be compelled to release their triumphs, so that anyone in the Game might find them, safe from intervention or forfeit. Think of it: every threshold would be open, every card would be free to turn and every move to be completed. There would be prizes for all.'

'Not everyone in the Game is after a triumph,' said Flora slowly.

'No, indeed.' The man fixed his shining eyes upon

them. 'There are many hopes sought in the Arcanum. But given the right card for the right venture...why, even a fool could play to win.'

'Tell us how to release you,' said Toby. His voice was strained. It was obvious that they could no more untie him from the tree than pull down the pillar of stone at their backs. The very air they breathed was steeped in the power of the Arcanum.

'Whether by accident or design, fate or luck, the key to my tomb is only found when a Suite of Fools has entered play.' He sounded profoundly weary. 'Where, then, is the fourth?'

'I – we – we don't know.'

The floor of the chamber was now a carpet of dead leaves that, even as they watched, turned to filigree and dust. It seemed the man's voice had grown dustier also, his skin like ash. 'You must find him. A fool for every court and a court for every fool...' he murmured. 'And so it is that four throws of the die will open your way. My sacrifice is the Twelfth, but my deliverance shall be by the First. When the First of the Greater gives you the Firsts of the Lesser, then I may be set...set free...' His voice faded away as his head sunk down onto his chest. The last leaf had fallen from the barren tree.

As they padded out of the chamber, its spindly branches were silvered in frost.

*

They returned the same way they came, through the mirrored wall, the shuttered house, back across the park and into the polished drawing room. According to the clock on the wall, only half an hour had passed.

Each was holding a card from the room with the gold curtain. On their return journey, the card in the centre of the table, the one around which the other four were arranged, had become the Triumph of the Magician. Moreover, the moment they had each reached for one of the four other cards, the motif of wheels had merged, briefly reshaping into colour and form before fading to blankness. The last card retained its abstract patterning. Cat had slipped it into her jacket, while Flora took the Magician and Toby the die. Nobody commented on this, just as nobody had said anything about what their card had shown. In fact, nobody had spoken since they'd left the crypt.

'Well,' said Toby at last, 'looks like we've got ourselves a quest.'

'Or a wild-goose chase,' said Cat. She didn't mean it though. The fleeting image revealed on her card, the Triumph of Justice, was still seared on her mind's eye. What had once been a faint hope was now a promise. *There would be prizes for all… Even a fool could play to win…* 'Can we have another look at that Magician?'

They moved under the light to inspect it properly. A man in red and white robes stood over a table displaying the symbols of the courts. His right hand raised a magician's staff towards the sky, his left pointed towards the earth, where roses and lilies were entwined. The back of the card was marked 'I'.

'The Hanged Man's the twelfth triumph, he said, and his "deliverance" will come from the first. That's this card here: Thoth, the mage and magician! He's the First of the Greater Arcana, and it's up to the three – four – of us to find him.' Flora's face blazed with conviction. 'It's *destined.*'

'I still don't see how we can do anything about anything,' Cat warned. 'Destiny aside, the fact remains that us chancers can't meddle in the Game. Not without paying a nasty price.'

Flora jabbed at the card in exasperation. 'Don't you see? This is different. This makes *all* the difference. For the first time ever, we have a card of our own to play, one that hasn't been dealt by any of the kings or queens. Which means that while we can't mess with them, they can't mess with us. And then once we've found the Magician and released the Hanged Man, everything and everyone will be set free. Greater and Lesser alike! Any chancer, knight or knave will be able to walk through the Arcanum and win a prize, and there won't be any stupid rules or forfeits to stop them.' Her face was alight with longing.

'If that's true, then we'll be making the Game Masters feel pretty twitchy,' Cat said.

'I suppose,' said Toby, 'the Game Masters *have* to be at some kind of collective risk, however unlikely, else there wouldn't be much of a thrill in playing. And, you know, the Hanged Man's story about how the lottery and so on developed makes perfect sense. I remember at school—' He stopped, and frowned.

'What?' Cat asked.

'Never mind.' Toby had turned his attention to the unmarked die. It was a tetrahedron with four triangle-shaped faces, and made of the same gleaming dark metal as the threshold coins. ' "Four throws of the die will open your way"…I bet this is what we need to create a threshold. Now, I wonder…' He threw it up in the air, nearly fumbling the catch. 'Gotcha!' With a flourish, he showed it to the others. One of the sides was now printed with a little silver zero, the sign of a Fool. Toby immediately tried again, but without producing any further transformation.

'Here, let me.' Flora took it from Toby's unwilling hand. 'Oh!' she exclaimed, as a second side revealed another zero. 'Go on, Cat – it's your turn.'

A third throw, and a third side revealed its marking. But no matter how many times they passed the die round again, the fourth face remained frustratingly blank.

'It must need the missing chancer,' said Toby gloomily. 'He said there should be a fool for every court, remember. Find the chancer, complete the die and throw it to make a threshold. But tracking him or her down could take *months*.'

'Not…necessarily,' said Cat.

'What are you saying?' Flora asked sharply. 'Do *you* know this person? Or how to find them?'

Cat waited before she replied. There had been something niggling at the back of her mind and now she wanted to set it straight. 'I think so. First off, though, I want to know why you didn't tell us you'd already tried the key.'

'What do you mean?'

'I mean that I was watching you during our trip to the crypt. And I reckon what we found there didn't come as a total surprise.'

For a moment it looked as if Flora would tough it out. Then she seemed to think better of it. She even gave an embarrassed sort of shrug. 'All right,' she said. 'All right, I'll admit that I didn't see any reason to tell you two about finding the key. Not at first. So yesterday I went to Temple House by myself and tried the key in the door.'

Cat folded her arms across her chest. 'And then what?'

'I went down the stairs and into the little room. But the

cards in the middle of the table – well, they were different. Four Fool cards, one at each corner of the Triumph of the Moon. Then I thought back to the other person in the move, and the coin coming up with a zero, and I realised that this wasn't something I should be doing on my own. When the Arcanum gives you a sign, you'd better listen to it.' She gave a slightly shaky laugh. 'In the end, I didn't even look past the curtain. I went straight back up the stairs, and decided to come back only after I'd found you two.'

'Does this mean you already knew what the Hanged Man was doing down there?' Toby demanded.

'No. Anyone who's ever flicked through a Tarot pack would recognise his card, of course. Knowing its role in the Game is a different matter entirely. And there have been whispers over the years about a card that never gets dealt, that opens all thresholds and is exempt from all rules… But most of the rumours in the Arcanum are bogus – players don't tend to share secrets or swap tips, and you shouldn't trust them if they do.'

Cat snorted.

'Look, I'm sorry I wasn't straight with you. But as soon as I realised the key, and the crypt, was something that involved all three – four – of us, I knew I'd been wrong not to share it. I didn't want to tell you that I'd started out on my own because I wanted you to trust me. And I *am* worth trusting. I swear.' Flora widened her eyes in appeal.

'OK, fine.' Cat kept her voice level. 'But if I'm going to try and find our AWOL chancer, and if we're going to take this…thing…any further, we need to be straight with each other. Swapping and sharing and all the rest of it.'

'You're right, and I'm sorry,' said Flora penitently.

'We're a team now,' put in Toby. 'Team Arcanum!'

'Exactly.'

Cat caught her own eye in the splintered mirror above the mantelpiece. She had already seen where the remains of a broken tumbler had been stuffed in the wastepaper basket, already remembered the crashes and shouts they'd heard from Flora's perfect white bedroom. What had Flora's card promised her? What had the image on Toby's revealed?

The first principle of a game of strategy was that no one revealed their hand.

CHAPTER ELEVEN

Cat began her search for Blaine at the service entrance to the Hotel Excelsior. At 7 am the yard was bustling with the arrival of those on morning shifts and the taking in of deliveries. She decided to start with a burly man who was supervising the unloading of crates of fruit from a grocer's van. 'Scuse me, I'm looking for someone who works here. His name's Blaine and—'

'This isn't a lost and found, dearie. Nor a dating agency.'

'I only want—'

'I want doesn't get; didn't your mother tell you? So unless you're here on official business, you can clear off. Go on – hop it.'

'Miserable old sod,' muttered a woman walking past with a clipboard. 'Blaine, was it?'

'That's right.'

'I know – does some washing up and that occasionally.

Strictly off-record, of course.' She winked broadly. 'If you can wait a bit, Malek will be coming off shift. He might know. I'll ask him to have a word.'

Cat did the rest of her loitering in the street. A quarter of an hour later, a small man in a cleaner's uniform, his dark face tinged grey with fatigue, stopped alongside. 'You look for Blaine?'

Cat nodded.

'Why you want?' he asked warily.

'He…he did some odds and ends for my uncle a while back. Stocktaking. We might have a bit of work for him, that's all.'

Malek didn't reply at once, but continued to look her over carefully. Whatever he saw seemed to satisfy him. 'OK. Blaine he sometime stay in Langdon Street by Turkish shop. Place down the underground.'

In the basement, presumably. Cat felt a rush of optimism: Langdon Street was in Soho.

The air by the Turkish coffee shop was warm and fragrant, mounds of pastries glistening in the window within a garland of red tinsel. To one side was a small hardware store, to the other a boarded-up office. Judging by the layers of flyers and posters plastered on every inch of surface, it looked as if it had been empty for some time.

However, in the dank little space down by the

basement Cat could see chinks of light between the boards and hear, faintly, the sound of voices. She knocked on the door.

Immediately, the voices stopped. She knocked again.

There was a minute or so's wait until the door eventually creaked open a few inches. It was Blaine. The recognition on his face was instant, and almost as instantly wiped clear. 'Yeah?'

'My name's Cat.'

'So?'

'Malek – from the hotel – said you might be here.' His hostile expression didn't waver and she had a flashback to Flora, playing dumb in the church and badass in the Arcanum. She wasn't going to let herself be stonewalled again. 'I want to talk to you.'

'What about?'

'This.'

She thrust the fourth card into his hand. The movement took him by surprise and he took the card before he'd realised what it was. As the interlocking wheels shifted into an illustration Cat couldn't quite make out, his face abruptly changed, its wariness replaced by something hard and resolute.

'You OK there, bro?' Someone else had come to stand behind Blaine; a very thin, very tall white guy with dreadlocks that had been dyed a startling flamingo pink.

Blaine cleared his throat. His sleeves were pushed back, and his free hand was tracing a ragged scar along the outside of his right arm. He hadn't taken his eyes off the card, though its face was now blank. 'Yeah. Just some kid.'

Cat felt a flash of annoyance: this boy couldn't be much more than a year older than her. She fixed him with her chilly grey gaze. 'So, are you going to talk to me or not?'

He shrugged. 'Looks like I don't have much of a choice.'

Same here, she wanted to say. The Six of Cups had seen to that. Somewhere, perhaps, in the ever-changing world of the Arcanum there were other cards with other means of discovering who killed her parents, and why. But now she had been offered another way – a way to play on her own terms, which could lead to the Triumph of Justice and the righting of wrongs – it was hard to keep her mind on anything else. Disclosure, judgement and punishment.

Yes, she knew how Blaine felt. No choice about it.

Cat had arranged to join the others at the greasy spoon Toby was so fond of. Their meeting wasn't meant to be much more than a progress report; she had not expected to recruit Blaine so quickly, and though she knew the others would be surprised and elated by her success, the closer they drew to the cafe the more apprehensive she felt.

Meanwhile, Blaine loped along in silence, hands thrust deep in his pockets, hoodie pulled low. Despite her own reticence, she was surprised by how much his unsettled her. She had kept her explanations as short as possible, as if brevity could reduce them to something manageable and matter-of-fact. But he showed little or no reaction to her account, and accepted her offer to meet the others with a terse nod.

Even so, her curiosity got the better of her. 'I know you were in the Triumph of the Moon,' she ventured. 'Does that mean you were at the Lottery, too?'

'Lotteries are a pile of crap.'

'But Temple House—'

'Temple House is an even bigger pile of crap. Garden parties! Fairy lights! Chitchat over the canapés.' He snorted. 'Makes me want to vomit.'

'I know what you mean.'

'Do you now.'

'I know that everyone involved in this is either desperate or lunatic or both. And it's stupid to pretend otherwise.'

'Yeah? So which are you?'

Cat ignored the remark. 'If you didn't get to the Moon through Temple House, you must've found its threshold in the city. The one we used to come back, in the underpass.'

Blaine gave a grudging nod. Then, somewhat to her

surprise, he went on to explain. 'I go out looking for them. I had this idea… I thought if I found enough thresholds, I might be able to work out a pattern. For where and when they turn up.'

'And have you?'

'No.' He grinned, and the shadows in his face briefly lightened. 'But since when does this Game of ours go to plan?'

They were approaching the cafe now, and Cat could see Toby and Flora in the window. Toby, a trilby perched on his head and biscuit crumbs down his shirt, was talking and gesturing excitedly while Flora, pretty in pink, pretended to sip a mug of stewed tea.

Toby was the first to spot Cat and who she had brought with her. 'I can't believe you've found him already!' he exclaimed. 'Wait – I mean – this is *him*, right?'

'Blaine, meet Toby. Toby – Blaine. And that's Flora.'

Flora was staring, fascinated, at his frayed cuffs and dirty fingernails. However, she soon rallied. 'Pleased to meet you,' she said in her most winning manner. 'It's awfully good of you to come.'

Blaine turned to Cat. 'Is she always like this?'

Flora's airs and graces might annoy her, but Cat wasn't ready to exchange conspiratorial asides about them. Not with Blaine, anyway. She compromised on a noncommittal shrug.

Toby broke into the increasingly awkward pause. 'Look, why don't you two sit down and we can get some more coffee or...' He looked doubtfully at Blaine's thin wrists and dark-rimmed eyes. 'Would you like, er, something to eat...a hot meal...?'

'How kind. Maybe you can knit me some socks and take round a collecting tin while you're at it.'

The air of embarrassment grew stronger. Blaine stretched and yawned enormously. 'But seeing as you're offering, I'll have bacon, egg and chips. And a large tea.'

'...so, basically,' Toby finished, 'we need to create a threshold and find the Magician. Then he'll help us get the Hanged Man down from the tree. Cool, huh?'

The dour cafe owner plonked Blaine's plate down with a disbelieving grunt, and went off shaking his head.

Blaine didn't look too impressed either. In fact, he seemed more interested in concentrating on his food, shovelling it in with speed and efficiency. When it appeared they were going to get no further response from him, Cat stepped in.

'See, we reckon the die will only work after you've activated the fourth side. And once that's done, we can get into the Arcanum whenever and wherever we like. We won't be tagging after some knight. We'll have our own card, our own threshold, and no king or queen to answer to.'

But again, Blaine showed no reaction and Cat ground to a halt.

'If it's all the same with you,' said Flora, who had moved on to inspecting her own fingernails, 'I'd prefer to put off any excursions until after Christmas. Would it be frightfully difficult for people to get away on Boxing Day?'

Conversation descended into the wrangling over places and timings that occurs when any kind of group outing needs to be organised. Blaine didn't contribute to this, either. But as the others were debating Cat's suggestion of meeting at Piccadilly Circus at three o'clock, Boxing Day, he turned from staring out of the foggy window.

'There's no sense in rushing things,' he said suddenly. 'It's not like the future of mankind is at stake. We don't even have to save the world from the Forces of Darkness.'

'Well, no,' said Toby, 'but rescuing the Hanged Man…'

'Let's not kid ourselves we're doing it for his benefit.'

Nobody had anything to say to this, aware of the blank cards they each carried, held close as a promise. Blaine looked slowly round the table. 'How did you lot get into this gig, anyway?'

Caught off guard, Cat found herself stammering. 'It – it began when I sort of – of – stumbled into someone.'

'I…erm…overheard a conversation,' Toby said

reluctantly, feet tap-tapping under the table.

'By following a thread,' said Flora, eyes defiant. 'And you?'

'I read a book.' Blaine pushed his plate away and got to his feet. 'Full of information, aren't we,' he remarked sardonically. 'See you later…team.'

The other three stared after his departing back. 'It looks like you've got some competition for that "enigmatic loner" tag, Cat,' Toby observed. 'Funny, he doesn't particularly sound like a street kid.'

'And how're street kids supposed to sound?'

Toby took the question at face value. 'Cruder. More…*guttural.* Hey, do you think he's in a gang? I'm sure that was a tattoo I saw on the back of his neck.'

'It was probably dirt,' said Flora, wincing at her mouthful of cold tea. 'Frankly, as long as he turns up and does his stuff, he can be gun-running for the Taliban for all I care.'

After leaving the cafe, Cat decided to kill a bit of time on Oxford Street, even though her Christmas purchases – chocolates for Greg, posh face cream for Bel – had been made long before. London crowds no longer alarmed her; she had recovered her knack for losing herself in them without getting lost. As soon as she got to Oxford Circus, though, she regretted it.

Every inch of pavement was seething with people, their bodies muffled in sludgy winter layers, their faces set, elbows, bags and feet all jostling for position. Every inch of shop front glittered with fake stars and sterile snow. Their promises were plastic too: Magic! Romance! The Perfect Present! A Better Future! Set in lights above Regent Street, characters from the latest Disney film gambolled in the air. A roast nut stand wafted a stale syrup smell through the traffic fumes, along with blasts of fried onions from a hot-dog vendor. 'Sinners spend but Jesus saves!' admonished the evangelist with a loudspeaker. 'If you shop till you drop, who will catch you when you fall?'

'It seems the End is Nigh,' came a voice in Cat's ear. It was Alastor, the King of Swords, wearing a long black coat with the collar turned up, and lounging beneath a slew of sale signs.

Cat started, but managed to reply steadily enough. 'Doing a spot of Christmas shopping?'

'As a matter of fact, I was hoping you'd spare the time for a little talk.' He nodded towards an unmarked black car that had just pulled up in the bus lane.

'There's no way I'm going anywhere with you. I'm not *daft*.' She began to back away.

'Oh, don't worry – you'll be quite safe. I'm as anxious to avoid any rule-breaking as you are. Please,' he said gently, 'I'd be very grateful if you'd get in.'

At this, although she wasn't quite sure how or why, Cat found herself climbing into the back seat. The interior smelled of expensive leather and the driver was shut off from his passengers by a sliding panel of tinted glass. The next moment, the car had moved off into the stream of traffic.

'God, what a slum this place is getting to be,' Alastor remarked, settling more comfortably beside her. He winked at her with lazy charm. 'So much nicer on the other side of town, don't you think?'

Cat looked out of the window. They had just turned down Regent Street, but the crowds and fumes and garish Disney characters had disappeared. The Christmas lights strung between the buildings were now a cascade of hearts, clubs, diamonds and spades, flashing black and red on white against a sunset sky. And as the car purred on, the majestic buildings lining the street slipped past in a seemingly endless curve.

She felt for the handle on the door. It was locked. At once, Alastor raised his hand in a gesture of reassurance. 'I told you I am not here to threaten or obstruct you. I will respect the rules.'

'Yeah – and who makes the rules?'

'The Arcanum operates according to its own principles. These will always endure. But without the rules that the courts impose there would be no strategy or structure, no restraint. And who would want that?' He arched his brows at her. 'After all, everybody who enters the Game does so freely, and for good reason. Even – or perhaps especially – those who claim it to be by accident.'

'I don't reckon accidents figured much in your career. The way I heard it, to get to be a GM, you have to grab every triumph in the deck.'

'And give them back each time, remember. Move after move, prize after prize, risking everything over and over... Why, Cat, don't tell me you're ambitious to be queen?'

'Not bloody likely.'

Alastor laughed indulgently. 'The last triumph I had to win was held by a queen, you know. Once I captured it, her court was mine. She had ruled Swords for a very long time; I think she may even have been one of the first Masters. And she put up a fine fight at the end.

'Of course, the final triumph is always the one that costs the most to win. A Game Master can't put their prizes to use outside the Arcanum. And in my last moments of struggle, renouncing the ordinary world seemed a heavy price...' Briefly, his face darkened. 'But, as they say, Fortune favours the brave. Since then, it sometimes feels as if I've only been playing for a few hours, sometimes from the beginning of time itself, yet every moment has the savour of my first victory.'

'Bet you wish you didn't have to share that victory, though.'

'What do you mean?'

'I mean that you'd prefer to be the one and only Grand High Game Master. Ahab told me how you're all angling to be top dog, even though nobody seems to know how to pull it off.' She thought back to the abandoned office and the eerie flicker of its computer screens. 'He reckoned there's a way of winning that means one Game Master gets to control luck and fate and the rest of it. Like playing God.'

'Well,' said the King of Swords softly, 'that would be a triumph indeed.'

Cat wondered what had happened to the queen who Alastor had deposed, and about the life he had given up to rule the Arcanum. What kind of man had he been, living in what kind of world? They're all fools, she thought. For all their swanky speeches and scheming, it's the Game that plays *them*.

She turned and looked out of the window again. The sky was bruised purple streaked with orange. A spiral of hearts flashed before her eyes, spinning into cups at the final moment. Behind, a tumble of spades was now an arch of dancing swords.

'So if you're not here to make threats, what's this about?'

'What an abrupt girl you are,' he said. 'I rather thought you were enjoying our chat. Still, I suppose impatience is a virtue of sorts.' He leaned forwards to rap on the driver's partition, and the next moment they were drawing up at Piccadilly Circus.

Cat felt even more uneasy once she got out of the car. The statue of Eros that presided over the intersection had been replaced by an effigy of Justice with her sword and scales. Seated on the steps below the fountain were the other king and queens – Odile in white, Ahab, sombre-suited, Lucrezia swathed in furs – all as motionless as the statue itself. Under the shimmer of the vast advertising panels, where Samsung and Coke had changed to alternating symbols of the four courts, the king's languid face pulsed white light and dark shadow, then neon red.

'The Game gives us the chance to make our own luck, Cat. To change our fate. To win our most secret desires, against all logic and reason, against all odds. And yet you are set on a course that will rob it of its most enduring standards.'

'Rob you of your powers, you mean. Is this where you tempt me over to the Dark Side? Promise me triumphs? Heroism and happy endings?' she mocked.

At that, he gave an odd sort of half-smile, reaching across to lightly touch her hair. 'Poor kitty-cat... If I drew you for my court, you would make a fine knight, I think. For today, Cups holds Justice. Tomorrow, who knows?' He tilted his head towards the three figures on the steps. 'We are all Fortune's fools, and it is not my place to halt the spinning of her Wheel. But do not forget the Game's imperative is *every player for himself*. Remember this, the next time your friends coax you through unmarked doors, or make their promises, or ask you to take their word on trust.'

Now the king leaned in nearer, his voice very low, breath sweet as cinnamon, as the sky was lit by the acid dazzle of swords.

'And there is something else, which is not a threat but a warning, the only one I may make. The Hanged Man has another, older name. In times past, he was called the Traitor.'

With great effort, Cat dragged her eyes away. The world reeled and sparkled but somehow she managed to straighten her shoulders and shake her head. 'If he betrayed you and your mates, then good for him. And seeing as the Arcanum works its own rules, I reckon it'll be able to get over any challenge to yours.'

Black, white and red flared against her eyes. Alastor laughed softly. 'Then face the odds and take your gamble, as we all must do.' He took out a coin and spun it high in the air. 'Happy Christmas, Cat.'

And by the time the coin returned to his palm, she was standing under the Statue of Eros, once more alone in the crowd.

CHAPTER TWELVE

Cat and Bel's Christmas began the same way as it always did: not with stockings, but with working their way through a box of crackers. Greg was spending the day with his aged mother out in Rotherhithe, so it was just the two of them. Over a ready-made lunch – hoisin duck and pancakes for Bel, roast chicken and trimmings for Cat – they turned on the stereo to drown out the interminable drum 'n' bass from next door, and drew the curtains so that they ate under the glow of the fruit lights. Rain pattered cosily against the windowpanes.

Cat felt treacherous for wondering how this Christmas could have been different; how it might have been if she still had her mum and dad. Bel would be there too, of course. They'd all be squeezed up close round the table, chatting and laughing. There would be stockings and home-made mince pies and a real tree. A family Christmas, Disney-style. Rose-tinted thinking,

Cat told herself. *Get over it.*

Bel was in a very good mood. She'd bought them both feather boas, pink for her and purple for Cat, and insisted they get dolled up, adorning Cat's face with swoops of silver eye shadow. She even made Cat wear her trophy from the crackers: a plastic four-leaf clover on a chain. Afterwards, she produced a set of keys with a flourish. 'Greg left them with me. I reckon it's time you had a backstage tour of the palace.'

'I thought you said it's a hole.'

'Hole, sweet hole. But there's a karaoke machine left from the Christmas party, as many crisps as you can eat, and widescreen telly in the bar. It'll be fun. Like sneaking round school after hours.'

For the second time in a week, Cat was shown into the Palais Luxe's dingy lobby. This time, however, they headed to the gaming floor, which was dominated by three blackjack tables and three roulette wheels. A plastic Christmas tree leaned drunkenly against a rank of slot machines. The paisley carpet was dark with grime, the ceiling low, and the air stale with a lingering smell of sweat.

Bel turned on the lights and sound system, flooding the room with Andy Martin crooning about Paris skies. The slot machines twinkled into life. 'Our own private party palace,' she said cheerfully, going to the bar to help herself to a rum and Coke. She came back with a can of lemonade for Cat, and an armful of snacks. 'C'mon, what do you fancy – Roulette? Poker? James Bond brooding in a corner?'

'Game of tiddlywinks is all I'm fit for.'

'We'll see about that.' Bel flicked her feather boa over her shoulder and sashayed over to the nearest roulette wheel. 'Would Modom care to place her chips?'

Cat gave in. She opened a packet of peanuts and placed three on the table layout to the side of the wheel. A straight inside bet, number eight. Eight was the Triumph of Justice.

Bel spun the wheel in one direction and launched the ball in another. 'No more bets!' she called, as the ball got ready to drop from the outside track of the wheel towards the numbered slots. It whizzed around some more, bounced and settled. 'Unlucky,' she said, placing a marker on the green '0' square on the layout and scooping up Cat's peanuts. 'Try again.'

But Cat was still staring at the wheel, where an image of the Queen of Cups leaning over the slots had flashed before her eyes. 'No,' she said, with sudden vehemence. 'That's enough.'

Her aunt laughed. 'All right, puss-cat. You keep hold of your peanuts. There was a bloke here yesterday – bloodshot eyes, probably hadn't changed his clothes all week – and I watched him lose ten grand in an hour. Ten grand! Course, you can't stop them, and they wouldn't thank you if you tried.' She frowned, her effervescence suddenly fizzing away. 'You know what I heard? Back in the old days, Lady Luck was a girl called Hecuba. That's the Queen of Witches.'

Cat's mouth felt dry. 'Who told you that?'

'Oh…just someone I used to know.'

'A gambler?'

'Yeah. They're a superstitious bunch.' Bel cleared her throat. 'Got a meeting with Leo set up after the holiday – you remember, from that poker tournament. The manager at Alliette's. Anyhow, he reckons there might be an opening for me there.'

Cat looked at the opposite wall, and its posters of soft-focus couples laughing as they placed their bets. They didn't bear much resemblance to the solitary, dead-eyed figures she had seen waiting outside the Luxe's doors. 'D'you think it'll really be that different to here? I mean, it would be bigger and flashier. Obviously. But underneath, it's…it's all the same, isn't it?'

Bel acted as if she hadn't heard. She moved towards the blacked-out windows, flexing her hands restlessly. 'When you first start handling the chips, it stretches your fingers. Makes them ache. I don't even notice it now…' She was still frowning. 'I'm a good dealer, Cat: slick with the cards, quick with numbers. The punters like me. At Alliette's they have proper training schemes, for management and that. There wouldn't be so many night shifts. And after all the chopping and changing and starting over...well, it could be my lucky break. *Our* lucky break, you know?'

'Yeah,' said Cat softly. 'I know.'

On Boxing Day, Cat got a call from Toby about an hour before she was due to meet the others. She nearly didn't answer it, feeling unable to cope with premature effusions about the adventures ahead. *The odds are ag-gainst you,* murmured the stranger in her dreams, and she had woken up to find her eyes swollen and gluey, as if she'd been crying in her sleep.

However, when she finally picked up, Toby sounded unnaturally subdued. 'Cat,' he said. 'There's something I need to tell you. I'll be at Piccadilly Circus in five – can you come and meet me?'

She supposed it was better then spending the next hour brooding in her room. But although it was a relief to get out of the flat – where Greg and Bel were drinking gin and jeering at the television – the grey quiet of the city, deep in its post-Christmas torpor, felt just as oppressive. Toby's serious tone had shaken her more than she liked to admit.

'What's all this about then?' she asked, as briskly as she could make it.

Toby took a while to answer, hunched over himself and frowning. 'Boarding school. I used to go to one, you see.'

Cat didn't see, but she nodded all the same.

'Nowhere smart. It was just outside London – small and arty and full of luvvie types. There was this secret club: the Chameleons. They gave people dares.'

'Dares?'

'Yeah. It was quite silly to begin with. The challenges were supposedly connected to film titles; anyone who got *Mrs Doubtfire* had to turn up to assembly in drag – that sort of stuff. Towards the end of term, though, things were different. Dares lasted a whole week. People were afraid to turn them down. And it was becoming…well, there was one called the *Invisible Man*, and the girl who got it wasn't allowed to speak to anyone and nobody was allowed to speak to her for the duration. It was like she didn't exist. Even the teachers seemed to stop noticing her.

'Another time, two people each drew a dare called *Brief Encounter* and they actually *went out*, had this passionately intense one-week relationship. And after their time was up, they went back to their original boyfriend and girlfriend.'

'Jesus, Toby. That's pretty sick.'

'Yeah, but it was also exciting. Which kind of bears out the Hanged Man's lottery story, doesn't it? The attraction of risk and all that.' His expression was dreamy. 'You have to understand that boarding school is this hyper-cliquey, claustrophobic world…those dares were a chance to throw out the rules, to see the old hierarchies turned upside down. No wonder I – we, I mean, got obsessed by them.'

There was a pause; Toby seemed unsure of how to begin the next stage of the story. 'OK. Anyway…there was this girl…a couple of years ahead of me, part of the popular crowd. Mia wasn't a snob, though. She was different to the rest. In fact, she was really nice.' Now he was blushing beneath his freckles. 'One evening I was staying late in the art studio, finishing off some coursework. And I'd just turned off the lights in the back room when I heard her and the art teacher, Mr Marlow, come in the main door. Mia sounded really agitated. She was saying she'd had enough, she was in over her head, they had to settle this once and for all. So I thought there was some, y'know, *affair* going on. Especially as Mr Marlow was this total sleazebag, the kind of teacher who thinks he's cool 'cause he smokes dope with the sixth form.

'But then they starting talking about drawing cards, and a duel, and how there wasn't anything in the rules about how it had to be fought. And I figured this must be some Chameleon dare thing. It wasn't that surprising Mr Marlow was involved. It was just the kind of thing he'd get off on.

'Mia suggested they settle the duel by tossing a coin, there and then. And Marlow laughed, very snide, and said there was no way he'd fall for *that*. No, he said, if they were going to flip for it, they'd go into the Arcanum and call the Game Masters as witnesses.'

'God. They were *both* in the Game.'

'Exactly. Of course, I still thought it was all Chameleon business... Mia sounded really reluctant, but Marlow was insistent. So in the end they agreed to meet at midnight in the clock tower. I guess there must've been a threshold still active there, because their move – the duel – hadn't been completed.

'Now, the clock tower was the oldest bit of the school and right the other side of the playing fields. It was out of bounds and all spooky and rackety, the perfect setting for a secret society. I knew this was my big chance to see who was in the Chameleons, how the dares were organised and so on. I thought that they might even let me join, once they'd seen how I'd tracked them down.

'It wasn't that hard sneaking out. Like I said, it was a pretty lax sort of school. Anyway, I got there just before midnight and found the door at the bottom of the tower was open. I went up the stairs, right to the top. I heard shouting, and a crashing sound, and then Mia screamed.

'It was obvious it was just the two of them and Marlow was...I don't know...*attacking* her. So I started to yell and pound on the door, shouting that they were in big trouble and that the police were on their way. I hoped he'd think I was the caretaker or something. There was utter silence. I couldn't get into the room, so I ran downstairs to go and fetch help.

'And just as I got outside, the tower began to shake. The bricks didn't look solid any more. They sort of…shivered in the air, as if the whole building was made of silk. I wasn't even particularly scared. I was transfixed.

'The next moment, Mia came flying out of the door, face blazing white and a gash in her forehead. "It's too late," she said, "it's too late." She ran off before I could stop her. Then the shaking stopped, and everything looked real and solid for a moment, before there was this awful groaning, cracking noise and the roof of the tower collapsed.'

'With – with Mr Marlow still inside?'

'No. Afterwards, there was no sign of him. He must've changed sides at the threshold in time.'

'And Mia?'

'They found her wandering around the edge of the playing fields. Quite calm, though there was still blood on her forehead. She said Mr Marlow had lured her out to the tower, and tried to attack her, though they'd both got out before it collapsed. She never mentioned me – and in all the confusion, I'd managed to sneak back into the main buildings unnoticed. Not surprisingly, she was immediately carted off to be treated for shock and stuff and after the police enquiries were over she didn't come back to school. It was the most tremendous scandal, especially since Mr Marlow was never found. Even the press got involved.'

'So which card did you find?'

'The Knight of Pentacles. Mia dropped it as she ran off. I knew I should hand it in as evidence, just like I should have come forward as a witness, but somehow my gut instincts were against it. And the next evening, just before my parents were due to come and take me home, I went back to the tower. It was fenced off with big "Keep Out" and "Danger" signs, and crime scene investigation tape, and there was a woman standing there, all dolled up in leopard print and high heels. At first I thought she was some kind of detective, or maybe a journalist. She was looking at another card. Later, I realised it was the Ace of Pentacles.'

By now, Cat was familiar enough with the deck to understand what this meant. 'The Root of Earth,' she said slowly, working things through. 'Marlow must've used the card to summon up an earthquake. He was the Knight of Pentacles, and Mia was Cups. They were dealt each other's cards and so had to fight it out. But Mia escaped before the ace did its worst…'

'I know. It must have been me hammering on the door that put him off, and bought her some time. Still, the queen – it was the dark-haired one, Lucrezia – didn't look too annoyed with me. She said, "I thought I might find you here", and sort of laughed to herself. Then she sashayed over and put out her hand, and before I knew it, I was handing her the card I'd found.

'There was a shout from behind – one of the coppers had come to warn me off the crime scene or whatever they thought it was. So I had to go. But before I left, she tucked the card back in my coat pocket. I could've sworn it was the same card I gave her, but when I got it out later, it was the Fool, with an invitation on the back, and a coin…'

'Didn't what you'd seen put you off? Scare you?'

'I was nervous about getting in over my head. Of course I was. I knew I couldn't afford to make any mistakes; that's why it took me such a long time to try out the Arcanum. I wanted to be properly prepared. Even so, I never doubted that it was, y'know, "meant to be".

'Look, it's obvious you and the other guys each have your own top-secret mission with a Very Important Prize at stake. And I'm just a – a hanger-on. I do see that. But it's not so terrible to want to be *involved*, is it? With something bigger than me, I mean. Something bigger and better and more exciting.'

Yes, she could see it all. The princess in her tower, rescue and romance… Which was all the Game would ever mean to him, Cat thought bitterly. Whatever was driving Flora and Blaine, it was plain that they were under some kind of imperative, perhaps even feeling the same kind of desperation as her. Meanwhile, Toby just wanted to play heroes.

'Why are you telling me this now?'

He started twisting his hands. 'Because – because after we said goodbye on Christmas Eve and I was going home, I swear I saw Mia. Walking down the street.'

'What did you do?'

'Went up to say hello, of course. We're both in the Game now, after all, and it'd be fun to catch up. But when I turned the corner, she'd disappeared, and the Queen of Pentacles was there instead.'

Cat exhaled sharply. 'I got the King of Swords. And a lot of fancy speeches about how I was making a big mistake.'

'Same here!' Toby's face brightened. 'We've obviously got them worried, and that's a good sign. But…Mia being there…it must have *meant* something… A kind of omen.'

'It was smoke and mirrors. Scare tactics. That's all.'

'Maybe,' he said dubiously. 'D'you reckon they tried to scare off Blaine and Flora as well?'

'Bound to.'

'In that case…well, I'm sure it's fine but…shouldn't the others be here by now?'

It was true it was nearly quarter past three. But the next moment, a taxi drew up and Flora got out. 'Gosh, I'm *so* sorry I'm late,' she said breathlessly. 'We had one of Daddy's golf cronies over for lunch and it went on and *on*… Did everyone have a nice Christmas?'

Although he hadn't announced himself, Blaine had also arrived at the east exit of the Tube, just behind Cat and Toby. His hooded top was pulled low over his face and he was swigging from a can. At Flora's words, he spat on the pavement.

Flora wasn't easily cowed. 'Hello, Blaine,' she said sweetly. 'How was your day?'

'Super. I robbed a little old lady and spent the money on crack.'

Her smile didn't slip. 'If you're trying to shock me, I'm afraid you'll have to do better than that.'

'That's assuming I give a toss about what you think.' He chucked his can into the gutter. 'Now we've got the banter over with, isn't it about time we made our move?'

Since it was the card alone that determined what they would face in the Arcanum, Cat had assumed that their meeting point would be where they'd create the threshold. She liked the symmetry of it, too: Piccadilly was where she'd first met the Knight of Wands, and where the King of Swords had taunted her with the effigy of Justice. However, she wasn't the only one who wanted their threshold's location to have some scenic or symbolic significance. It emerged that Flora wanted to move up to Mercury Square while Toby preferred to walk down to Admiralty Arch – 'I've always thought it's got a triumphal sort of feel about it.'

'Give us a look at the trinket,' Blaine said abruptly.

'Careful,' said Toby. 'Once you've thrown it, the faces will be complete and – we hope – ready to work their magic.'

Blaine flicked the die into the air. Sure enough, as soon as he caught it, the final face was marked by a zero. 'Nice. So all we need to do is give it a roll and, Open Sesame, a threshold appears.'

'I think so, but we don't want—'

Too late. Blaine had already stooped to send the die skittering down the pavement. Its triangular shape meant that it moved oddly, more of a bounce than a roll, yet the motion had a strange sense of purpose to it. As they watched, it tumbled over from edge to edge in a rough circle, before coming to a stop. This time, each felt an unmistakable throb on their right palms, as the four faces of the die glowed silver, then returned to blankness. Now it was just a lump of dark metal.

Flora's breath hissed. 'You irresponsible *jerk*.'

'Oh, get over it. If I'd left it to you lot, we'd be debating postcodes till next Christmas.'

'So where's the threshold, then?' asked Toby. 'And can I be the one to raise the coin?'

'Be my guest.' Cat pointed towards a fast-food outlet a few feet away on Shaftesbury Avenue. The lit-up 'Hot Food' sign in the window had a wheel worked into the first 'o'. A few seconds later, Toby was proudly brandishing his coin.

'Look, it's got our zero on it as well! OK, team – time to rock 'n' roll.'

'What, no big speeches?' Blaine jeered. 'No gathering round for a Condemned Man's Last Burger?'

'You want to make a speech, go ahead,' Flora replied. 'Please. I'm sure it would be most inspiring.'

Cat looked up from where she'd been staring at the pavement. 'I dunno about last meals or big speeches and that, but it seems to me that if any of us are having second thoughts about this…thing…we're doing, now's the time to say so. Because once we throw the coin, it'll be too late.'

She waited. A motorbike roared past, a woman giggled into a mobile phone, pigeons pecked for crumbs in the gutter. Nobody spoke. Slowly, carefully they met each other's eyes. Slowly, carefully, they each gave a brief nod.

'All right then. Time to go.'

CHAPTER THIRTEEN

They were in a city of ruin: of ragged walls and blind windows, bones of buildings in a starless night. Even the air tasted stale. The only sign of life came from the threshold, and the glow of the burger bar's menu – an incongruous token of the other side.

But they had only been peering around them for a moment or two when a jumble of light and music began to seep into the night. It seemed to be coming from what had once been Great Windmill Street. Near the turning, Cat realised uncomfortably, to her own flat.

'Sounds like a party,' said Toby, nonchalantly setting off in its direction. Flora and Blaine followed more slowly.

Cat was the last to move. Greg's flat, with its plasterboard walls and damp ceiling, might not be up to much, but she didn't want to see it reduced to rubble. She was even more uneasy once she'd turned the corner and was faced with the Palais Luxe, lit up like a schizophrenic

Christmas tree. Only it wasn't the Luxe any more: according to the ultraviolet lettering above the door, it was a club called Hecuba's.

Its sooty brick façade was the only intact structure on the street. A dance beat pumped out of windows pulsing with technicolour, and an enormous bouncer stood guard outside, his arms folded menacingly across his chest. 'No card, no entry,' he growled.

His expression didn't soften when Flora held out the Magician card in her best party manner. However, after clearing his throat in a resentful sort of way, he condescended to unhook the rope from across the entrance.

Before Cat could go in, Blaine stopped in the doorway. 'There's a redhead who works at the Luxe. She's some kind of relation of yours.'

'My aunt. How did…?'

'Soho's a small neighbourhood.' He stepped into the lobby. 'You never know; a bit of insider's knowledge could come in handy.'

It was true that, thanks to Bel's tour, Cat was familiar with the layout of the Luxe. The casino's safe was in a strongroom in the basement. Customer facilities were on the ground floor; the gaming hall and bar were one flight up, while the third floor was for surveillance and staff offices. But although Hecuba's might have had the same basic structure – and the same shabby paisley carpet in the entrance – that was where the resemblance ended.

For one thing, it was packed; a smoky fug of people, some of whom were in fancy dress. A Japanese geisha, a trio of men in Second World War RAF uniform, a woman in an elaborate powdered wig, an old gent in a toga…

'Who are all these people?' Toby asked.

Flora shrugged. 'Optical illusions. Ghosts of players past. God knows. They're just part of the scenery; it's the Magician who *counts*.'

'For illusions, they feel pretty solid,' Cat grumbled, as a girl in leather hot pants crashed past, squealing endearments at a man on the other side of the lobby. 'Somehow I don't reckon Mr Abracadabra will look much like the mugshot on his card. Which means we'll have to work our way through the rooms and hope we'll know him when we see him.'

They began with the basement, which had been set up with a stage where showgirls writhed in costumes of tattered feathers and diamanté. Puffs of dry ice swirled around the tables that crammed the floor. If the Magician was there, he was keeping a low profile, and after five minutes of knocking into tables and getting sworn at for obstructing the view, they retreated back to the stairs.

As they moved up the building, the din intensified. What had been the Luxe's gaming hall was now an amusement arcade, where shooter and racer games were packed alongside pinball and slot machines. Everything blared with noise and colour as players pushed coins into slots, pulled levers and furiously hammered on buttons.

'This is completely *mad*,' Flora called out, pushing back a strand of sweaty hair. There was something about her expression – something glinting and reckless – that reminded Cat of how she'd been the first time they met at Temple House. Perhaps the excitement of the place was catching. At any rate, Cat couldn't take her eyes off all those whizzing, blinking panels. Her heart raced and ears rang. Was this how the punters at the Luxe felt, as they waited for the roulette wheel to spin? For a confused moment, she could have sworn she saw Bel, tilting her head back and laughing, and she had to steady herself against a slot machine. Focus, she told herself, *focus*.

'What's the matter with you?' It was Blaine, glowering at her.

'I thought I saw someone I knew. Just for a second.' Come to think of it, one of the dancers in the basement had looked very like the blonde from the strip joint down her street. And that fat man lighting a cigar was a dead spit for her old geography teacher.

'Me too. It's not real, though. Don't let it get to you.'

Blaine's hooded top had been pushed back, and under the glaring lights Cat saw the remains of a bruise on one cheek. She was gripped by the absurd notion that if she were to put a fingertip to it, and the purplish smears under his eyes, she could rub out the markings, as lightly and easily as if she were using an eraser on pencil.

'What?'

She realised she had been staring and looked away, confused.

The upstairs dance floor was the source of the techno beat thudding through the building, yet the couples beneath the glitter balls swayed in sleepy embraces, as if moving to some faint melody that only they could hear. On the other side of the floor was the way through to the bar. Behind a mirrored counter, bartenders juggled bottles and glasses with dizzying ease. Cat grabbed a tumbler of ice and held it against her hot cheeks.

It was less busy here than in the rest of the club, with most of the crowd concentrated in the centre of the room. Some sort of demonstration or performance was taking place. A man in a top hat and tails was presiding over a card table while his audience called out incoherent instructions and encouragement, interspersed by raucous cheers.

Cat thought she recognised the game. She'd seen a version of it played on street corners, where gullible passers-by could be waylaid, and a quick exit made at any sign of trouble. It was known as 'Follow the Lady'. To begin, the dealer would place three cards face down on a table. He'd nominate one of the cards – usually the Queen of Spades – as the target card, and then quickly rearrange the cards to confuse the player as to which was which. The player was invited to choose one of the three cards. If it turned out to be the Queen, he'd win an amount equal to the stake he bet; otherwise, he lost his money. Of course, thanks to the dealer's sleight of hand, and all manner of misdirections and diversions, the only sure thing was that the player would lose.

'Care to place a bet, my friends?' The man looked at them craftily. His eyes were black and very bright, his face creased and yellowish. 'It's the easiest game in the world!'

He spread out the Three of Clubs, Seven of Diamonds and Ace of Hearts and waved a red silk handkerchief over the table. Now they were their Game of Triumph equivalents. 'Three! Seven! Ace! But where's the Lady?' With a wink, he reached behind a pretty girl's ear and pulled out the Queen of Spades. He tossed all his cards in the air; when they fell face down on the table there were only three again. 'Pick a card, any card!'

'The Twelfth,' said Blaine.

The whole room seemed to freeze. Heat, noise, movement all drained away into a ringing silence. Then, as if at the flick of a switch, the party resumed, although the Magician's smile had vanished. 'No more bets!' He gave a hasty bow, before backing away from the table. 'The entertainment is over, ladies and gents, and the game is played! Thank you for your time!'

Pushing through his former audience, the Magician headed for a door marked 'Staff Only' at the side of the bar. The four chancers hurried after him, into a storage space stacked with crates of bottles. Ahead of them was a set of steps leading to another exit, through which their man had disappeared in a whisk of coat-tails.

They found themselves on the roof, in a small flat space between the gables. It was furnished with a bench and a sprinkling of cigarette butts. A string of tropical fruit fairy lights sagged overhead. The Magician was standing at the very edge of the roof, staring across the skeletal city.

'Excuse me, sir,' Toby began. 'The four of us are chancers, right, and the Hanged Man gave us your card – in a manner of speaking – so we were hoping…'

'I know, I know,' he muttered, gnawing at his lip. 'The Twelfth. And you are set on his undoing, and the undoing of all. But what can I do?' He began to twist his hands in agitation. 'If the Wheel has turned that way, then I must follow it. *Fortunae te regendum dedisti, dominae moribus oportet obtemperes…* So it was at the beginning, so it has always been.'

'And you *were* there at the beginning, weren't you?'

Flora said, looking at him intently. 'Thoth, the mage, and first maker.'

His forehead creased, as if he was trying to remember something. 'I was once, perhaps... But I have had many names, and the cards many makers. The man of whom you speak, I first met by the gates of Atlantis. Or was it Babylon? There was a temple in Thebes, I recall, and a cherry tree... *Haec nostra uis est, hunc continuum ludum ludimus—*'

'Yeah, whatever,' said Blaine roughly. 'Question is, will you help us release him?'

At this, the Magician shot him a sly look; the showman's gleam was back in his eyes. 'I must do as I am bid, young sir. Oh yes indeed. See how my Lady plays her tricks: once I was a god, now I am a mountebank... Still, I have kept a few trappings of my craft. Behold!'

He opened out his coat to reveal all manner of pockets sewn into its faded scarlet lining. From one he produced a shot glass, from another a steel paper knife. Patting his outer pockets, he drew out a cigarette lighter and, digging deeper, a plastic poker chip.

With a flourish, he spread his red handkerchief on the bench and laid out his trophies. 'As above, so below,' he told them, with one of his quick crooked smiles.

They might have looked like a load of junk, but the objects did correspond, in a skewed sort of way, to those shown on the Magician's card.

'Four aces, my friends – that's what you'll be chasing, if you wish to bring about Yggdrasil's fall.'

'Yggdrasil…is that a demon?' Toby asked breathlessly.

The Magician laughed. 'It is a tree, young master, and one you saw in the place of sacrifice. Axis Mundi. Yggdrasil. Etz haChayim… It has nearly as many names as I, for many seeds may fall from the one fruit. To reap its harvest will take the powers of the earth and air, fire and water.'

'Elements…like the aces. The first cards of the Lesser Arcana,' said Cat. She remembered the shining blue of the Hanged Man's gaze, how his voice had faded with the leaves on the tree. *When the First of the Greater gives you the Firsts of the Lesser, then I may be set free.*

'Bravo. A big hand, please, for the lady in the corner!' The Magician tipped his top hat in her direction.

'Behold the Ace of Pentacles, Root of Earth.' Taking the poker chip, he spun it on the trestle. When it settled, they could see the disc was no longer plastic, but made of clay. 'Ta-da!' He spun it again, faster and faster, until its blur crumbled into a little scoop of dust. A puff of his breath and it was gone. 'Next Cups, Root of Water.' He held up the shot glass, which transformed into dripping ice that melted in his hands. 'Swords, Root of Air.' At this, he picked up the knife and threw it over Flora's head.

Instinctively, she ducked, but as it flashed through the air it turned into a bird that swooped upwards and away. 'And lastly, Wands, Root of Fire,' he announced, flicking open the long black lighter. The next moment it shot skywards in an explosion of rainbow sparks, as the Magician took a bow and looked round for applause.

'But – where have they gone?' Flora asked.

'Back into the Game, of course! Now, in order to play my card you had to roll a die, did you not? I would like to see it.'

After a slight hesitation, Blaine passed it over. 'I don't think it works any more. The little symbols vanished once the threshold showed.'

'Did they indeed?' The Magician took off his top hat, put the die inside, and placed the handkerchief over the brim. He then passed the hat to Cat. 'Click for luck.'

Feeling like a kid at a birthday party, Cat snapped her fingers over the red silk.

'Expertly done, Madam.' With a wink and a smirk, he brought out the die again. 'Ta-da!' All four sides were once more etched with a silver zero.

'Now then,' he said briskly, 'a die rolled in the Arcanum can take you through the Game, but not out of it. You will have to find an ordinary threshold for that. Instead, I have loaded this die so that each throw will take you to where an ace can be found. And four aces to gather means four moves to play.

'Since you do not belong to a court, the kings and queens cannot intervene until your round is over, and the final venture begins. Even then, they may not oppose you except through the rules of forfeiture. So my advice to you is this: have a care with your meddling. Other than that, your path is clear.'

Four blank faces stared back at him.

'Tsk. Do you *still* not understand? The objects you saw just now were only the shadows of what you seek, just as the tree you saw in the crypt was the shadow of a greater tree – as above, so below, remember. I have put each ace back into the move and the hour where it was last played, and where you may win them back again.'

'And what do we do once we've won them?' Toby asked.

'Why, then you will return to Yggdrasil, and plant each root. For you must follow the aces, ladies and gentlemen, follow the aces!'

'Uh, that's really cool, but…couldn't you just give them to us?'

His laughter was mocking now. 'And where would be the fun in that? I have shortened the odds, my friends, but now you must throw your die and take your chances.'

Blaine glanced at the other three, shrugged, and bent to roll the die for a second time. As soon as its strange circular tumbling was over, a threshold wheel flickered into life on the door behind him. This time, however, the corresponding symbols on the die didn't disappear. 'No point hanging around,' he said.

'Indeed not.' The Magician's gaze had drifted back to the ruins all around. 'So many fair cities, and their endings all the same,' he murmured. 'Players too, and yet... *Tu uero uoluentis rotae impetum retinere conaris?* The show is over, and my part is done.'

CHAPTER FOURTEEN

The other side of the Magician's threshold was an oak tree in a park. This wasn't much like the orderly lawns behind Flora's house, however, for the landscape had the unkempt feel of moorland, and the buildings at its rim were a faraway blur. Swollen black clouds glowered overhead, though here and there a frail blue was beginning to peep through.

They had come from ruin, and here was wreckage of a different kind. The oak they were standing under had been split in two, the ground around it scorched, its branches blackened. Fallen trees were tumbled on every side. A pram had been caught in one of the half-toppled giant's branches; the flotsam and jetsam of litter bins and abandoned picnics was strewn like grubby confetti across the grass.

'"Behold, the blasted heath",' Flora murmured. 'Looks like the Ace of Swords has done its worst.'

'Which means we're on the right track.' Toby didn't sound particularly enthusiastic. 'It's a shame we couldn't have had a bit of downtime at Hecuba's first, though. Let's face it, it'll be years before I get a chance to visit a club like that again. And some of those showgirls were *hot*. Right, Blaine?'

Blaine didn't return his smirk. As usual, he was standing a little apart from the other three. Now he pointed towards a hill about half a mile ahead. Something was glinting on its top: a greenhouse or conservatory. Its ornate structure looked out of place in the middle of a common, but the Arcanum was full of things far stranger, and by unspoken agreement they set off in its direction. It seemed the only thing to do.

Before they got there, however, there was another hill and what looked like the remains of another greenhouse. Smashed windowpanes glittered in the watery afternoon light; the hothouse plants trampled in the mud were already smelling of rot. A cracked cherub statuette pouted in a puddle.

They poked around for a bit, just in case the Ace of Swords had been discarded somewhere in the undergrowth. 'I still don't see why the Magician couldn't have just given us the cards,' Toby grumbled.

'That wouldn't have been very epic-worthy. I thought you were a fan of impossible quests,' said Cat.

'Looking for playing cards in the mud isn't epic,' he retorted.

'Are we even looking for a card?' Blaine asked. 'After the Wizard of Odd's performance, I should've thought the Ace of Swords is just as likely to be a bird. Or that knife he pulled from his trousers.'

'We'll have to hope we recognise it when we see it,' said Flora. 'He said the die was "loaded" in such a way as to take us to the right move, at least, so it's got to be here *somewhere*.'

'What would be our chances of finding all four aces without the die?' Toby asked.

'Slim to nil,' she answered. 'The Triumph of Fortune card turns up regularly – Lotteries are fairly frequent, after all – but finding an ace in the Arcanum is much rarer. I don't think even the kings and queens can control when and where they pop up, or who gets their hands on them.'

'I saw a knight use the Ace of Wands,' Cat said slowly. 'He tore the card in half and – *kaboom*. A towering inferno in seconds.'

'Well, I hope he put it to good use,' Flora replied. 'You'd only play something as powerful as an ace as a last resort.'

Blaine grunted. 'So why was this one used?'

Nobody had an answer for this. And as they resumed

their walk, Cat found she was hanging back again. It wasn't just because of Flora's remark about last resorts. Their destination – an octagonal conservatory crowned with a cupola – appeared to have weathered the storm unscathed. Glossy leaves and flowers bloomed within, its floor-to-ceiling arched windows were gilded by the emerging sun. The flowers, the sunshine, the shining glass…it reminded her of the Six of Cups, and not in a good way.

As with many places in the Arcanum, the conservatory's interior was bigger than it had looked from the outside. A black and white mosaic path wound its way through the beds and bowers; classical music was playing somewhere, and mingled with the tinkling of a fountain. The air was warm and deliciously perfumed. There could be no greater contrast with the bedlam of Hecuba's, or the desolation they had walked through before and after.

Flora, Toby, Blaine and Cat filed along the path, under swathes of pink blossom. By the time they had reached a circular space below the cupola, they all had a scattering of petals in their hair.

'My dears! I am so *very* pleased that you could come!'

An elderly lady was smiling up at them from a wicker armchair. She had an elegantly faded face and a great quantity of silver hair, held up in a chignon. It looked as if she had been doing some gardening, for a pair of pruning shears and a basket of cuttings were next to her slippered feet.

Flora eyed the teapot and four cups on the table beside her. 'You were expecting us?'

'But of course. After all these years, I like to be the first to welcome visitors. Offering a little refreshment is the least I can do.'

'It might be poisoned,' Toby muttered.

The old lady's laugh tinkled as merrily as the hidden fountain. 'Poisoned! Why ever would I want to poison you? It's not often that I receive guests, you know – and when they do arrive it's always *such* a treat. Now, do stop fussing and sit yourselves down.'

In the end, they each accepted a cup of amber tea, though nobody intended to risk drinking it. Flora perched gingerly on the other wicker chair, the others hunkered down on the little wall winding around the flowerbeds. Blaine looked especially awkward with a dainty china cup balanced on his knees.

'Isn't this nice!' Their hostess sighed contentedly. 'So quiet and comfortable, and far away from those meddlesome courts.'

'But there is a card in play here, isn't there?' Cat asked.

'To be sure – and a very pretty card, too. Now, where did I put it…' She patted the folds of her embroidered bed jacket. 'I had it just a minute ago… Here we are. My Nine of Pentacles.'

It was, indeed, a pretty picture. A richly dressed lady was enclosed in a luxuriant garden, with a bird on her arm.

'How time flies!' their hostess said with a chuckle. 'It's hard to believe I was only a few years older than you when I was dealt it.'

'So you are – were – a knight? A knight playing for a triumph?'

Her face clouded briefly. 'I suppose I must have been – I daresay it seemed highly important at the time. All that struggle and risk and aggravation! No, I'm much better off as I am… It took me a while to settle in, of course, but there are my plants to keep me busy, and the occasional guest for entertainment. You'll see.'

Toby cleared his throat. 'About those guests. We think someone came here quite recently. A knight who used the Ace of Swords. You probably noticed the, uh, hurricane thing…'

'Oh, but it's always nice and sunny in here.'

'Please,' Flora tried, 'this is important. We need to find whichever player came here last, or at least see where they went. We think they might have left a card behind.'

'Young folk these days, forever dashing about!' The old lady tutted. 'It was the same with the last fellow. Ah, well.

If it's really so important, I'd best put you in the right direction – people do tend to lose their way among the paths.'

Everyone got to their feet, Toby taking the opportunity to tip his tea into a potted lily. Their guide led the way, somewhat stiffly, to the foot of miniature wrought-iron bridge. The little pool below was sequined with darting fish, the path on the other side led to a brick wall and a white door. 'That's where everyone goes. Are you quite sure you won't stay for another cup?'

'I'm afraid we can't,' said Flora. 'But thank you very much.'

'Goodbye, my dears.' She stood on the other side of the stream, waving at them fondly. 'And remember: people in glass houses shouldn't throw stones!'

The door led to another conservatory, apparently identical to the one they had just left. There was the same faint melody of violins and splashing water, and the same mosaic path meandered around a profusion of leaf and blossom. Birdsong warbled and petals fell.

Pleasant as it all was, Cat was beginning to feel slightly claustrophobic. The interconnecting wall between the two buildings was the only section of the octagon not made of glass, but from where they were standing, the windows to either side were half-obscured with foliage, half-misted up by the moisture in the air. She pushed her way through the greenery, towards the view of open skies and rolling heath. Except the view had changed.

'Uh, guys...I think we have a problem.'

Their conservatory was no longer connected to the old lady's. It was on its own little hill. One hill, among many. One conservatory, among many. At least a hundred self-contained bubbles of glass, glinting and winking in the sun.

At once, Blaine hurtled back to the door they had just come through, closely followed by the other three. It was nothing more than a painted panel nailed to the brick. A marble nymph peeped out from the shrubs nearby. Blaine seized the statue and, staggering slightly, flung it against the nearest window.

The glass wasn't even scratched.

They were trapped.

At first they refused to accept it. They went round each of the conservatory's eight sides, inch by inch, hope against hope, like flies buzzing against a windowpane. But by the time they ended up where they had started, they hadn't found so much as a chink or chip in the glass.

'That evil witch!' Toby fumed. 'I *knew* we shouldn't have trusted her! A sweet old Arcanum granny – of *course* it'd be a trap!'

'She said that she'd been dealt the Nine of Pentacles when she was only a few years older than us,' said Cat weakly.

Flora's eyes darted between the three others in horrified disbelief. Cat knew what she was thinking. *These same people in this same place. For the rest of my life.*

'Oh, God.' Toby had had the same thought. His face went blotchy. And in spite of everything, in spite of the claustrophobia, and the bewilderment, and the surging fear, Cat felt a tiny stab of satisfaction. It was about time Toby realised the Game wasn't such a glorious romp.

Blaine was silently, and ferociously, stripping the petals off an azalea.

'Ugh!' Flora suddenly smacked her forehead with the palm of her hand. 'We're being idiots. It's fine. I mean, we're not fine exactly, but we have the die, remember? We can't use it to leave the Arcanum, but it means we can create a threshold to the next move whenever we want to.'

Of course! How could she have forgotten? Cat felt almost sick with relief; from the looks on the others' faces, they felt the same.

'But,' Flora went on, 'this move here is our only chance to get the Ace of Swords. If we don't find it before we leave, we might as well give up on the whole thing.'

Toby nodded, though he was still looking a little green. 'I guess we know what its airy powers were used for, at least: "To huff and to puff and to blow the house down…" And, as happens, I think we're exactly where we need to be.'

'How d'you mean?'

He pointed to an orange tree behind Cat; a small gilded cage hung from one of its branches. Its latch was open. 'There wasn't any birdsong on the heath, or in the other conservatory – did you notice? In fact, the last time I saw one of our feathered friends was with the Magician at Hecuba's. And if he was serious about shortening the odds, he'd put the aces back into the Arcanum in as accessible a way as possible.'

As if in answer, a bird trilled. Accessible or not, it seemed to Cat that the sound had a faintly taunting note.

'Time to go catch us an ace.' Blaine got to his feet.

'Wait – where are you going?' Cat asked. 'The sound came from that way.'

'No, it didn't, it came from behind us,' said Toby.

'I'm sure it was in those bushes over there,' said Flora.

They stopped still, listening.

Silence.

'You know,' Cat said reluctantly, 'splitting up is probably a bad idea but…'

'…it's not like we have much of an option,' finished Toby. 'OK. Last one back to the birdcage is a loser!'

But before he could charge off, Flora took hold of his

arm. 'Just a minute. Before we all disappear in different directions, perhaps we should take a moment to consider – well, to consider our various responsibilities.'

'How do you mean?' he asked impatiently.

'Oh, well, only that it might be a good idea to check exactly who's looking after what. In case anything goes wrong, you know.' She smoothed down her hair, keeping her voice carefully casual. 'For example, Blaine's still got the die…'

Blaine gave a bark of laughter. 'What, you think I'm going to run off with it into the bushes and never come back? Sneak ahead to grab all the aces, then flog them half-price down Temple House?'

'Of course not; I only thought we should—'

'Fine. I get it.' He felt in the pocket of his top, and threw something at Cat. 'Catch.'

It was the die. 'Hey, *I* don't want it.'

'Tough. Her Ladyship seems to think it belongs in more trustworthy hands.'

'For goodness' sake! You're *deliberately* misunder—'

But he had already sauntered into the flowerbed behind them, whistling, 'Here, birdie birdie…'

Flora pursed her lips, before heading up the path in the opposite direction. Toby and Cat were left looking at each other.

'You want to take the left or the right?' he asked.

'Whichever.'

She ended up going right, and at first made good progress. She could hear cooing only a little way ahead, and once or twice she was sure she glimpsed a flutter of white feathers. The sounds of the others blundering about faded the further into the greenery she went. The plants in the beds grew denser than she would have thought possible; in fact, the glass dome of the conservatory was almost completely obscured by the mesh of branches overhead.

Maddeningly, the piped music was playing a melody with flutes in it, whose ripples were very close to birdsong. She couldn't hear the fountain any more and the black and white check of the path had also disappeared from view. The air grew more humid, its sweetness darkened by the scent of compost and decay. Her feet squelched over fallen fruit. Bugs squirmed, flies buzzed.

Soon she was sticky with sap and sweat; her hands were torn from when she'd had to struggle past a tangle of crimson roses. The wretched flute music had stopped, at least, but now she was aware of all sorts of uncanny noises – little rustles and scuffles and creaks in the undergrowth. She called out, hoping to hear Toby, or Flora, or even Blaine, but nobody answered.

At last, she came to a thicket that seemed impenetrably matted. She hunkered down in a small hollow among a clump of ornamental ferns. The earth here was dry, and very soft. If she could just get her breath back, have a little rest…she would worry about finding the others later… she would worry about everything later… Cat curled up and closed her eyes.

Twoo-tweet…

It was her ears playing tricks again. An echo of something that wasn't there.

Twoo-tweet, twoo-tweet…

Tweet, tweet…

Her eyes snapped open. Preening itself on a branch just the other side of the ferns was a small white bird.

Hardly daring to breathe, making her movements as slow as possible, she sat up. Cat and bird regarded each other. Its feathers were snowy, its eyes beads of red. An albino.

Twoo-tweet…

Her quarry half hopped, half flew to the ground. Now it was less than three feet away. Oh God. Any sudden movement or noise, and it would fly off, out of sight and out of reach. What she really needed was a net. Perhaps she could lure it to her with something…but with all these seeds and berries, it wasn't likely to be hungry.

And yet…the way the bird was cocking its head, the tentative little hops as it sidled along… It seemed almost as interested in her as she was in it.

A thin shaft of sun had filtered through the canopy,

making something on her top sparkle. The pendant from the Christmas cracker! She'd forgotten she was still wearing it; up until now, it had been hidden by the collar of her shirt. It was just a bit of tat: a plastic four-leaved clover, coated in gold glitter. Glitter that twinkled in the sun.

The bird hopped closer.

Weren't magpies supposed to be attracted to shiny things? This wasn't a magpie; it wasn't any kind of ordinary bird. But it was worth a try.

With agonising slowness, Cat inched her hand up and around her neck to undo the clasp of the chain. Very slowly, very gently, she lowered the pendant into her hand. 'Like the bling, don't you,' she crooned, soft and coaxing. 'Come and get it then, you little horror. Because I'm going to take you down; yes, you and your king bully and all his loony court.'

And the bird swooped into Cat's opened palms.

She gasped in shock, but reflexively closed her hands around its body. The bird didn't struggle. She could feel its heart beating, warm and steady within the frail puff of feathers, as it looked up at her, its eyes bright as blood. The Root of Air was cupped within her hands.

Shakily, she stood up. To her immense relief, the foliage jungle had thinned, and she could see the path only a few steps away. Cat stepped out from under a canopy of jasmine, to find the others were also emerging: scratched, sweaty, bleary-eyed.

It seemed impossible that they could ever have lost their way among these fragrant bowers and neat paths. The orange tree and cage were exactly as they'd left them, the water still babbled and the music played. Cat walked up to the cage and carefully placed the bird inside. Her captive seemed perfectly content, cooing softly as she fastened the latch. Close to, she saw that the cage was octagonal, to match the conservatory, with a little dome on top.

'And now,' Cat said, her voice trembling a little as she reached for the die, 'let's get the hell out of here.'

CHAPTER FIFTEEN

The clock had stopped at five minutes to midnight. Moonshine illuminated the pearly glass panels of the giant dial, which, at about twenty feet in diameter, dominated the bare brick room.

'OK, so this is weird,' said Toby. 'Weirdly familiar, I mean.'

'You know this place?' Blaine asked.

'A very watered-down version of it. The clock tower at my old school got pulled down by the Ace of Pentacles.'

'Well then,' said Flora, after a slightly confused pause, 'given the scenery, I suppose the card here could either be the Triumph of Time or the Tower.'

'Looks more tardy than triumphant,' Cat observed. The bird in its cage cooed, as if in agreement.

The Nine of Pentacles already felt far away. After Cat had thrown the die, they had found the threshold sign carved in the bark of the orange tree. Here, it was welded to the axis of the hour hand. This was made of wrought iron, as were the Roman numerals around the clock's rim. It didn't look as if it had moved in a long while.

Broken cables – presumably once connected to the bell at the top of the tower – lay in a tangle of plaster and fallen masonry. The inner workings of the clock were visible in the room below, since a spiral staircase ran between the shafts that attached the mechanism to the hands on the dial. The section of the stairs that continued up to the belfry had either rusted or been wrenched away and came to a jagged end about two feet off the floor.

Toby peered out of the clock face. A number of panes were missing; beneath the tower, bare sands spread in every direction. 'On clear days, you were supposed to be able to see London… It feels all wrong not to be looking down on a cricket pitch.'

'*Everything* about the Arcanum feels wrong,' Cat muttered, shifting the cage under her arm. She'd only been carrying it for five minutes and it was already doing her head in. 'Look – there's writing around the frame of this thing. More Latin slogans.'

'"*Infima summis, summa infimis mutare gaudemus*",' Flora read aloud slowly. '"We make the lowest…turn to the top, the…highest to the bottom."'

'We delight,' said Blaine.

'I'm sorry?'

'*Gaudemus*. We delight.' Blaine's voice was deliberately colourless. 'You missed it out. Fortune, the "royal we", or Time – or both – *delights* in making the downtrodden rise and the stuck-up fall.'

'Um…yes. Right. How…?'

He smiled slightly. 'So now I know what it takes to shock you.'

After a brief hesitation, Flora swept on as if she hadn't heard, although her cheeks had reddened. 'We need to start looking for the ace. Toby thinks the Ace of Pentacles has been played here, but if that bird is anything to go by, it could be in a variety of forms: a poker chip, a piece of clay…even a handful of dust.'

'Best hope not, seeing as we're in the middle of a desert,' said Cat.

'I'll check the other room,' Toby volunteered, his hands already on the broken rail of the stairs. The other three continued to poke around the dial but there wasn't much more to see, and a few minutes later Cat went to join him.

She descended the rickety spiral very cautiously, her movements hampered by the birdcage she was carrying. The stairs ended in a walkway over the middle of the clockwork, with ladders down to the aisles on either side.

Cat wasn't the technical type, but even so she was impressed by the size and complexity of the mechanism, an intricate system of weights, wires, wheels and drums. It was contained within a cast-iron frame that took up most of the space in the room.

'Impressive, isn't it?' Toby had got out his pocket torch, and was shining it across the frame. 'See – there's three series of interlinked gears: the time train, the striking train, and the chiming train. That one should be connected to the bells. And there's the handle for winding it all up.'

Cat ran her hand along a dusty brake-shaft, imagining what the works had been like when in motion. A sharp-edged engine of ticks and turns: not just for measuring time, but driving it…

'Got anything?' Blaine thumped carelessly down the stairs and along the creaking platform.

'Toby's giving a lecture on gear-trains.'

'And talking of lectures,' Toby said, 'what was with all the gaudy/gaudier/gaudiest stuff back there? Had you seen the slogan before?'

'No.'

'So you really could translate it?'

Blaine looked about to snap back, then seemed to think better of it. 'I used to live with a teacher,' he said shortly.

'A Latin teacher…whoa. That can't have been much fun.'

'You could say that.' He moved his hand absentmindedly towards his right arm, and the line of scarred flesh beneath its sleeve.

'What's this for, Toby?' Cat asked, sensing the need for distraction. She gestured to a ten-foot rod with a circular weight at one end.

'Duh – it's the pendulum.' He pointed his torch, and they saw the ledge made by the weight had two neat stacks of coins on it. 'Pennies! That's how they adjust the timekeeping in Big Ben's clock. You add or subtract coins to speed up or slow down the pendulum; it's not the weight of the coins that makes the difference, but the height of the stack. It moves the centre of gravity, you see.'

'Fascinating.' Cat suppressed a yawn.

But Toby was looking thoughtful. 'More coins… It can't just be a coincidence. I wonder if…' He leaned forwards and shone the torch directly on the stack. 'A*ha*. The one on the left isn't a coin at all! It's our Ace of Pentacles!'

'Toby, wait. We should—'

It was too late. He was already reaching to pick it up. A second later, the pendulum began to swing and the gears shifted into reluctant life.

Toby looked confusedly at the small clay disc in his hand. 'But it shouldn't make any difference – it's not the pendulum that drives the clock.'

'Since when did the Arcanum make any sense?' Cat snapped. She had a bad feeling about this. 'We've got the second ace, so it's time to make our exit. Flora!' she called, as her free hand fumbled for the die. 'Let's get out of here!'

'All right, all right, I'm coming,' said a voice from above. 'What on earth have you lot done to the clock?'

Flora began to climb down to join them. When she was about three or four steps from the platform, a bell began to toll. First one, then two, then a whole cacophony of them. Midnight.

Toby didn't need to tell anyone that this shouldn't be happening. They'd all seen the broken cables. And the sound of the bells themselves was wrong, too: harsh, discordant, thunderous. The Triumph of Time had struck.

Flora cried out as the stairs began to shake, reverberating in time with the clanging bronze. There was a sound of smashing glass from upstairs, and a sandy wind came whipping through the stairwell. For a few moments she pitched and swayed above the mechanism, clinging to the rails like a sailor to a storm-lashed mast, before there was a great screech of metal and the stairs crashed onto the platform.

Somehow, Flora had managed to keep on top of the crush of iron, the whole weight of which had fallen onto the platform's thin rungs. It didn't look as if they could bear it for long – the slightest movement on her part could bring everything down into the thrumming, spiky mass of machinery below. All the while, the bells rang on, louder and louder.

'We have to jam it!' Blaine shouted. He pointed to one of the poles that drove the clock hands, and which originally ran parallel to the stairs. Their collapse had snapped it at the base, and it now swung crookedly from the ceiling, about a foot away from Flora's head.

The next moment, Blaine had climbed onto the lower bar of the frame, leaning dangerously far out to make a grab for the pole. Flora's white face stared out from the wreckage. Even if they could use the pole to seize everything up before the platform collapsed, there was no way of knowing how long the brake would hold. The mechanism, like the bells, had acquired a crazed life of its own.

Blaine lunged at the shaft, and missed. Only Toby grabbing at his waist kept him from tumbling into the clockworks himself. But with the next lunge he caught the end of the shard. Cat and Toby pulled behind him, adding their weight. By now, the noise of the bells was almost unbearable, and their faces were stinging from blown sand. The bird thrashed within its cage, half-maddened with fear.

Somehow, by dint of the three of them tugging, they managed to wrench the pole down so that it stuck, quivering, into the centre of a gear-train. With a shudder and shriek that could be heard even over the bells, the machinery ground to a halt. A second later, the platform finally gave way, tipping Flora forwards. Blaine was there to steady her, however, and she was able to scramble over the tangle of metal unscathed.

The clockwork might have stopped, but the bells, if anything, got louder. The noise was like a hammer striking at the flesh and brain, bursting through the blood, swelling unstoppably through the body. Sand was pouring in from the room above. In a blizzard of grit, thunder beating at their ears, Cat tossed the die for a second time. A silver wheel glowed briefly on the brick behind them; a few agonising seconds later it was all gone.

CHAPTER SIXTEEN

At first, they were afraid the bird was dead. Its eyes were closed and it was bunched up stiffly in a corner of the cage. But when Cat tapped on the bars, it croaked faintly and opened a crimson eye.

The bird wasn't the only one feeling battered by their recent experience. Everyone was ashen-faced; for a while they just swayed on their feet, waiting for their heads to clear and their ears to stop ringing.

They were in a stony mountain valley, under a sky blazing with stars that were much brighter, and more thickly clustered, than any they had seen before. Tiny white flowers formed the sign for the threshold and were scattered underfoot. Here and there were slabs of paving, presumably a relic of the city street on the reverse side. A series of pools glimmered before them.

'I think I know where we are,' Flora said dazedly. 'This looks like the Star, the triumph for healing.'

'It does seem sort of refreshing,' Toby agreed, sniffing the cool air. 'And I already feel a lot less knackered than I should do.'

'That doesn't mean there isn't a nasty surprise in store,' said Cat.

'And here it comes,' Blaine muttered, as a stumbling figure came into view.

He was a tubby, young-ish man in a pinstripe suit, clutching a small stone urn to his chest. When he saw the four chancers, he gasped, and staggered.

'No – you can't stop me!' he choked out. 'Stay away!' And he clasped the urn all the tighter, and began to back away, his eyes darting fearfully. 'Did Swords send you? Because the courts can't intervene, not now. I played it fair and square.'

The four of them exchanged glances. 'By "it", do you mean an ace?' Cat asked.

At this, the man looked almost petulant. 'The Ace of Cups was all I had! I didn't want to use it,' he whined, 'but it was him or me. Swords should never have tried to interfere – he gave me no choice...'

'Don't be afraid,' Flora said gently. 'If you're here for the Star's power of healing, we're not going to stop you.'

'I wouldn't let you!' he said defiantly. He looked down at the urn. 'I was the first to the grotto but he was the first to find the vessel. And I *had* to have it. It's the only way to carry the water past the threshold.'

'Water?'

'From the spring. The final test. My wife, she's ill – the doctors are useless – and I – I promised her – there was *no choice.*' He dragged one hand over his face, groaning. 'God forgive me…' But with his next words, the whine of defiance was back in his voice. 'Two rivals for the same triumph at the same time: there could only be one winner. If he'd had the ace, Swords would've acted as I did. You would have, too.'

Then he turned his back on them, and lurched on down the valley.

After five minutes' walk in the opposite direction, they found what the ace had been used for.

They had already passed two shallow pools, their surfaces silver with starlight. The third, however, was solid ice. Its depths were clear enough for them to see the man encased within: his hands petrified in a futile gesture of defence, his face frozen in a twist of fury and fear. His eyes stared out from his prison; it was horribly difficult to drag their own away.

'D – do you think he's still…alive?' Cat faltered.

'I dunno,' said Blaine. 'But I reckon we'll need to get him out of there if we're to have the ace.'

'We could hack the ice with a rock or something,' Toby suggested.

Flora shook her head. 'It will take more than that to break the Ace of Cups.'

'So what'll we do?'

'The knight had an urn of spring water. That's what they were fighting over, he said. It might just be a token to decide who gets the triumph. But if the spring has some kind of healing power…'

'…We can use one kind of watery force to cancel out the other.' Toby nodded. 'Makes sense. Well, the knight came from this direction, so if there is a spring, it must be somewhere up in the rocks over there.' He reached into his jacket pocket and brought out a hip flask with a Magician-like flourish. 'We can carry the water back in this.'

'Got any more tricks up your sleeve?' Cat asked.

'Sure. Torch, chocolate rations, compass, whistle…'

Blaine snorted. 'Camping stove, encyclopaedia, kitchen sink.'

Actually, Cat thought that Toby had the right idea. The torch had already come in useful, and she found herself wishing she'd equipped herself with more than a few tissues and a packet of chewing gum. 'OK, let's go climb some rocks.'

'Um, if you don't mind,' said Flora, 'I think I'll have to

wait for you here.' She smiled apologetically. 'My ankle is still a little weak from when I twisted it the other day, and I'm afraid I wrenched it again on the clockwork.'

'We can't just leave you! Look what happened when we split up in the other moves,' Toby protested.

'I'll be fine. The Star is one of the most benign cards in the deck.'

'Tell that to Frosty the Snowman.'

'C'mon, it won't take four people to fetch a bottle of water,' Blaine put in. 'Us two will go find the spring. Cat can stay with Flora.'

Toby passed Cat the whistle. 'In that case, you'd better have this. Blow three times for an SOS, and me and Blaine'll come to the rescue.'

'So you get to be boy scouts, and I'll play nursemaid,' she said, but under her breath. The truth was, she'd be glad of the rest.

By unspoken agreement, the two girls moved away from the tomb of ice, settling instead by a pool where the water was clear and fringed with flowers. Flora went down to the water's edge and set about washing her face and hands. Then she took a comb from her pocket, smoothing out her hair and tying it back in a neat ponytail. Finally, she applied a slick of cherry lip balm.

Cat watched in fascination. There was no doubt they were all in a state: grimy and dishevelled, speckled in scratches from the Nine of Pentacles, gritty with sand from the Triumph of Time. But given the circumstances, Flora's grooming routine struck her as wilfully perverse.

Flora caught her eye and held out the lip balm. 'Granny always told my mother, "Put some lipstick on and you'll feel better". And actually, I think she was right.' She laughed humourlessly. 'Of course, gin is Mummy's pick-me-up of choice.'

Cat remembered the wild shouting. The crack across the mirror, ugly as a scar... She swallowed, tasting the faint scent of cherry on her mouth. 'Is that why you're in the Game? Because of – of your parents?'

She didn't really expect to get an answer. But when Flora finally replied, her voice was very calm. 'No,' she said. 'I'm in the Game because of my sister.'

'Grace is seven years older than me, and beautiful. Clever, too. All the time she was growing up, she had that... shining quality, a kind of radiance, which people are drawn to without quite understanding.

'With such a big age difference, you might have thought that she wouldn't have much time for me. Grace had hundreds of friends, and all kinds of interests and preoccupations and the rest of it. And there I was, the little sister, always trailing after her… But it wasn't like that between us.

'When I turned ten, Grace invented a special game for us to play. It was our secret. We pretended that there was an enchanted land waiting around the corner, where there were fabulous cities and creatures, and dreams came true. Grace said the only way to enter the land was with a magic coin. I couldn't go there, however much I begged her to take me – I was too little, she said. But she used to draw me pictures of the adventures she had had, and tell me stories of kings and queens, knights and knaves. A word full of complex rules and fabulous quests.

'I was too old for make-believe, really. Far too old to believe my sister was having adventures in a different world. Even so, I was obsessed by our game. I used to go through her things, looking for a magic coin. I waited up for her when she was out late; I even tried to follow her a couple of times. Needless to say, I never got very far.

'A few days before Christmas, Grace seemed unusually preoccupied. Even our parents noticed that she was on edge. I think they thought it must be something to do with a boy. On the evening of the nineteenth, she came to find me in my bedroom. She was excited: fizzing with energy. But she was nervous, too.

' "I've been lucky so far," she told me. "I'm good at this

game, and the cards have been kind to me. And I'm so close, Flo – so close!"

'Then she started pacing up and down, biting her lip. "I've got a bad feeling about this next one, though. My fourth move and final test. I don't know…"

'I was just happy she was playing our game again. She hadn't talked about it for a while; I was worried she had become bored of it.

'When she found me, I was doing some homework on the Greek myths. We had to read the story of Theseus and the Minotaur. "Theseus had a test," I told her. "He got lost in a maze and had to fight the Minotaur. But the princess gave him a thread to show him the way, and he killed the monster and escaped and became king. You'll be like him: like a hero." Grace shook her head and smiled. "Sometimes the heroes came to bad ends," she said. I didn't beg her to take me on this new quest. I knew that wouldn't get me anywhere. But as a joke – though I meant it half-seriously – I gave her some red embroidery silk from my ribbon box. I told her it would help her find her way home.

'My sister laughed, and hugged me, and left me to my book. She was supposed to be going to a party that evening. A Midwinter Ball. Our parents were out too; I was staying at home with the housekeeper.

'I couldn't sleep that night. I kept thinking about

Theseus, lost and alone, and the half-man, half-beast with the head of a bull. In the end, I got out of bed. It had started to snow, and I saw that the door at the bottom of the garden was ajar. I'd never seen it open before and all of a sudden I was terribly afraid.

'Even though I didn't want to be alone in the dark, I felt I had to face this by myself. Like the heroes. So I put on my slippers and dressing gown and went to the end of the garden, and through the door into the deserted park. There was something – some*one* – lying on the path outside. It was Grace, all spread out in her scarlet evening dress. The snow was already settling on her face.

'I can't remember much of what happened immediately after. Everyone seemed to arrive at once: my parents, the paramedics, the police. The only thing we knew for certain was that Grace was in a coma. Nobody knew how she'd got there or what had happened to her, except for the fact that she never turned up to the party. She had no injuries, no signs of illness, alcohol or drugs, though they tested her for everything. She was…untouched.

'I didn't show anyone the card I had found by her side; the picture of a woman bound and blindfolded inside a cage of swords. I didn't tell them why Grace had a loop of embroidery thread tied around her index finger, either. I knew it was Grace's secret, and that she wouldn't want me to tell. At first, you see, we thought she would wake up.

'My parents left me at home while they went in the ambulance with Grace. And that morning, very early, I went down to the garden and out into the park again. It had snowed heavily during the night and everything was covered in white. I went to where I had found Grace, and walked all around, and that was when I saw something red fluttering by the park railings.

'It was a strand of silk. The one Grace had tied to her finger, like Theseus in the labyrinth. And I took up the end of the thread and followed it across the park, until I came to the summerhouse.

'A young man and a blonde were sitting there, drinking hot chocolate. I remember thinking how beautiful the woman was, all wrapped up in white fur. "I'm glad you could make it," she said, and took my card.

'"What have you done to my sister?" I asked.

'"She took a wrong turn," the man replied. That's all they would tell me. Then, or ever.

'My parents think their daughter has spent the last five years lying motionless in a hospital room. They have stopped talking about the day when she will come back to us. I know better. Because I know that Grace, the *real* Grace, is trapped in the Arcanum somewhere. That's why the threshold in the park is still there. Whether my thread helped or hindered her, it was an intervention, and it changed her move. A move that remains empty and incomplete.

'And as long as the threshold remains, I know my sister can still be saved.'

Flora's narration had been so matter-of-fact as to be almost expressionless. Cat didn't know what to say. She wasn't used to heart-to-hearts or receiving confidences; perhaps it would have been easier if Flora had broken down and cried. At least then she would have had a cue.

Cat recognised the card that Flora described as the Eight of Swords. She thought of the Arcanum's other prisoners – the inhabitants of those gilded greenhouses, the knight trapped beneath the ice, the Hanged Man and his tree – and wondered what all-consuming hopes and fears had driven them into the Game. Cat now knew what Flora was playing for, but what about Grace – Grace the radiant, Grace who had everything? And what about her mum and dad? If they had had the chance to play, what prize would they have chosen?

'I'm sorry,' she said at last, and inadequately.

Flora didn't seem to hear. 'Of course I've kept looking, but not as hard as I could have. I'm afraid, you see, that if I go into the Arcanum too often I'll discover why my sister loved it so.' Then she gave her head a shake, as if to wake herself up. 'Really, Cat, I can't think why I'm boring you with all this. It's certainly not your problem.'

'My parents were mixed up in the Game. They got killed because of it.'

God – why had she blurted it out like that? Just because Flora was going all confessional… Cat could feel herself turning red.

'Then I am sorry, too.' And Flora gave a small, bleak smile.

Toby was the first to return, zigzagging breathlessly past the boulders, and brandishing the hip flask above his head.

'Hey, guys! Look what I've got! Jeez, it was a total *nightmare* climbing over the rocks – until we got to this really cool grotto with a naked goddess statue and everything… I think the water made my insect bites better. Or it could just be the placebo effect. How's your ankle, Flora? I wanted to try the spring water on it, as a test, but Blaine said we should save it all for the iceman. You know, if only we had a way of taking it past the threshold I bet we'd make a packet on miracle cures. Like the holy water that the monks flog at Lourdes—'

'Can we just get this over with?' Cat cut in. 'We don't even know if the water'll work its magic, let alone if there's an ace in it for us.' An unwelcome thought occurred to her. 'Hey – what about the hands-off rule? If the other bloke put this one on ice to win, we don't want to muck things about by getting him out again. "Have a care with your meddling"; that's what the Magician said.'

'This move's finished,' said Blaine impatiently. 'Knight Number One's already taken his water to the threshold. He'll be home and dry with the loot by now.'

He was standing at the ice's edge. The figure within, stuck in his moment of terror like a fly in amber, was all the more grotesque for being surrounded by the beauty of the valley and its diamond-bright sky. It was hard to imagine the ace's act of violence in such a peaceful place. Yet it had turned a quiet pool into a tidal surge, liquid into solid, life into death.

'I'd like to do it,' Flora said, holding her hand out for the flask. Toby looked disappointed but he passed it over. Steadying herself on Cat's shoulder, Flora unscrewed the cap and leaned over the ice, so that the water fell down in a sparkling arc.

It was as if she had poured a flask of acid. The ice hissed on contact and there was a burning, sulphurous smell as the water ate through its glassy surface, dissolving it into slush. The prisoner twitched, then began to flail about, choking and thrashing – and very much alive.

Blaine waded into the pool to pull him out. The man's

skin was mottled white and blue and he couldn't speak for shaking. But once they settled him on dry ground, the shudders subsided and the colour returned to his face with remarkable speed. In fact, Flora had only just begun to wrap her coat around his shoulders when he shook her off roughly and leaped to his feet.

'Where is he?' he shouted. 'What have you done with him?'

'It's fine,' Toby said soothingly. 'You're safe: the other knight's long gone.'

The Knight of Swords' face contorted with rage. 'All the triumphs in all the Game won't be any help once I've caught up with him. Dirty snake! I had the urn – I had it *in my hand* when he pulled his trick.' He grasped Cat by the shoulder. 'Where did he go, girl? Back to the threshold?'

'I'm not sure…'

But the man was already haring down the valley, still dripping and shivering, savagery in his eyes.

'You're welcome!' Toby called after him. 'Huh. What an ungrateful sod.'

'That's all the thanks we need,' said Flora, pointing. 'Our Root of Water.'

For the pool was evaporating before their eyes, until there was nothing left of it except a grassy hollow. A shard of ice was nestled in the centre. When Flora picked it up

CHAPTER SEVENTEEN

The sky was low and grey. Shabby buildings loomed around a threadbare patch of grass and shrubs enclosed by rails. A rubbish skip on the pavement overflowed abundantly, as if to compensate for the barrenness everywhere else. They were back in the garden at Mercury Square.

For Cat, it was doubly familiar. The exhausted-looking cherry tree in the centre of the garden was encircled by a ring of scorched earth. A crushed beer can lay underneath a bench where, until recently, a tramp had snored. Looking towards Temple House, she half expected to see herself doubled over by the railings, retching with shock.

Blaine was watching her. 'Seems just like yesterday, doesn't it?' he said.

It was the first time he'd acknowledged how they'd met. Cat still didn't know if, like her, he had wandered into the move by accident, thanks to Temple House's overlap with the Arcanum, or if his visit was deliberate, and part of some strategy. She was momentarily dizzy with the remembrance of it all: the helplessness, and the horror.

This time, however, there was no visible blurring between the two of sides of the threshold. The move in play here might not have required any fantastical shifts in scene, but was unmistakably part of the Arcanum landscape in the way that aspects of the familiar world seemed exaggerated, others less defined. It was shrouded in silence.

The quiet didn't last. A rustling by the railings made them draw together, faces tense, as a figure edged out furtively from behind a shrub. Cat immediately thought of the lads with the hooded tops and bats. However, whoever it was seemed even more nervous than they were. A boy of eighteen or nineteen, with a sharp bony face and close-cropped hair.

'You,' he said, half-accusing, half-panicky. 'You just come from nowhere. I seen you do it.'

'Er, yeah. That would be on account of the threshold,' Toby replied.

The new arrival stared. 'What's he talking about?' Then, plaintively, 'It's not right. Nothing's right. Why's it so quiet? Where's everybody *gone*? They must've been and closed off all the streets for miles around. Here,' – his face creased in alarm – 'you don't reckon we're in one of them terrorist alerts, do you?'

'He's a chancer,' said Flora wonderingly.

'But he can't be,' said Cat. 'There are only four of us in the Game. The Hanged Man said—'

'That comes later. We're back in the move where you and Blaine first met, aren't we?' Cat nodded: she had told Flora about their encounter when she'd agreed to try and find the fourth chancer. 'This boy might have been one of us last Saturday, but anything could have happened to him afterwards…'

'Hey – I'm not "this boy". I'm Liam.' He looked from one to the other, gnawing his lip. 'Who *are* you people?'

'We're like you,' Blaine said shortly. 'Tell us what happened. About what happened to you this afternoon.'

'I dunno!' he replied, exasperated. 'I dunno *nothing*. All I did, right, was follow this bloke – posh for a black guy, all suited and booted – to one of them big houses. Over there. And he left the door open, see, and it was all very nice inside, a class act, you know? So I thought I'd best go in and warn him about the security risk. Opportunistic theft. After all, you can't be too careful in this neighbourhood.' He sniggered a little. 'And then – then – all this weird stuff kicks off. There's crazies waving cards and droning about Fate and Forces and suchlike and

I thought, stone me, it's them doomsday cult nutters. So I exited sharpish and when I come out, things was different. Different like this.'

'How did—' Blaine was beginning, when his eye was drawn by movement at the end of the square. The light was fading fast, but they could just make out hooded figures gathering in the shadows of one of the streets leading off the north corner. The Knaves of Wands had returned.

'Quick. We have to get out of here,' said Cat urgently, hurrying to the gate of the garden and casting around for an escape route or hiding place.

'This way,' said the new chancer. He darted ahead and up to one of the windows of a shut-up house. One of the boards was loose, and he was able to prise it open without difficulty. 'Got no idea what's going on, but I knows trouble when I see it. Pretty good at getting out of it, too.' And he grinned, flashing a mouthful of yellow teeth.

One by one, they squeezed through, clambering down from the sill into the disarray of an abandoned office. It looked as if it had lain undisturbed for years. The tops of the filing cabinets and desks were furry with dust.

Cat put her eye to the gap in the boards and watched as the four knaves swaggered into the dusky garden. One squatted down to inspect the scorched earth around the cherry tree, while the others muttered in a huddle.

Flora came to join her. 'I think we're OK; they're here for the knight, not a few stray chancers. The trouble is, if we're to get our ace, I think we need to find him too.'

There was a yelp from behind. Liam was sucking a finger and staring balefully at the birdcage, which Cat had set on top of an ancient photocopier. 'I didn't know birds bit! Usually travel with your budgie, do you?'

'It's our team mascot,' said Cat distractedly. 'Listen, did you see anyone else before we, uh, arrived?'

'Nobody but some old wino. That's how I knew to come in here – I seen him scramble through the window.'

'So the knight must still be in the building!' Toby exclaimed. 'That's brilliant.'

'If you says so.' Liam appeared to have got over his earlier fears. In fact, he looked almost cheerful. 'Now then: I can see how you're anxious to avoid the crew out there. But there's no harm in us having a poke around the place, right? You never know what the removers might've overlooked – could be some good gear lying about.'

He was already moving towards the dilapidated reception area. But after picking their way past stacks of mouldering folders and broken computer equipment, they found the main stairs were blocked by a fallen bookcase. It looked as if their explorations were confined to the lower levels of the building.

'Here, Cat,' Blaine murmured in her ear. 'About our

first time in this move: how many knaves did you see?'

'Uh…four, I think. Plus you at the other end of the garden – though when you came up to me later, I figured you were, you know, ordinary. From the home side.'

'But I was never in the garden. I was staying well clear, behind that skip.'

'Oh.' She thought back to the boy who'd been throwing pebbles at the cat, and had stared at her with such intensity. A vague shape in a baggy sweater, too far away to distinguish his features properly. She had just assumed that he and Blaine were one and the same. 'OK, then: there were five of them. That makes better sense. Five of Wands, like the card.'

'Yeah. So why're only four out there now?'

'Shhh!' Flora hissed from ahead, as they shuffled past a series of storage cubicles and yet more filing cabinets. Light glimmered from a door just a little way down the passage, behind which a slurred voice was raised in song.

'Luck – *hic* – be a laaady toniiiiight…'

Liam turned to look at the other four huddled behind him, his face flickering in the gleam of Toby's torch. He put a finger to his lips and winked conspiratorially, before turning the handle on the door.

It opened into a small concrete room lit by a single bulb. A man was slumped on the floor in a heap of ragged clothes and wild grey hair. His hands and feet were bound with an old electrical cord. 'Wha – wah?' he mumbled, blinking up at them with bloodshot eyes.

'Brought you some company, old man,' said Liam. He grinned. Then, in one swift shocking movement, he drew out a knife and held it to Cat's throat.

'You three: against the wall by Pentacles,' he rapped out. 'And don't think of trying any tricks.'

The blade stung coldly against Cat's neck. She swallowed, and felt the metal prick into her skin. The warmth and weight and smell of Liam's body were pressed against her in horrible intimacy.

'Time to lose Tweetie Pie. Set it on the floor – nice and slow, now.'

Cat bent her knees and, holding the cage with one unsteady hand, sank towards the floor. Liam bent down alongside her without loosening his grip. She set the cage a little distance from her feet; when she stood up, the bird beat its wings in agitation against the bars as if to echo the leaping of her heart.

'What've we here, hmm?' Keeping his knife to her throat, Liam was using his other hand to search her clothes, and had found the die. 'Very nice. Four little zeros for four little fools. Well, I ent no fool, nor chancer neither, and I don't need none of your tricks.' And without more ado, he kicked it through a rusty grate in the floor.

Meanwhile, Flora, Blaine and Toby had lined up along the wall behind the knight. His song over, he appeared to have passed out, and was filling the air with rich bubbling snores.

'You've already got your man,' Blaine said tightly, 'so fetch your mates and finish the move. We've got nothing to do with this, and nothing to do with you.'

Liam sneered. 'Typical gutless chancers. You're an even bigger waste of space than Pentacles here. The boozing idiot gets his hands on an ace, one of the powerfullest cards in the deck, and practically throws it away – didn't even have the sense to use it to seal off the threshold and make his escape.' He spat on the floor.

'Three hours I kept watch on his little bonfire. Three hours! Soon as it started to die away I could've gone for backup. But no, I knew better'n that. I waited. And I watched, just like I'd watched this one,' – he leaned into Cat, so his breath tickled sourly against her cheek – 'go all weak-kneed at the threshold. I got a feeling in my gut her move wasn't finished, and in this Game, it's gut instinct what gives you the edge... Course, a whole gang of yous turning up was an unexpected surprise.'

'So what do you want us to do?' Flora asked coldly.

'Easy. I want one of you fine ladies and gents to deliver the Knight of Pentacles to the Knaves of Wands.'

'But – but he's already your prisoner. You can set your

thugs on him any time you want.'

'Ah, but I got somebody else in mind for the job. A chancer. A chancer what'll bring the power of Wands down on Pentacles, and win this move for my court. 'Cause you know what that means, don't you?'

Nobody answered.

'A knave what catches a chancer meddling gets set free from his forfeit: that's the rule.' Liam sniggered at his own cunning. 'Thanks to the intervention you'll be so kind to make, *I* goes back to being a knight, while one of *you* gets to be the King of Wands' shiny new knave. Bonus points all round.'

'Wait,' Toby tried. 'You don't need to do this. The four of us are on a quest. We're going to overthrow the—'

'Shut it.'

'But—'

'I said, shut it. Chat, chat, chat, hoping to distract me… I weren't born yesterday. No, I'm the one what's doing the talking, 'cause I'm the one in charge. I want a volunteer in the next thirty seconds. And your little friend better pray,' – his eyes glinted dangerously – 'that this here ent a case of every player for themselves.'

At this, he pressed the knife tighter so that Cat felt warm blood trickle on clammy skin. She stared out at the concrete cell with unseeing eyes. Was this how her mum and her dad had felt, waiting helplessly as the stranger raised the gun? It wasn't just her life that was at stake, either. To save her, one of the other three would have to give up their freedom for enslavement to the Court of Wands.

'P'raps,' Liam mused as he drew the blade – lightly, teasingly – towards her ear, 'you're thinking I'm the type for idle threats. P'raps I should start off with a little nibble of the knife, just to show how easy—'

'I'll do it,' said Flora. She looked at the others' stricken faces and shrugged dismissively. 'It's fine: I'm bored of being on the sidelines as it is. Who knows, I might even get a career break like Liam here. And a knave's one up from a fool, wouldn't you say?' Then she pushed herself off the wall and stepped over the drooling body of the knight, giving him a contemptuous kick on the way.

Liam tensed and pressed the blade against Cat's throat again, but Flora barely glanced at them. Instead, she bent down and picked up the birdcage. 'I'll have one advantage, at least,' she said briskly. 'There are few knaves who have a real live ace up their sleeve.'

'Ace?' said Liam, frowning. 'That card's been played. And put that thing down, I don't—'

Too late. Flora flicked open the gilded door and, swinging the cage through the air, flung the bird at his face.

It might have been a creature of the Arcanum,

conjured by a magician, and forged from the raw element of air. But it was also just a bird. A frightened bird, in a squawking, scrabbling fluster of beating wings and beak and claws.

Instinctively, the knave put up one of his arms to protect his face. He didn't release Cat, but his grip slackened. Even so, he would have recovered from the distraction in seconds if it wasn't for the knight, who suddenly swung his bound legs up and across the floor, jackknifing into the backs of Liam's knees.

The next minute or so was all confusion as Cat scrabbled out of the way and the knight and knave flailed about on the floor. The knight had somehow managed to work his hands free, but his legs were still tied, and Liam had the knife. However, the knight was neither as old nor as drink-sodden as he had first appeared: there was bulk beneath his tattered layers of clothes and a ruthless gleam in his eyes. Before the others quite knew what had happened, Liam's head had hit the concrete ground with a crack and his body collapsed limply.

'Little bastard,' said the knight with satisfaction. He took the knife to cut the remainder of his cords, which he used to truss up his former captor. 'Still breathing, more's the pity.' He then produced a battered version of Toby's hip flask from within his layers and took a hefty swig.

'You all right, Cat?' Blaine asked quietly.

Cat nodded. She had backed into a corner of the room, and was holding one hand around her throat.

'Let me see.' He reached to take her hand away, then touched, very gently, the scratch made by Liam's knife. 'There,' he said, as if his touch could rub out the mark, lightly and easily, like an eraser on pencil. Their eyes met, as they had that first time in Mercury Square. It already felt like a lifetime ago. The bird swooped down from its perch on a hook in the wall and settled on her shoulder, cooing contentedly.

Toby was still gawping. Flora looked similarly stunned.

'Here you go, princess,' said the knight, holding out his hip flask. 'This'll put some colour in your cheeks. Pass it round, if you like.'

Flora managed a weak smile. 'Not for me, thank you. Though you're very kind.'

'D'you think Wands could make the case that Fl – our – involvement has won this move for you?' Blaine asked the knight, leaving Cat's side to rummage through Liam's pockets.

'Hmm.' The man rubbed his bristly chin. 'I'm not home and dry yet, remember. Got to get back to the threshold for that. As for this little weasel…well, all knaves are cheats and losers. I reckon I could've taken him down on my own, but I can't swear to it. Either way, it's a close call.' He took another swig from the hip flask and belched loudly.

'Too close for comfort,' Toby fretted. 'At this stage of the Game, the kings and queens will use any excuse to take one of us out of play.'

'So it's just as well Liam was carrying this, then.' Blaine held up the thin black lighter that the Magician had conjured into the Ace of Wands.

The other three chancers heaved shaky sighs of relief. 'Thank God,' Flora whispered.

'Y'know,' mused the knight, 'I never come across *one* chancer before, let alone four. I never saw a bird like that one, neither. A quest, you said…' He squinted round at them with shrewd wet-rimmed eyes, then gave a hoarse chuckle. 'I know: don't ask, don't tell. Gotta keep my mind on the job in hand, anyhow, if I'm to get to that threshold with all my bones intact.'

'What if those other knaves catch up with you outside the Arcanum?' Cat was thinking of the desperate chase through Soho.

'Nah, knaves don't cross thresholds. Not unless a knight tries to scarper home before their move's played out.' He went to the door of the room and looked up and down the corridor. 'Still, this particular gang can't be the cream of Wands' crop, if they bunked off to leave our rat-faced friend here in charge of surveillance. I reckon I've a decent enough chance of pulling through.'

'We should get moving too,' said Blaine. 'It's a shame we've lost the die, but it's not like it'd be of much use from here on, anyhow. We've already got everything we came for – and Temple House is only three buildings to the right of this one.'

'Off to HQ, eh? You'll just need to keep going through the basement; as far as I can make out, it's all joined up on this side of the threshold. And, like any rat-run, there's some useful bolt holes.'

Taking a final gulp from his flask, the knight tucked it away, stretched enormously, and rubbed his hands through his dirty grey hair. 'Time to be up and at 'em. Cheerio, chancers.'

Striking a match from a box in his pocket, he turned left and sauntered into the darkness, singing under his breath. '*Luck be a lady tonight…*'

'Come on.' Flora wearily turned in the opposite direction.

'What about him?' said Cat, prodding Liam with her foot. The knave stirred slightly and let out a faint groan.

'Leave him for his crew to find,' Blaine replied. 'We've got other priorities.'

They nodded, grim-faced. They were so close. But they didn't dare hope. Not yet.

The knight was right about it being a rat-run. Their corridor soon diverged into a jumble of nooks, crannies and crooked passageways; after a while the office clutter changed to household junk but the dust and dilapidation were the same. Some stretches had bulbs that flickered into sallow life; in others Toby's torch was the only light they had to guide them. The Ace of Wands remained in Blaine's pocket.

Cat dropped behind to talk to Flora. 'Thank you. For what you did back there, and the risk you took.'

'Obviously, none of us would have stood by and watched you get your throat cut. I happened to move first, that's all,' Flora said calmly. 'Though it was... unfortunate the knight was involved.' She bit her lip. 'I'll just have to hope we get to the Hanged Man before the forfeits get to me.'

'We won't let that happen – to you or anyone. We're in this together.'

'No, we're in this for ourselves,' the other girl replied. 'Don't get me wrong – I don't want anything bad to happen to you or Toby or Blaine. Of course I don't. That's why I acted as I did. But at the end of the day, the four of us have to look out for each other because that's our best chance of survival, and our only chance of success.'

Cat knew Flora was right. She only had to let her guard slip for a moment and she would be flooded with a terrible hunger for the memories awakened by the Six of

Cups, and all-consuming grief for what came after. It had taken consistent struggle to keep these feelings in check so that she was able to concentrate on the task in hand. But expert as she was at suppressing her own hopes and fears, Cat was beginning to find that blocking out other people's was a different matter.

Toby's voice broke into her thoughts. 'This is it, team. We're standing beneath Temple House.'

She had been wondering how they would be able to tell, as it was nearly impossible to keep track of dimension and distance in their subterranean progress around the square. Now she saw that this latest partition had a gate in the middle – a gate that had the design of the wheel worked into its rusting bars. A number of low chambers lay before them on the other side, though unlike the Hanged Man's crypt, the walls were plastered in peeling whitewash and the air smelled of damp.

'You say our…uh…enchanted tree thing is growing below this cellar?' Blaine asked, scuffing the paved floor with his feet.

Toby nodded solemnly. '*Far* below. It felt like miles when we were climbing the stairs.'

'Which must be behind there,' said Cat, pointing the way through two low arches to the stone wall on the other side. They had come to the end, not just of Temple House's basement but, it seemed, the chaotic underground warren that had led them there. 'Got the key, Flora?'

'All present and correct.' Flora flourished the little silver key that she had carried ever since the Triumph of the Moon.

Everyone's spirits lifted. They had beaten the cards and won their round, and now they were right where they needed to be: just a few floors below the mirrored door that would take them to their prize.

CHAPTER EIGHTEEN

When they emerged from the basement, it was to find that the interior of Temple House had undergone another one of its kaleidoscopic shifts in space or time. The dustsheets and junk mail of their last visit had disappeared and the musty smell had gone. Lustre gleamed from every surface, a drowsy richness warmed the air. The chequered hall was deserted and the golden curtain pulled close.

Even so, there was something unsettling about the stillness. As they began to climb the stairs to the second floor, it felt as if the whole house was drawing its breath.

'This place is equal to all players, remember,' Flora said, as if to reassure herself. 'We can do what we like.'

'Oh, my dear,' said the Queen of Pentacles, 'that's where you're wrong.'

Lucrezia had emerged from behind the black-and-gold doors at the head of the stairs. Her expression was amused, and a little indulgent: an adult surveying fractious children. She was dressed in another of her voluptuous evening gowns, and its emerald skirts rustled like paper as she moved. 'For as long as the courts hold sway, every one of us must obey the rules. One of which is that all play is suspended while a Lottery takes place.' She smiled dazzlingly. 'And since we have a Lottery this evening, I'm afraid you'll have to wait.'

Her three companions were close behind. Alastor, looking sleepy and rumple-haired, was the last to emerge. As he did so, he took a blank card from within his coat and passed his hand over its face. When he held it up, they saw a leering thief-figure. 'Seven of Swords,' he said with his customary nonchalance. 'Or, if you prefer, the Reign of Futility.'

Behind him, the doors to the ballroom quivered, then melted into a solid wall. They took the only route to the Hanged Man's tomb with them.

'But – but the Lottery hasn't even *started* – you can't *do* that!' gasped Toby in outrage.

Ahab regarded them dispassionately. 'It appears we just did.'

Blaine moved as if to challenge him, but Flora put a restraining hand on his arm. 'It's fine,' she said, tight-lipped. 'We'll just wait until the Lottery's over. They can't delay us for much longer.'

None of the kings and queens looked in the least concerned. Alastor swung ahead, whistling under his breath. They continued down to the hall and through the curtain without so much as a backward glance at the four chancers.

The square outside was thronged with people and the Game Masters' arrival was greeted with a ripple of applause. The table and wheel from the ballroom had been set on the centre of the lawn; the cherry tree behind was a cloud of white blossom in a rose-flushed sky. As the kings and queens took their seats, the voice of the doorkeeper raised itself above the murmur of the crowd. 'Ladies and gentlemen, princes and vagabonds, players all…'

The four chancers slumped on the front doorstep. For the interim, at least, they had no choice but to sit it out.

'Where are we, anyway?' Cat asked disconsolately. 'Are we still in the Five of Wands move from last Saturday? Or has Temple House taken us back to…well…*now*?'

'Was it snowing last Saturday?' Toby asked.

'Er, no.'

'Then we're back to the present.'

He pointed to the far side of the square where, just past the lace of spring leaves and twinkling lights, the rosy sky darkened to black. Flakes of snow were spiralling onto the pavement. A lone pedestrian, muffled-up against the cold, didn't give the interior of the garden a second's glance.

'It's still not right.' Flora frowned, this time sounding more bewildered than angry. 'The Magician said they couldn't oppose us except through forfeits. I don't understand how they can block our way like that. I just don't understand...'

'We could do something with our aces,' Toby suggested. 'They're supposed to be super-powerful.'

'Not in the form they're in now. What are you going to do – set fire to the King of Wands' hair with the lighter? Shove an ice cube down the Queen of Cups' neck? No, our only hope is to get them to the Hanged Man's tree, and that's that.'

Nobody had anything to say to this. Instead, they lapsed into glum silence. The energy and agitation that had kept them going this far had all ebbed away. Even fear had faded. As the bird preened its feathers, and the audience laughed, clapped or sighed as events required, Cat could feel a gentle lull stealing over her.

'Uh –?'

Somebody – Blaine – was shaking her out of her daydream. 'They've called for us. Come on.'

Groggily, Cat rubbed her eyes, rose to her feet. The birdcage felt unusually heavy, and dragged at her arm. The other three looked equally disorientated as the crowd parted to let them through. The line of faces was like one long pale snake filled with eyes. It seemed to take an inordinate amount of time to cross the lawn to where the Game Masters were waiting.

Ahab was the first to speak. 'It appears,' he said ponderously, 'that the courts are due recompense. An unlawful intervention has been made.'

The audience seethed with scandal and delight.

Cat was wide awake now. 'No,' she said, her voice sounding childishly high and thin. 'No, you're wrong. That knight would've got free of Li – of the Knave of Wands without any of us having to do anything. You can't know if us being there made a difference to whether he won his move or not. Not for definite.'

'I entirely agree,' Lucrezia purred. 'The whole business is *far* too complicated to bother disentangling. Both Wands and Pentacles have agreed to put the issue aside.'

'The case in question here,' Odile said in her light, precise voice, 'is a petition brought by the Court of Cups.'

The doorkeeper stepped forwards. 'Let the Knight of Cups bear witness.'

A plump, anxious-looking young man came out from the crowd. It was the first knight from the Triumph of the Star.

He pointed at the four chancers with a trembling hand. 'You,' he quavered. 'You four released Swords from the ice. He caught me at the threshold, and in the struggle the vessel was broken and all my water spilled. You ruined *everything*.'

There was a stunned pause.

'But you had *ages* to leave the move!' Toby exploded. 'Why the hell did you stay hanging around the threshold?'

'I needed time to gather my strength,' the knight said aggrievedly. 'I was an emotional wreck – you saw me. I thought I was safe, that I'd *won*. And I had, too, until you intervened and—'

'The situation is clear,' Alastor interrupted, looking up from swirling the ice in his glass. 'These four cost Cups – or possibly Swords – the success of his move. All are liable for forfeit.'

'Indeed. And since the intervention in the case of Wands versus Pentacles is unresolved, I would like to propose the allocation of one knave to each court,' said Ahab.

'Agreed,' said Odile. 'Lucrezia?'

'Oh, absolutely.'

'But you cheated,' Flora was saying furiously. 'We were about to go to the Hanged Man and you—'

'The courts respect the rules of the Game,' Alastor's voice cut in, cold as steel. All his indolent charm was gone. 'We have given you the opportunity to complete your venture. *Fortunae te regendum dedisti, dominae moribus oportet obtemperes.*' He pointed to the wheel. 'Let play begin.'

The doorkeeper stepped up to turn the wheel. By the time its spinning came to an end, all four chancers would be bound to the courts until their forfeit had been paid. No longer fools, but slaves.

Time slowed. Cat saw the others frozen in disbelief: white-faced and staring-eyed.

Elsewhere, the audience buzzed with anticipation while the Game Masters lounged and yawned. Above them, the cherry blossom ruffled, as if moving to a wind that only it could feel. A man at the front of the crowd tipped his hat at her, mockingly…

Ta-da!

Round and round whirled the wheel, faster and faster, building to the moment of reversal…

As above, so below…

The shadow of a greater tree…

Return to Yggdrasil, and plant each root…

It was like the other time at Mercury Square: her voice had rusted and her gestures dragged clumsily, as if she was moving underwater. 'The tree,' she croaked, fumbling with the catch on the birdcage. 'As above – the tree – it's the *same one* – as below—'

Toby was the first to understand, and the first to act. As

the wheel spun into a blur of speed, and the world around them seemed to revolve too, he took the clay disc from his pocket and crushed it in his fist. Lurching past the table, he hurled his handful of dust beneath the tree.

At once, the ground began to shake. A mound of earth buckled, sending the wheel crashing down. As the crowd, tumbling into disorder, cried out in fear, the tree groaned and swayed, its roots exposed by the heaving of earth. The tremors subsided. It was crippled, but its slender trunk stood firm.

The kings and queens were standing also, although their table had been toppled with the wheel. Their faces blazed but they did not move or even cry out in protest. Alastor had spoken the truth when he said that the courts obeyed the rules.

Cat could feel a roaring in her ears; the blood sang in her veins. A fierce delight surged through her: so *this* was what it felt to win. The moment of triumph! She flung her head back and laughed as Flora stepped forwards, grasping her shard of ice over the twisted roots so that the water dripped from her hands. As the roots shrivelled, the blossom turned dirty brown and the bark oozed with the stench of decay.

Blaine flicked open the lighter and touched it to a branch. For a moment every twig, every petal, bloomed rosy-gold, before the tree burst into a crackling, spitting inferno that burned and burned but did not die.

Only one thing remained.

Cat had opened the door of the cage. For the last time, she held the Root of Air, warm and soft within her hands, before she launched it into the sky.

The bird flew straight into the heart of the blaze, where it came to rest and opened its throat in song. As if in answer, a great wind came and roared through the tree of flame, blowing its sparks everywhere and nowhere, until they were nothing but ash; soft, white ash, thick as blossom, as snow, that drifted all around.

A man emerged from the blizzard of whiteness. His face was both old and young, his eyes shone innocent blue. '*Ave Fortuna.* Behold, my deliverance has come!'

The spiralling flakes were as hot as embers, but in a very little while their sting became the coldness of snow. The wind had scoured away the spring leaves and rosy light, leaving winter and darkness in its wake. And an ordinary cherry tree. But Mercury Square still flickered between the two sides of the threshold as the players thronged around. They were in far greater numbers than before, although now their presence was as quiet and shadowy as ghosts. Among them, Cat thought she glimpsed faces that she knew: the costumed revellers from Hecuba's, a ragged tramp, an old lady in an embroidered bed-jacket...

The man advanced towards the chancers. 'My four wise fools! What marvels you have worked! And so together we embark on the final play.'

They looked back at him, uncomprehending, past the power of speech, movement, thought…anything.

'For now is the round of new turns and reversals, as the Lady of Fortune sports with the Lord of Misrule.' He turned, exultant, to where the kings and queens were standing. 'You have had a fine run, but the Wheel has turned and your hand is played out. Will you renounce your triumphs?'

The Queen of Pentacles answered through bloodless lips, 'We will.' All four were already curiously diminished: bleached of colour, their faces showed new lines and hollows. Their shoulders shivered in the dark.

'Then take your banishment: back into the lost years of the Game and the past moves of your knighthoods. You were common players once, and in exile you will be again. This time, though, you will relive defeat, not victory.'

Somewhere in the rush and roar of the wind, the wheel had righted itself so that it stood in its former position beneath the cherry tree. '*Sum sine regno*,' said the King of Swords, with a ghost of his old smile as, of its own accord, the wheel began to spin. There was a great sighing from the crowd; in one revolution the kings and queens were gone.

The new Game Master raised his hands. 'Now every card is free to turn, every die to roll and every move to be completed. My friends, it is time to play freely and fairly. Pick your card to claim your prize.'

Cat looked down on the crumpled card in her hand. The card she had carried out of the Hanged Man's tomb, with its promise of justice. The card that was still blank.

'I – I already have one,' she faltered.

'Of course you do!' He laughed delightedly. 'From here on, therefore, it is yours for the playing. The right card for the right venture, as I promised you beneath Yggdrasil's shade. Behold!'

At this, four metal objects came rolling across the grass towards their feet: a die each, this time with a silver wheel on every side, ready to create a threshold for their next moves.

'But remember, a card has two faces, a dice four or six. A man, even more… And each has its place in the Game.'

As if on cue, the audience broke into applause, the rippling thunder of a thousand, thousand clapping hands. The sound seemed to come from very far away. And suddenly Cat's card was flooded with shape and colour, until she was once more looking at the stern-faced woman with her sword and scales.

Toby, Flora and Blaine were also gazing, transfixed, at their prizes. She saw that Blaine clutched the Knight of

Wands, and Flora the Eight of Swords. Toby held the Chariot, triumph of heroism… Around their axle of stillness, the shadow of the Arcanum began to whirl.

'At last,' said the Lord of Misrule, as his smile slanted and his eyes burned with blue fire. 'At last, the true Game of Triumphs may begin.'

AUTHOR'S NOTE

Playing cards are believed to have arrived in Europe from the East at some point in the fourteenth century. There are many theories about the relationship between our modern deck and Tarot cards, and I have touched upon some of the most colourful in my story. One of the inspirations for this came from reading about the trick-taking game of Tarot, where using the Fool card ('the excuse') exempts one from the rules of play.

The Rider-Waite Tarot deck is probably the best known of the classic Tarot designs. Its illustrations of the Major (Greater) Arcana are based on early Renaissance playing cards, which themselves drew on mythological, religious and heraldic themes; the scenes on the Minor (Lesser) Arcana derive from traditional divinatory and occult symbols. This is the deck that most closely resembles the cards dealt in the Game of Triumphs.

I Trionfi, a poem by the fourteenth-century Italian

scholar and poet Petrarch, describes the triumphs of Love, Chastity, Death, Fame, Time and Eternity in similar terms to the Allegory of the Triumphs in Temple House. Scholars still debate the connection between Petrarch's poem and the early Tarot decks.

Fortune and her Wheel are an enduring motif throughout history. The Latin epigrams quoted by the Magician and the King of Swords, and inscribed in the Triumph of Time, are taken from speeches given to Fortune in a sixth-century work by Boethius, *De Consolatio Philosophiae* (The Consolation of Philosophy). The verse at the beginning of the book is from the Burana Codex, also known as *Carmina Burana,* a thirteenth-century collection of poems and songs set to music by Carl Orff in 1936. Among the literary and mythological sources I have used, the Hanged Man's account of the origin of the Game owes a particular debt to a short story by Jorges Luis Borges, *The Lottery in Babylon* (1941).

The writer Italo Calvino described the Tarot as 'a machine for telling stories'; when all speculation and superstition is put aside, this is, of course, their true magic.

Laura Powell, 2009

ACKNOWLEDGEMENTS

Contrary to popular belief, books aren't written in isolation. These are the people I would like to thank for helping me make this one.

My agent, Sarah Molloy, for her unflagging good-humour, patience and enthusiasm.

My editors, Kirsty Skidmore and Sarah Lilly, and their Band of Triumphs at Orchard Books.

All the people – you know who you are – who endured my ramblings about the Wondrous World of Tarot and listened politely.

My sister, Lucy, who read the first few chapters and said, 'More, please.'

My parents, for everything.

LOOK OUT FOR. . .

THE
LORD OF
MISRULE
BY
LAURA POWELL

THE THRILLING SEQUEL TO

THE
GAME OF
TRIUMPHS

COMING SOON. . .

TURN THE PAGE
TO READ AN EXTRACT!

Flora struggled on through the mêlée, trying to concentrate on the thread she still followed, trying to ignore the damp heat of her coat and the chafing of her shoes.

It was then that she saw her.

A slope of white neck. A loop of golden hair. The scooped back of a scarlet gown.

Grace.

Grace.

She was weaving her way through the throng, untouched by the mayhem all around. Flora, however, couldn't move. She was rooted to the spot, though shaking so violently it seemed impossible that the whole building wasn't trembling with her. The far side of the room opened onto a small stairwell. When Grace reached it, she looked over her shoulder and smiled at Flora. It was the first time Flora had seen her sister's eyes open or her face mobile in five years. The smile was one of serene welcome. Then Grace turned her back, and glided on.

Flora found she was clutching the thread so tightly it cut into her palm. She was terrified she'd drop it, that the silk would fray or snap beneath somebody's heel before she could catch up with her sister. She called her name but her voice was immediately swallowed up by the din. Finally, she began to push against the barrier of hot, obstinate flesh, until she was kicking and struggling, shouting obscenities... And all the while, the strange yet familiar people carried on swaying and embracing and bellowing, just as if it was she who was the illusion, not they.

At last, she fought her way to the stairwell, just in time to see Grace disappear through a set of doors on the second floor. It was a relief to close them behind her and shut out the sights and sounds of the party. She was now in an area of the building that was completely unfamiliar to her; either because she had never ventured this far in her visits to the clinic or, more likely, because she had reached a part that was entirely constructed by the Arcanum.

Flora padded down a long curved corridor whose carpeting was so soft and thick that she strained to hear Grace's footsteps ahead. She came to another corner and another staircase. It was steep and spiralling. Up she went, higher and higher, until she felt dizzy from all the turning and her heart banged in her ribs. She couldn't hear the party any longer, but there was another sound: a whirring and clacking…

Something had happened to the embroidery silk. As she climbed the stairs, it darkened in colour, from red to burgundy to a kind of burnt maroon. It felt thicker and more fibrous, too. By the time she reached the top of the stairs, the line of thread running under the gap between the door and the floor was black. And the whirring noise was much louder.

The turret room was small and bare. In front of the window, three women were grouped around a spinning wheel. The youngest, who didn't look much older than Flora, was turning a crank to keep the wheel in motion. A woman of her mother's age was feeding raw yarn into the spindle, while an old lady wound the spun thread into little bundles. In spite of the antiquated nature of their task, they looked as if they belonged to the party downstairs. All three were identically kitted out in black cocktail dresses, lipstick and pearls.

Flora took all of this in without really registering it. The only thing she could think about was the fact that Grace was not there.

'Where's my sister?'

'I'm afraid you've taken a wrong turn,' the spindle-woman replied coolly.

The girl turning the wheel smirked into her sleeve.

Whirr, whirr, clack, clack.

'The thread led me here. There must be a reason for it,' Flora said, taking care to keep the tremor from her voice.

'Then I'm sure you'll find it,' the old lady said peaceably, as she straightened one of the bundles on her lap. Her face was creased like rumpled tissue paper, but in spite of her age, she was upright and trim and wore the same cosmetic flourishes as her younger counterparts. Their lips were painted in a crimson Cupid's bow, their faces powdered white, their eyebrows pencilled in a thin black arch, and each wore their white-blonde hair coiled high around their heads. All three were regarding her with their heads slightly tilted to one side, mouths pursed, an identical glint in their bright black eyes. As if, Flora thought uneasily, she was being measured for something...

MORE BRILLIANT NOVELS FROM ORCHARD

Knife	R J Anderson	9781408303122
Stargirl	Jerry Spinelli	9781846165993
Love, Stargirl	Jerry Spinelli	9781846169250**
Milkweed	Jerry Spinelli	9781843624851
The Haunting of Nathaniel Wolfe	Brian Keaney	9781846165207
Jacob's Ladder	Brian Keaney	9781843627210
Weirdo's War	Michael Coleman	9781846166013*
The Cure	Michael Coleman	9781846163456
Little Soldier	Bernard Ashley	9781860398797*
Flashpoint	Bernard Ashley	9781846160608
Horowitz Horror	Anthony Horowitz	9781846169694
Juby's Rook	Michael Lawrence	9781846166211

All priced at £5.99 except those marked * which are £4.99
and that marked ** which is £10.99

Orchard books are available from all good bookshops,
or can be ordered direct from the publisher:
Orchard Books, PO BOX 29, Douglas IM99 1BQ
Credit card orders please telephone 01624 836000 or fax 01624 837033
or visit our website: www.orchardbooks.co.uk
or email: bookshop@enterprise.net for details.

To order please quote title, author and ISBN and your full name and address.
Cheques and postal orders should be made payable to "Bookpost plc."
Postage and packing is FREE within the UK (overseas customers should add
£1.00 per book)

Prices and availability are subject to change.